AN ILL WIND BLEW

AN ILL WIND BLEW

Jack Gayton

To Jan
with Best Wishes
[illegible]
2004

The Book Guild Ltd
Sussex, England

First published in Great Britain in 2004 by
The Book Guild Ltd
25 High Street
Lewes, East Sussex
BN7 2LU

Typesetting in Baskerville by
Acorn Bookwork, Salisbury, Wiltshire

Printed in Great Britain by
Antony Rowe Ltd, Chippenham, Wiltshire

A catalogue record for this book is available from
The British Library.

ISBN 1 85776 754 3

With thanks to my wife, Penny, for her constant encouragement and to Franco Colosimo for his early assistance

PROLOGUE

The sun was just raising itself above the horizon and its golden rays were highlighting the fortress at the entrance to Calvi harbour. The bright light was reflected from the mass of windows of the old Corsican town with fiesta-like brilliance. Until the car started the only sound was the rattle of halyards against the masts of the yachts and the harsh cries of the sea-gulls as they wheeled overhead in search of an early breakfast.

The Englishman was slumped in the back seat. The Arabs on either side pressed against him and the knife was sharp on his ribs. He had made an unforgivable mistake and now he must pay the penalty. He was on his own, there would be no one coming to his rescue. He leaned back and closed his eyes, flinched, but made no protest, as the knife jabbed into his side in response to the movement. He would not give them the satisfaction of witnessing his fear.

He was oblivious of the breathtaking scenery around him. Instead he tried to figure a way out of the mess in which his foolishness had landed him, but the only image that flooded his mind was of the girl standing naked in the companionway of the boat, her beautiful body highlighted by the moonlight which streamed through the hatchway. He still felt the desire for her, even though she had destroyed him. He felt aroused as he remembered her silken skin, the way the long black hair fanned out on the pillows and the passion as she had made love to him. He could taste again the cognac which he had drunk as they lay at rest afterwards, the cognac that *she* had poured for him – that was what had sealed his fate. After the cognac there had been nothing until the water splashed onto his face and he had woken heavy-eyed to see the huge muzzle of the gun inches from his forehead. His head throbbed painfully from the effect of the alcohol he had consumed the evening before and even more from the drug she had administered. He wondered pointlessly what she had used. He should have tasted it – he knew that now – but the wine and the sex had dulled his senses.

The girl had gone. Instead the stocky Corsican stood over him, leering face just visible in the weak morning light. 'Get up, Englishman, the fun is over. Now you pay and the price is high. She's good at her job is that little bitch, Maria.' The English was strongly accented but there was no mistaking the meaning. There had been no need to stress it by dragging the foresight across the man's face – that was just the act of a sadist and the Englishman saw it as such. As the blood trickled down his cheek and he tasted the saltiness at the corner of his mouth, he looked at the other with a feeling of loathing. The man laughed. He was shorter than average but his width made up for that. His hair was dark and cut short, receding at the front and thinning at the back. A seemingly permanent sneer contorted his dark-skinned face, and was accentuated by the unshaven jowls.

'I need to get dressed,' said the Englishman, as much distressed by his nakedness as by his danger.

'You don't need clothes where you're going. You're just going to take a short ride.'

The Englishman shrugged. There was no betrayal of the fear which was beginning to build up inside him. 'I'm sure that the sight of a naked man crossing the waterfront is an everyday occurrence in Corsica and no one will remember it. But if they do, that's your problem.'

The Corsican screwed up his swarthy face in anger, then laughed cruelly. 'Okay, get dressed then. Maybe it's better – you're going to need your pants on, you bastard. We don't want shit all over the car, do we?' He continued to chuckle at his warped joke.

The Englishman pulled on his shirt and trousers, and reached across for his jacket, which was lying on the deck. All the time he was alert, watching for the slightest chance, but none was given – his adversary was a professional too.

'That's enough. You're not dressing for dinner.'

Even so, the man picked up the jacket and shrugged into it as the gun prodded him painfully.

'Get moving.'

He led the way up the ladder to the cockpit, ready to kick backwards into the evil face behind but soon realized that the Corsican had not come alone. As he shielded his eyes from the bright sunlight he saw the Arab with his gun steadily pointing at him, and cursed silently. He should have expected it.

They were taking no chances. While the Arab kept him covered, the Corsican went ashore and stood guard for them to cross the gangplank onto the quay. In much the same way they made their way into the car, which was waiting with engine running, the driver already in his seat. The Englishman recognized the familiar features of the driver even in the early morning light, but the recognition gave him no pleasure. A second Arab standing alongside the car opened a rear door and climbed in, sandwiching the Englishman between him and his compatriot.

The car started away with a jolt as the driver let in the clutch too quickly and the prisoner gasped as the knife in his side cut through flesh. In the front seat, the Corsican cursed the driver. 'What are you trying to do? I thought you knew how to drive.'

The driver muttered something about not knowing the car, then fell silent, his fear of the other man plain to see. No one spoke as the car made its way steadily across to the east coast of the island and into the large town of Bastia, which was almost deserted at such an early hour.

At the old port the car stopped and the Corsican got out. 'Keep alert, you lot. Watch him closely, he's a tricky bastard.' With that he disappeared into a dark doorway in one of the old buildings which surround the port.

The prisoner thought about causing a disturbance to attract attention, but quickly discarded the idea. There was no one around to help and he would invite a knife in the side all for nothing.

After about ten minutes the Corsican emerged from the building and climbed back into the car. 'Okay. We go ahead as planned. The boss has agreed.'

He settled back and closed his eyes as the driver swung the car round and headed south towards Solenzara. As they travelled, they could make out the fertile coastal plain with its backdrop of grey mountains. The smell of wild herbs was heavy in the air – a smell that had fascinated the Englishman on his arrival in Corsica but now nauseated him as he made what would, in all probability, be his last journey. His only hope had been that the Corsican's boss would want to do a deal, which would gain him precious time. The visit to Bastia had finished that. He shuddered involuntarily. He had learned to face death and it no longer frightened him – it was the manner of his dying that really scared him.

Just short of Solenzara the car turned right off the coast road, away from the blue Mediterranean, and headed up the narrow road into the mountains. The large sign by the roadside informed travellers that the pass was open because the winter snows had long since given way to the summer sunshine. The road was narrow and the surface rough making the car jolt violently. With every jolt the knife jabbed into his side and he could feel his shirt sticky with blood. Try as he might, he could not suppress a cry of pain but his captors ignored him.

The prisoner wondered where he was being taken. He knew the road well and had travelled it on happier occasions. As they climbed so the road narrowed until there was barely enough room for two cars to pass. On the left side the cliff rose nearly vertically and on the right it fell away almost as steeply to the mass of trees below, its slope covered with a blanket of shrubs. The smell of the herbs was everywhere. If only a vehicle were to come from the other direction, he might have a chance. Even as the idea occurred to him he felt the knife dig deeper into his side as warning. However, it was not to be – no one was moving through the mountains so early in the morning.

Eventually, the road widened and, on the grunted instructions of the Corsican, the car pulled across and came to rest close under the cliff. The Englishman realized that this would be his last chance to make a break. By parking so close to the cliff, it was impossible for the two people on that side of the car to get out: the odds had been halved. Again the Corsican grunted instructions in a patois that he did not understand, but he tensed himself, ready to make his move. The tall, thin Arab on his right opened the door and started to climb out. As he did so the Englishman whirled, the side of his left hand chopping the other Arab in the throat. The blow had been aimed at the nose and top lip – a killing blow – but the result was effective and he felt the knife fall away as the man's hands flew upwards and he gasped for breath. The prisoner did not hesitate but launched himself forward at the other Arab, who was taken completely unawares, flattening him on the rough road. Sensing freedom ahead of him, the Englishman did not hesitate. He clambered across the fallen body and dived forward towards the edge of the road, leaping into space regardless of what might lie below. His spirits soared as he flew through the air. He had done it. He had made his break and, against all odds, he was going to win. Better to lie injured in the trees than submit himself to the cruel tortures of the Corsican and his friends. They would take a while to get down to the valley and with luck he could give them the slip in the thick woods and shrubs. The thoughts flashed through his mind as time seemed to stand still, but he never knew that it was all in vain, for, even as he jumped, the huge bullet slammed into his back, shattering his spine and leaving a large hole in his chest as it ripped its way clear. It took with it pieces of flesh and bone, and life itself. The body crashed down and came to rest among the trees that were to have provided shelter.

The Corsican pushed his smoking revolver back into its holster and scowled at the Arabs. 'Imbeciles! I warned you the man was good. I told you to take care. Now we have lost him for good.'

The driver spoke for the first time. 'Shall we go down and look for him? He may not be dead.'

'He's dead.' It was a plain statement of fact.

'Since he won't tell us where it is, we'll have to search the boat again.'

'He's hidden it well. We searched thoroughly last night while Maria entertained him in the bar. No, we won't find it that way.'

'Why don't we just take the bloody boat out and sink the damned thing and all that's in it?'

'Because, you fool, it may not be on board. Then we'd never know. The boss won't be satisfied until it's in his hands, and until it is we are all in danger. Your future in particular is very shaky – very shaky indeed. No, we must wait until they send someone else to collect it and try again. Maybe it will be someone easier. If I were you I would pray hard.'

1

Harlow read the signal for the fourth time, then swore softly and let the flimsy piece of paper fall to the desk. The paper was stamped in red 'TOP SECRET – FOR UK EYES ONLY' and the news it contained could hardly be worse. Beardsley had been a strange bastard and hard to get to know, but Harlow had liked him. He thought of him now in the past tense, although the death was not confirmed. He had missed three reports and no one had seen him for several days. Now he had missed a pre-arranged rendezvous. That was enough. Agents in the Department did not miss reports, certainly not three, and they did not fail to keep a rendezvous unless they were in serious trouble. In spite of everybody being so well trained, on paper the department did not exist – it could not exist in this age of freedom of information. The Director reported to the Prime Minister directly and no one knew where the finances came from. Even the Public Auditor would not have been able to work that one out.

Harlow was sad about Beardsley. He had been in the Department for a long time and they had worked together in the field on many occasions. This would have been Beardsley's last assignment, if he had completed it. Then he would have been put out to grass, because he was very much the practical agent and a desk job would not have suited him. Looking back, Harlow remembered how the drinking had become more obvious in recent months and how he had always had difficulties passing up a willing woman.

From a personal point of view Harlow was not looking forward to reporting to the Director. The mission had been an unofficial and unauthorized one. Harlow had stuck his neck out to help a friend in French Intelligence. It had seemed a straightforward job, as straightforward as anything in their world. The trouble was that the whole thing was centred on Corsica and that was French territory and, as such, was out of bounds to the Department unless there was a very good reason. He drummed his fingers on the table and considered his options. He could keep his mouth shut and hope that Beardsley turned up or he could face the wrath of the Director. He read the signal yet again and braced himself. Oh, hell! He might as well get it over. The old man had probably seen the signal and, anyway, ignoring it hadn't really been an option.

He stood up and stretched. He was close on six feet tall and his well-built body was in superb condition. His short, dark, curly hair needed little attention, which was fortunate, because he didn't care much about appearances. His ruggedly handsome face was clean-shaven and tanned from his constant outdoor activity. Whenever possible he would take a break in his home country and spend the time in fighting the fast-flowing Welsh rivers in his canoe. He'd tried growing a beard once, but had never managed to get over the itchy feeling. To him cleanliness and comfort were all important; fashion was a non-runner – much to the disgust of his boss, an Old Etonian. Harlow's school had been a State one in Swansea and nothing could rid him of the accent, not that he ever tried to lose it. He took a deep breath and shrugged into the leather jacket, which his boss despised so much. He scooped up the paperwork from his desk and locked it in the safe in the corner of the sparsely furnished office. Then he glanced around the room, windowless in the name of security. He listened to the hum of the air-conditioning. He hated it. The dry air gave him a sore throat – much better his old office with its ever-open window looking out over the park. They had moved to these cells because their security branch had warned them about long-range cameras and listening devices. It all seemed so pointless now, not like the days of the cold war. He often hankered for those times, when he had been younger and active in the field, when they knew who the enemy was. Now you could never be certain; it seemed to chop and change daily. Allies now, enemies tomorrow and viceversa. There was talk of a federal Europe with Britain as a member and Eastern European countries included. He was not a politician but it sounded crazy to him that Europeans should be tightening their bonds when most of the other federations in the world were tearing themselves apart – usually with lots of blood-letting.

With a last look round he left the room, checking that the door locked behind him, and went along the passage. He came to a halt in front of a heavy mahogany door and grinned as he remembered the Director's insisting that he wouldn't leave behind his previous office door – if he had to work in a cell at least the entrance would be respectable. He rang the bell, waited to be identified on closed circuit television and pushed the door open as he heard the buzz of the lock releasing. The middle-aged woman sitting at the desk was quite attractive in an elegant way and her smile was warm. She liked John Harlow and his down-to-earth approach to life. He made a refreshing change to the rest of these men in grey.

'Hello, John. You look tired – it's time you took a holiday.'

He grinned. 'Oh, for the chance. There's just too much paper-work in the world. One day we'll float away on a sea of it.'

'I have noticed you are doing your best to reduce it. There are several files logged out to you that appear to be stagnating. The registry is getting quite upset. However, the Director awaits you. I'm afraid he's seen the signal and he's not very pleased so I hope you're well prepared.'

'Oh, I'm prepared, but I hope he had a good night's sleep and a hearty breakfast, because this will be a little difficult for him to swallow.'

'Ouch.' She grimaced and pressed the intercom on her desk. 'John Harlow is here, sir.'

There was no reply, but the door in the wall slid open silently.

Harlow walked through and was waved to a chair in silence. The Director sat with both elbows on the desk, his chin resting on his hands and looked at him. Then he spoke softly. 'Jesus Christ, John. What the hell have you been up to? I know you're not keen on the European Union, but are you trying to break it up all by yourself? We've got an agent almost certainly dead and we've been operating under cover in allied territory – and French territory, of all places. My opposite number over there will blow his top. Just when I'd got back on speaking terms with him. It couldn't be worse. If this leaks out the shit will hit the fan, that's for sure. For God's sake, have you taken leave of your senses?'

As Harlow tried to interrupt, he raised his hand. 'I don't want excuses. Just tell me the whole story – and I mean the whole story, not a Harlow edited version. I've got to go cap in hand to the PM on this and I don't want to be tripped up by awkward questions. You know what he's like. He tries to pretend that he doesn't want to know the details but that's just a front he puts on to keep his yard-arm clear.'

Harlow grinned. 'Basically it started out as a favour for a French colleague, but as things progressed it became clear that it involved us too. So you can say that we were actually working for them and not against them.'

He went on to detail the operation in depth, as instructed. The Chief listened intently without interruption. Harlow had to give him that: he was a good listener. When he had finished the Chief again sat in silence.

'Why didn't your froggy friend do his own dirty work?'

'Several of his operatives have already been compromised and he didn't know who he could trust, so he wanted a complete outsider.'

'Why didn't you ask me for authority?'

'Because you wouldn't have given it.'

The Chief smiled slightly. 'That's for sure. As for you saying that we were working for them, that's debatable. If this thing is what you claim, we could be working against a lot of very influential French politicians, not to mention a large part of their judiciary. Now what the hell do we do? If we could find the damned thing and hand it over to the French, maybe we could get away without too much egg on our face. What about the agent you have out there already? Surely he knows where the damned thing is hidden.'

'Unfortunately, he doesn't. Beardsley told no one, not even him. I don't want to use him unless it's absolutely necessary, or we'll blow his cover. We may need him later.'

'So, I repeat, where do we go from here?'

Harlow decided he'd stuck his neck out so far he might as well go the whole distance. 'I feel we've got to get something out of this operation, if only to justify the loss of Beardsley. In order to do that we must get the boat back to this country and, if necessary, take it apart to the last plank and nail. I feel sure he'd have hidden it on board.'

'What if it's not there any more? What if Ricard has found it already?'

'I think not. I checked out a few things before I came to see you. He's still keeping watch on the boat. If he'd got it he wouldn't give a damn about the boat.'

'Okay. I'll give you that. How do we go about recovering the vessel? Send a detachment of the Special Boat Squadron? The French would really love that.'

'Too true. The cat would really be out of the bag and the tabloids would have a heyday. No. We must be a bit underhand. We must send in someone who appears entirely innocent. We have to give the impression that there's nothing of value aboard and we are just tidying up loose ends.'

The Chief raised an eyebrow. 'And who might this gullible man be?'

'I thought we might offer Nick Byers a holiday in return for services rendered.'

'What!' The Chief lurched forward in his chair, his face went scarlet and he stared at Harlow in amazement. 'That amateur. I can't believe you're really suggesting this. Now I *know* you've taken leave of your senses. If you think I'll sanction that, you must think I'm as mad as you are.' He sank back into the chair and covered his eyes with his hands. 'It's my fault. I'm obviously overworking you. Tell me you weren't being serious, please.'

Harlow stuck to his guns. 'Sir, I was being dead serious. Think about it. He has all the qualifications. He knows how to sail and he's resourceful. What's more, he'll look innocent, because he *is* innocent. And, most important, if the story gets out and the papers learn anything, he's nothing to do with us.'

The last part really caught the Director's attention and he sat in silence for a while considering the options, before nodding slowly. 'You mean that we keep him in the dark. You're a hard bastard at times, John. I thought the man was a friend of yours.'

'Oh, I like him, there's no denying it. However, this could be a big break-through and if we have to make sacrifices it's worth it.'

'You have to break eggs to make omelettes, eh? Okay, John. It's absurd, but I can't think of a better alternative. Do it. God help all of us if it misfires.'

2

Nick Byers was a big, easygoing kind of man. In his late thirties, he was still superbly fit and intended to stay that way. His fair, curly hair was a little on the long side, maybe as a rebellion against the years he had spent as a naval officer, but he drew the line at a pony-tail. He strode along the cliffs above Kynance Cove and, as always, admired the beauty of the Cornish coastline. There was something timeless about it; those cliffs had been a bulwark against the stormy sea for thousands of years. His German shepherd, Karl, bounded on ahead, chasing a rabbit that quickly fooled him by going to earth.

Although the tourist season had started, there were no walkers to be seen so early in the day. Somebody had ignored the sign saying 'NO CAMPING' and pitched a tent in the corner of the car park. Nick chuckled to himself as he thought of the reaction of the car park attendant. Fred's wife gave him a rough time at home and he was pretty intolerant first thing in the morning. Rebuking the campers would make a good start to his day.

Nick made his way down into Caerthillian Cove, scattering the birds which had settled on the rocks. On entering the Lizard Village he called the dog to heel and made for his cottage. Stone-built, it had belonged to his aunt for many years. On her death it had been left to him and was now his real home. At the gate he met the local postman, who was his usual moody self.

'Don't know how you find the energy to go out walking at this hour every morning. If I didn't have to be up and about, I'd still be asleep in bed.'

'That's because you stay up in the pub until closing time – and a bit. I'll tell Peter to throw you out earlier. I'm always ready to help.'

'That's the only bit of pleasure I get. You wouldn't want to stop that, would you? Otherwise it's sitting at home with the missus watching the bloody telly. Anyway I've got one letter for you. Look's like it's from the Government.'

Nick laughed. 'You don't want to read it too, do you?'

'No need to be like that. I'll be on my way. Can't stand here talking to you all day.'

Nick waved goodbye and leant back against the wall. He couldn't think what department of government was writing to him. He'd paid his income tax as instructed at the end of January, so it couldn't be that. Well, there was one way to find out and he slit open the letter to read the contents with mounting excitement. He thought for a while and wondered how Sarah would take it, which brought him down to earth with a bump. He would have to break the subject to her tactfully, and he'd have to wait until she was in a good mood. Maybe he could take her out to dinner and raise the subject there.

Deep in thought, he made his way indoors and through to the small kitchen at the back. Approaching Sarah from behind he put his arms round her and kissed her long, flowing, black hair. She turned round and reached up to kiss him on the lips.

'Did you have a good walk? Karl looks as if he enjoyed himself.'

'Yes, he certainly did,' Nick replied, bending down to ruffle the dog's head before wandering through to the dining room where Sarah had laid the table for breakfast.

He usually had a healthy appetite and enjoyed a cooked breakfast. But now he prodded at a sausage absent-mindedly with his fork as he wondered how to break the news to Sarah.

At last she could stand it no more. 'Are you going to tell me what the letter was about?'

Nick looked up in surprise. 'Which letter?'

'The one you got from that old misery, the postman.'

'How did you know there was a letter? Are you related to Sherlock Holmes or something?'

'I don't have to be. When you got up this morning you were full of the joys of spring. I saw you walking back along the lane. You were swinging along happily then. Now you are subdued to the point where you can't eat your breakfast. I'm sure I've said nothing to upset you. The only thing you've done is to chat to the postman and he's got nothing useful to say, so, *ipso facto*, it was something he *gave* you that changed your mood.'

'The trouble with you, Sarah, is that you're too damned clever. Okay, read it for yourself.' He dug the letter out of his pocket, passed it across and watched apprehensively while she read it.

Sarah looked up at Nick. The air of friendly banter had vanished. 'You're not seriously considering this are you?'

'It sounds a great idea, sailing a nice big yacht back from the Med. I can't think of a better way to spend the summer. You'll love it. He says there's no hurry to get back so we can visit the French coast and the Balearics. It would be great.'

'No, no, no. No way will I go anywhere or do anything for that man. It's probably stolen or something. He's so devious he doesn't know himself when he's telling the truth. Not that he ever does. You can't really mean you want to cancel our holiday in Scotland to do what he wants.' Sarah's beautiful face, normally full of humour, was now flushed with anger.

'I don't want to do it for him. I want to do it because I think it will be fun. Anyway, it's not *his* yacht; he's acting for a friend. He says he's only trying to make amends for the last time.' Nick wasn't sure he believed it himself, but he knew he wanted to sail the boat back from the Mediterranean to England. It was too good a chance to miss – and get paid a ferrying fee. He just had to go.

Sarah snorted. 'He just wants to make amends for nearly getting us killed – for getting us on the hit list of a psychopathic killer. Thanks to him we were chased all over the Scillies, hounded out of London and you were damned nearly crippled –

all so that he could catch his man. You really believe he wants to make amends? You must be mad. You go. Me? I'm going to have a nice quiet week at Glencoe.'

They continued to argue for most of the morning, but Sarah was adamant. Nick realized that, if he wanted to go, it would have to be by himself. They tried to change the subject but it remained between them.

Sarah was in her late twenties, tall and quite stunning. Her Chinese mother's looks showed in the high cheekbones and long black hair, which shone with purple flashes. Her English father had provided the startling blue eyes. Her figure was superb, with long legs tapering to slender ankles. All told, it wasn't surprising she was in great demand as a model. She had met Nick in the Isles of Scilly while he was diving on an old Dutch East Indiaman, which had sunk a couple of hundred years before, laden with all kinds of treasure. That was where they had become involved with Harlow and his shady, cloak-and-dagger world and become the target of a political killer. Nick was some ten years older than Sarah and had served a short service commission as a naval pilot, flying Sea Harriers. He was a well-built man, over six feet tall with powerful shoulders and narrow waist. The brown eyes in his tanned face twinkled in keeping with his easy smile. He maintained his fitness by lots of exercise on top of the many hours of diving. However, his last little adventure with Harlow had landed him with a severe spinal bend. Although he suffered no noticeable after-effects, other than a slight limp, he had decided to take a break from diving and rest for a while in his cottage on the Lizard peninsula. It was because he was getting a little bored with the inactivity, that they had arranged the holiday in Scotland. But that was before Harlow's invitation.

Sarah walked slowly along the track across Glencoe, oblivious of the wild hills around her. There wasn't a soul to be seen and she felt terribly alone: not because of the absence of people but because of the absence of Nick. Even the weather seemed to match her depression. Dark clouds were gathering and a storm was building up over the hills. She walked slowly because she was deep in thought, not because she was tired. Indeed she, like Nick, was at the peak of physical fitness and most men would find it hard to keep pace with her should she wish to stride out.

She had been walking most of the afternoon and when she returned to the hotel she tried to relax in a hot bath, but to no avail. She was troubled. Wrapping herself in a bathrobe, she gazed out of the window. She shouldn't have gone there by herself – she should have been with Nick, especially if he was heading into some kind of danger and, with her knowledge of Harlow, she firmly believed that to be most probable. His world seethed with intrigue and all kinds of skulduggery. The strange thing was that she couldn't help liking him, although she would never admit that to Nick – but she would never trust him.

When she had left for her holiday, they had parted on fairly friendly terms but there had been a tension between them – a tension that had never existed before. He had driven her to the railway station and kissed her farewell on the platform. She had almost turned back then but it was not until she settled down for the long journey north that the real loneliness had set in. The journey should have been an exciting car trip, Nick driving his old Lancia HPE just a touch too fast and she rebuking him – but loving it nonetheless.

As she gazed across the purple heather she smiled. If Nick called and asked her to join him she would go at once. She sighed – if he only would call. Having decided that, she felt better. She turned back into the room and let her bathrobe fall to the floor. She gazed into the mirror and felt quite satisfied with what she saw. Nick was a red-blooded man, and she knew all about those voluptuous Mediterranean beauties. Yes, she would go to him before he got himself into trouble.

It was early afternoon when Nick's aircraft touched down at Ajaccio. He had been well looked after by the attractive French air hostess, much to the chagrin of other male passengers sitting nearby. However, he had not really noticed the attention nor had he registered the fact that Harlow had provided him with a first-class ticket and its concomitant comforts. His mind was hundreds of miles away in that lonely Scottish hotel.

'Hell,' he thought. 'I'm a bloody fool. What if she falls for one of those damned Scotsmen with their fancy kilts?' Visions flashed through his mind of a massive, kilted Scotsman tossing a caber over and over while Sarah gazed on mesmerized. As soon as he arrived at Calvi and saw the boat he would telephone her. If he could say the boat really existed and was all that Harlow claimed maybe she would change her mind and join him. The bell drawing attention to the notice for passengers to fasten their seat belts brought him back to reality.

The first thing Nick noticed as he disembarked into the warm sunshine was the smell of the wild herbs. He had heard somewhere that Napoleon had always claimed he could recognize Corsica if he were blindfolded, just from the smell. He could well believe it. The next thing was the dry heat, eased by a gentle breeze. When he had left London early that morning it had been damp and dreary. His spirits rose. This was going to be an exciting adventure – as soon as Sarah joined him, as he was sure she would.

He lost no time in finding a taxi and gave the driver the address of the Bar des Sports in Calvi. The man's eyes lit up at such a long fare. 'It's at the other end of the island, monsieur. I will have to charge a double trip.'

'That's okay. Someone else is footing the bill.'

Nick's French was limited to the bare essentials but the driver spoke excellent English and kept up a running commentary as he made his way northwards along the rugged coast, blue sea on the left, rearing mountains up on the right. The road was narrow, and twisted and turned as it clung to the cliff, so the driver was forced to keep his speed down and Nick had plenty of time to drink in the scenery. He could see why the French called Corsica the Island of Beauty. At one point the car hugged the cliff side and out towards the sea stood the most fabulous collection of rock pinnacles. As he gazed out at the unspoiled landscape he felt contentment and anticipation.

Calvi is a cocktail of architectural styles. The old fortress stands guard over the entrance to the harbour; there is a wide water-front with the busy yacht moorings and, opposite, a scattering of cafés and bars. A couple of narrow lanes lead up into the small town. Across the bay a series of new hotels has sprung up, indicating the start of the inevitable tourist invasion. Nick wondered idly why it hadn't happened before. Maybe it was all the stories of bandits and feuding – the road signs were peppered with bullet scars. He had asked the taxi driver about them but had got no satisfactory explanation. He shrugged his shoulders; bandits were no concern of his. He had no intention of getting mixed up with anything of the kind. He chuckled as he thought of Harlow getting involved with hoodlums.

The Bar des Sports was not a particularly inspiring place. Situated in a row of classy, sophisticated cafés it seemed to shrink from view in understandable embarrassment, its dowdy colours suiting the general demeanour of the place. The row of tables outside was unoccupied, except for a few dirty glasses. He slung his one large bag over his shoulder and entered the bar. After the bright sunshine the interior was dark. As his eyes adjusted he could make out a long, zinc-topped bar down the left side and a scattering of tables throughout the rest of the room. The floor was of mosaic tiles, many of which were cracked, and the walls covered with posters of bullfights and football matches, long since forgotten. Nick could just imagine adverts describing the bar as 'unspoiled' – often synonymous with seedy. The place was deserted. He knocked on the bar and called loudly. 'Hello, hello.'

He heard shuffling footsteps and a tall, stooping man appeared from a doorway behind the bar. His head was almost bald, with just a grey fringe and the pale skin was stretched tightly over his high cheekbones. With his prominent hooked nose he gave a passable imitation of a vulture. His eyes were almost black and seemed devoid of any expression as if he'd given up all feelings or ambition years ago. He wore a stained, once-white apron over a grubby T-shirt and a cigarette dangled from the centre of his mouth.

He stopped in front of Nick and stared at him before speaking. 'Monsieur?' As he spoke the cigarette wobbled up and down.

Nick was a little surprised by the curt welcome. He'd been told that the patron was expecting him and that he spoke good English. In his schoolboy French he started to explain. 'Monsieur, je suis Nick Byers, et je suis arrivé d'Angleterre pour le bateau *White Albatross*. Je . . .'

The patron removed the cigarette from his mouth and stubbed it out against the edge of the bar before interrupting. 'Passport, monsieur, please.'

Nick felt in the pocket of his tunic and produced the document which the other man examined carefully. When he was satisfied he handed the passport back and reached under the bar to produce a set of keys. He then held out his hand.

'Welcome, Monsieur Byers. Please forgive my rather ungracious suspicions, but when I was given the keys I was told to be very careful, since other people were interested in the boat.'

At once alarm bells started ringing in Nick's head. Perhaps Sarah had been right; maybe Harlow had fooled him. Then he shook off the feeling. The patron was probably exaggerating; he'd probably misunderstood the instructions. Nevertheless, a slight uneasiness remained. 'Who actually sent the keys and the message?'

'Mr Beardsley's agents in London telephoned and told me you were coming. The Australian who looks after the boat handed over the keys to me. I think he has another set of his own.'

'Mr Beardsley is the owner?'

'Yes, didn't you know?' The man's voice was suspicious again.

'No, I've never met him. I only dealt with his agent.'

The other man relaxed again. 'I understand that you plan to sail her back to England.' Nick nodded. 'You should have no trouble, she is a fine boat.'

'Do you know her well?'

'Only as a visitor. Monsieur Beardsley sailed it into Corse about one month ago, but I have been on board several times to drink wine with him.'

'The Australian guy who looks after the boat, do you know him?'

'Of course. Everyone around here knows Steve. I don't know where he is just at the moment, but he'll probably be here this evening.'

'How about Beardsley, do you know where he is now?'

'Not exactly. I was given to understand that he had returned to England on business and had fallen sick there. Now, monsieur, if you will forgive me I must get back to work.'

Nick raised an eyebrow and gestured around the bar. 'You're not very busy here, are you?'

The patron shrugged. 'It's the siesta. Only the tourists are out in the afternoon and most of my trade is for the locals and, of course, the sailing people who appreciate the good atmosphere of the bar. So many bars these days are flashy, with no ambience – and they charge too much money. They cheat the tourists, but the locals know better. Now I am preparing food for this evening, when we will be very busy. If you come in you will see and maybe will meet Steve.'

Nick looked about him at the scruffy surroundings and the badly stained bar. He had watched fascinated while a cockroach spiralled its way up the flex of the single light hanging behind the bar. He decided that, if this was ambience, he preferred glitz. As he listened to the patron's directions for finding the boat, he made a mental note to eat elsewhere. He thanked him and walked out into the bright sunshine.

He had little trouble in finding the boat, moored stern to the quay in typical Mediterranean fashion. He stood for a while and admired her. She was a ketch-rigged boat of some forty-five feet overall with centre cockpit, wooden built with sparkling white painted topsides and varnished coachwork. The well-scrubbed planks of the deck were spotless and the bright work sparkling. Even the rope ends were cheesed down neatly. Nick guessed that she was about fifty years old but had been, and indeed still was, looked after with love and affection.

As he made his way aboard all misgivings were swept away in admiration and excitement. This was a real boat – the kind he had always wanted to own. It not only looked right – it felt and smelt right. He made his way forward to the cockpit and looked up at the towering mast equipped, he was pleased to see, with stainless steel rigging. The cockpit was spacious, with seating down both sides. The forward part was covered by a small doghouse while a large stainless steel wheel was mounted aft to give the helmsman a clear view of the rigging and sails. The after cabin was accessed by a hatch and companionway on the starboard side aft of the cockpit while another in the centre forward, protected by the doghouse, led to main accommodation.

Nick made a slow, methodical check of the boat, starting with the after cabin. It contained two full-sized bunks with stowage below. Between them, at after end, was a small wash-basin. At the forward end of the port bunk was a combined toilet and shower compartment. Everywhere was finished in glistening varnished mahogany. He pulled out one of the drawers under the bunk. In it there were neatly folded shirts and trousers. The locker under the wash-basin contained shaving-gear and tooth-brush. Beardsley had certainly travelled light back to England. Again Nick felt an uneasy prickling at the back of his neck. He decided to gather all the owner's belongings into one drawer and try to forget about them.

He made his way back to the cockpit, around the centre-placed compass binnacle and down into the forward accommodation. There, once again, the mahogany was prevalent. Aft on the port side a single berth ran aft under the cockpit, while on the starboard side was a navigating position with plotting tables. GPS navigation equipment was fitted above a powerful-looking radio set. Hingeing aside the companion ladder gave access to a diesel engine. On the port side, forward of the pilot berth, was another toilet/shower compartment. Next forward was the lounge area, with plenty of seating. The hanging-rack above the table could be freed to counteract the heel of the boat. Next came the galley. Finally, right in the bows was a small workshop area. To port was a work-bench complete with vice, on the other side a pipe-cot, which looked as if it had been recently used – obviously by the Aussie since Beardsley's possessions were in the after cabin. Right forward, against the bulkhead, was a rack holding four single Scuba sets and a small portable compressor. In the deck-head was a hatchway to the foredeck. Nick judged that the compressor would lift out through it without too much trouble, enabling the sets to be charged in the fresh air, free from exhaust fumes. He opened a locker to reveal a wealth of diving equipment from demand-valves to weight-belts. He had brought along a wet-suit jacket, just in case, and now the excitement grew at the thought of diving in the clear, warm water of the Mediterranean.

More than satisfied with what he had seen, he sat down in the saloon area to make out a list of things that he needed right away. Obviously, Beardsley had made preparations to sail because there were plenty of tinned and dried foods already in the lockers, but no fresh stuff. He had been pleased that the selection of sails in the forward compartment was good and, from what he could see, they appeared to be in first class condition. The fuel- and water-tanks were full and the batteries charged. The Aussie had done his job well. Nick reckoned he needed a couple of days to get used to the boat, a short sail around, and then he would be ready to leave.

As he was leaving to go shopping he noticed a red ensign on a short mast lying on the pilot's berth. He took it onto the deck with him and mounted it on the stern. He might as well let the Aussie know that he had arrived.

He strode briskly ashore feeling really pleased with himself. This was wonderful – what a boat! He was looking forward to the voyage. Only one thing was missing – Sarah – and, of course, she would come when she heard about the boat. On the other side of the waterfront he had spotted a telephone kiosk and now he headed for it, pulling out a credit card. With the modern dialling facilities he was connected to Glencoe in a matter of seconds, only to find that she was out walking. He left a message that he would call back and continued into town, feeling disappointed.

Sarah finished dressing for dinner and went down to the restaurant. As she passed through reception, the young girl behind the desk called to her. 'Miss Drew – a Mr Byers telephoned you earlier, but you were out. He said he'd call back.'

'Thank you. Did he say what time he would call?' The girl shook her head. Sarah was one of those people who hated waiting for the telephone to ring. You had no control over it, so it ruined the whole evening.

She carried on into the restaurant and settled down to order dinner. Now Nick was about to ring and he would certainly ask her to go out and join him. If he were suitably penitent she would agree – reluctantly, of course.

She had finished her starter and was about to tuck into a juicy steak of best Scottish beef, when the receptionist walked over to the table. 'Mr Byers is on the phone for you, Miss Drew.'

Aloud she said, 'Thank you. I'll come to reception to take it.' However, to herself she cursed quietly. How could he have been so thoughtless as to ring in the middle of dinner? She didn't consider that there might be a time difference, or that he might not know when she would eat. She made her way quickly to the phone booth in reception and lifted the receiver.

He made no apology, but instead talked non-stop about how good the boat was and how she must come out at once. How soon could she get there? Could she get a flight the next day? He just assumed that she would do as he wished. With her steak congealing in the restaurant, Sarah was furious. His attitude was the final straw. Her previous thoughts of flying out to see him faded.

'I haven't said that I would come. On the contrary, I'm having a great time here.'

'But of course you will fly out. Stop being silly.'

'I haven't decided yet. Call me tomorrow. Now I want to get back to my dinner, if it's not ruined.' She rang off.

Back at the table, she sat for a while but her appetite was gone. She pushed the plate away and left the dining room. How could she have been such a silly little fool? She desperately wanted to start again but had no way of calling him – she couldn't even remember the name of the boat. Tears began to form in her eyes and she hurried from the restaurant. Up in her bedroom, she threw herself face down on the bed and sobbed bitterly.

Nick was more hurt than angry as he made his way across to the yacht moorings. He had been brash and foolish with his approach, and he certainly hadn't been prepared for her reaction. He realized there was still a lot about Sarah that he didn't understand, and was still pondering the situation when he arrived back at the gangplank. It was only the young man standing there that brought him back to the present. At first he thought that it must be the Aussie, but when the man spoke he was clearly very English.

'Hello there, sir. Is this your boat?'

'It is for the time being,' Nick grunted. Still smarting from Sarah's rebuff, the last thing he needed was some public school smart-arse hanging around. The young man was about six feet tall and of slender build. His wavy fair hair was longish but neatly cut and his smooth complexion gave the impression that shaving was not a frequent requirement. For all that, Nick realized that he was not so young, probably about thirty.

'I'm terribly sorry for barging in like this but I saw the old red duster and it made me feel a little homesick.'

Nick softened. 'That's all right. Are you on holiday or do you work here?'

'Well, a bit of both really. I'm a writer and I'm doing an article on tourism growing on the island and the effect it's having. I'm afraid I'm not very good, but I keep trying.'

'Sounds interesting. Have you been here long?'

'A month and a bit. But I find it difficult to relax with people and I don't make friends easily so I've been rather lonely. By the way, my name is Peter Cassells.'

Shaking the proffered hand Nick responded. 'Nick Byers. Would you care to come aboard for a drink? I seem to have a pretty good selection.'

'Thanks a million, but I ought to go back and do some work. I find that mornings and early evenings are the best times. But if I might take up your offer tomorrow, I'd like to very much.'

'Of course. I plan to go to the Bar des Sports later this evening. If you care to join me there you'll be welcome.'

'Thank you. I won't promise, but I'll see how the work goes. 'Bye for now.' He walked away with a strangely positive stride. He was an odd mixture, Nick decided, with his cherubic features and hesitant manner, coupled to an obviously fit, athletic body and a purposeful gait. Still, the man was lonely and Nick could sympathize with that. He shrugged and made his way across the gangway and onto the boat. There was still no sign of the Aussie called Steve.

3

The room in the old part of Bastia was dingy and empty of furniture. As he looked through the dirty window-panes down to the old harbour he felt satisfaction. He turned round slowly and faced the girl who stood, cringing slightly, between the two Arabs.

'This is what we've been waiting for.' The thickset Corsican stared at the girl and she shivered as she looked back at the cruel black eyes. 'Do not fail – you know the penalty for failure. You remember Rosa. She failed. If you don't want to spend the rest of your life like her, you must not fail.' He laughed at the girl's shudders as she thought of the crippled, scarred girl who cleaned the nearby bar. 'Hopefully he'll go to the bar this evening. If not, you'll just have to find another way of getting to him. It shouldn't be too difficult for a slut like you. You've got the powder – put it in his cognac. Just as you did before.' He laughed coarsely. 'After he's sampled your delights he won't notice the taste. As soon as he's asleep come and report. We'll look after the rest. Now get out.'

The girl nodded dumbly and slipped out of the room. She shivered as she ran down the stairs and into the open air, knowing that if things went wrong he would crush her as he would a fly. She was scared, but there was no way out for she was committed to this evil man. What a mess she had got herself into. When she had first met him she had been proud to be with such a powerful man. He had bought her presents and treated her kindly. Then it had become a familiar story. Once she was wholly dependent upon him he showed his true colours – and she dared not disobey. First he forced her to have sex with his friends and clients. Then she had become an accessory to murder and now it appeared that she would become so again.

She went into a drab little café, ordered a coffee, sobbed quietly. No one interfered. The customers and staff knew Maria and the man who controlled her. None of them was prepared to get involved.

Nick poured a tumbler of cheap red wine and made himself a sandwich from the fresh bread and cheese that he had bought earlier, then sat down to a solitary supper. He missed Sarah badly. She had changed his life. In the old days he would either have appreciated being alone or else gone to the bar to find company. Hell, he thought, there's no reason why I shouldn't do just that. Maybe the Aussie would be there, as the patron had suggested.

He stood up and tossed back the remainder of the wine. The evening was still warm as he made his way ashore and the sky was full of stars.

The tables outside the bar were still empty but he could hear the hum of conversation and the odd laugh coming from inside. Making his way through the door, he was surprised to see a good crowd, mainly men, gathered there. Several were standing at the bar but most of the tables were in use. In the far corner a man was playing a gaming machine while his companion looked on. Just inside the door were two men dressed in blazers with white shirts and cravats. They looked strangely out of place among the casual, if not scruffy, attire of the rest of the clientele. As Nick passed he realized from their conversation that they were English and guessed that they were more than just good friends. One was probably in his late twenties, slim with fair hair and delicate features. His eyes were a very pale blue and his thin lips were compressed as if a smile would be alien to them. The other was older, possibly in his early forties, and much bigger. He had probably had a good body once but now it had run to fat. He had a ruddy complexion, and a big black beard. His black hair showed signs of thinning on top and probably owed its continuing darkness to Grecian 2000. Nick nodded to them as he passed. The older man forced a smile and nodded back, but the other ignored him.

Nick made his way to the bar and ordered a beer. The patron welcomed him and told him that the Aussie had not yet arrived. He carried his glass past a group of American yachtsmen to a free table at the back of the bar and sat down facing the door.

As he slowly sipped his ice-cold beer, he looked around at the self-contained groups in the bar and realized that he was cut off from them. He felt the depression of loneliness and sympathized with the young Cassells. He hoped that he or the Aussie would arrive to join him. He toyed with the idea of approaching the two Englishmen, but was not disappointed when they stood up, looked around the bar and left. At the bar the group of Americans were laughing loudly at some private joke. One of them, a well-built young man in his early twenties with an uncontrolled mop of blonde hair, was obviously feeling the effects of the local wine. He was reeling slightly, and his language was causing his companions some embarrassment. Nick decided that he'd wait another fifteen minutes for Steve or Cassells, after that it would be back to the boat.

His time limit had almost expired when the girl entered the bar. She was absolutely stunning: small with jet-black hair which shone in the lights of the bar. Dark brown, almost black, eyes sparkled from her dusky face. The long black skirt and loose red blouse couldn't hide the shapeliness of her body. The girl knew the effect she was having on the drinkers; that was clear from the swing of her hips as she walked, bare-footed, to the bar.

Before she could speak, the young American broke away from his party and staggered to her side. His long arms went round her shoulders and he hugged her to him. In spite of her protests, he pressed on. 'Come on, baby, have a little drink with me and be friendly.'

'I don't want a little drink with you. You are drunk and I want you to leave me alone.' The girl's English was heavily, but attractively, accented.

The American ignored her protests and pulled her tighter with his left arm while his right hand explored the front of her blouse. Nick realized that, unless the others stopped the boy, he would be compelled to intervene – much against his wishes. It was then the girl acted for herself. She broke free and swung a stinging blow to the boy's face and as his hands flew up to his cheeks she pushed him hard backwards across a chair. The boy sprawled onto the floor as the chair collapsed. He clutched at the table to stop his fall but that only served to pull it over on top of him, covering him with wine and glasses. He started back to his feet with wine running down his face, staining his white T-shirt. He pressed down on his left hand to lever himself up and cursed as a piece of broken glass cut deeply into the palm. His handsome face was screwed up in anger as he stared at the girl. He held his injured hand high in front of him but the thumb pressed hard into the wounded palm failed to staunch the flow of blood entirely. He moved towards her menacingly. She looked for a way out, but the boy was between her and the door, and the other customers stood stunned and bewildered. Then she spotted Nick rising from his seat. She ran towards him and flung her arms round his neck crying out, 'Oh, darling, thank God you are here!' Then she whispered in his ear. 'Please help me.'

As the American lurched towards them Nick placed his hands on the girl's waist and, lifting her like a feather, placed her to one side. He looked at the approaching boy quite calmly. He didn't want a brawl but he knew that if it came to it he could take this lad apart with one hand – drunk or sober.

'Push off, sonny. The lady is with me and you've gone too far already. Now, get lost and get that hand seen to. In future, try to act like an adult.' Nick's voice was calm and confident. The young American hesitated, uncertain now that he was faced with such a large soft-spoken adversary. Even in his drunken state he realized he was confronted with a situation he couldn't handle.

Nick didn't take his eyes off the boy but allowed a confident smile to flicker over his lips. In the background he could see one of the other Americans approaching. If he was going to join in that would be different. He hoped common sense would prevail. The other man stopped and put his hand on the boy's shoulder. He spoke sternly but quietly. 'Brad, get the hell out of here before I let the man take you apart – and I'm sure he can. Joe is on the boat – he'll dress your hand. You're lucky that's all you've got to repair.' He smiled at the boy but there was no humour in his eyes. 'Out. Now.' The two words cut sharply through the bar which had fallen quiet with expectation, and the boy hesitated only a moment before slinking away through the bar door.

The man turned to Nick and held out his hand. 'Please accept my apologies for the behaviour of one of my crew towards you and this charming lady. It was quite unacceptable and I will see that he receives the necessary chastisement. Can we just blame it on too much wine and the foolishness of youth, two things that do not mix?'

Nick readily accepted the apology. He took the proffered hand. 'Forget it. It wasn't your fault and maybe it's taught the young sod a lesson. Fortunately, the girl's got one hell of a right hook.' The man laughed, bowed slightly to the girl and rejoined his friends at the bar.

Nick swung a chair round so that the girl could sit at the table and grinned across at her. 'You're stuck with me now, at least until that lot leave. Were you really meeting someone?'

The girl smiled back shyly. 'I came in to look for some friends but they are not here. I'm so grateful to you and very sorry to have involved you, but I didn't know what to do. I'll get out of your way as soon as I can.'

Nick laid a hand on the girl's arm and the skin was silky and warm. 'There's no hurry. Since you're my girl for the time being, I'd better introduce myself. My name is Nick Byers. What's yours?'

The girl's deep brown eyes were fixed on his face. 'I'm Maria – just call me Maria. Everybody else does.' She giggled softly Her beauty and the husky voice with its appealing accent fascinated him.

'If you promise not to hit me I'll offer to buy you a drink.'

Maria chuckled and reached out to touch his hand. 'I only hit drunken Americans. You are my friend and I would like to drink a glass of red wine with you. I think that I'm glad my friends are not here.'

Nick felt a thrill at the touch of her hand. He hesitated a second, then called to the young waiter to order a couple of glasses of wine. He looked at the girl and said, 'Tell me about yourself and your island.'

'There is little to tell – I am just an ordinary girl. But I will gladly tell you about my island. How long have you been here?'

'I arrived today. I've come to pick up a yacht and take it back to England.'

'How exciting! Are you staying here for a long time, before you sail away?'

'A few days, probably.'

The girl's eyes flashed and she raised both her hands. 'Wonderful. Then I will not only tell you about the island, I will show it to you. I will bring my car tomorrow and we will go on a ... how do you say it? ... a sightseeing tour. Then maybe you will take me out for a trip in your yacht.'

Nick laughed at the girl's infectious excitement. 'That's a bargain. I can't think of anything I would like more.'

The two Englishmen had walked in silence since they left the bar. Now the older one spoke with a slight North Country accent. 'Well, James, he's arrived like you said. Now what do we do?'

The younger man's voice was cultured and clearly public school. 'We'll have to wait and watch him for a couple of days to see what he's like and how to approach him. He's certainly going to be no pushover.'

'Don't forget we're not the only ones to be considered. We can't afford to be too long about it, because Pierre won't wait for his money indefinitely.'

'I agreed. We may have to think again and find another way – I hope not, but it all depends on Byers. I don't think he's one of us, so we'll probably have to appeal to his greed. They say that every man has his price . . .'

'What if the price is too high?'

'Then we'll have to accept and cut our losses – or find another way.'

Nick and Maria had drunk a considerable amount of wine and talked and laughed freely throughout the evening. Now they were the only ones left in the bar. The young waiter had carried away all the dirty glasses and gone to the back room, while the patron polished the bar.

Maria smiled at Nick. 'Let us have a last glass of cognac and you can show me your yacht before I go home.'

'That sounds a great idea, but I'll have to escort you home. I'm old fashioned like that.'

'How wonderful! But first the cognac then your yacht.'

Nick ordered the cognac and the patron brought it to the table. He put the drinks down and hesitated a little before saying softly, 'Take care, monsieur.'

Nick had a feeling he had wanted to say more but had decided against it. He felt a bit uneasy – then he shrugged it off. The man probably wanted to tell them to go home so that he could go to bed.

They finished the cognac quickly and left the bar. The night air was chill as they walked across the waterfront and Nick put his arm round the girl and drew her close. She snuggled against him. As he had suspected, she wore nothing under the thin blouse.

They crossed the gangplank onto the boat and it gave slightly under their weight. She fell against him and, as he caught her in his arms, she looked up into his eyes, reached up and kissed him softly on the lips. They lingered together for a brief while before she broke away and made her way to the cockpit.

'You have two cabins. Which one will you show me first? I know, this one.'

Nick felt a flash of guilt, but she opened the unlocked hatchway to the after cabin and went quickly down the companion steps. He followed. At the bottom she turned and reached up to put her arms round his neck. Her lips found his and softly explored them. He reached for the buttons of her blouse and, as if by magic, it fell away to reveal her small but beautifully shaped breasts. He ran his fingers gently over them and the nipples hardened to his touch. She felt down to her waist and the black skirt fell away. She stood naked and the moonlight through the hatchway highlighted her beautiful body.

Nick was torn apart by desire and guilt. He desperately wanted this girl and he could feel himself harden with desire, but he loved Sarah and to be unfaithful to her would mar their relationship for ever. He knew that he could not live with that guilt. Others might be able to, but he wasn't that type. He could not spoil everything for this girl, however desirable she might be.

'I'm sorry, Maria, I'm really sorry, but I just can't,' he whispered hoarsely and dropped his arms to his side. The girl pressed her body against him and reached to unbutton his shirt. Her hands ran over his chest, as light as a breath of wind. His breath came faster and he knew that he must be strong and stop it, before his will gave way.

'No, Maria. I mean it.' He held her firmly and eased her away from him. 'Get dressed and I will take you home.' He began to button his shirt, while the girl stared in astonishment.

Maria could not believe this was happening. She had been so sure of herself. 'Why? Why are you doing this? Do you not find me beautiful? Am I not desirable? You have led me on and excited me. Now you wish to cast me aside. Why?'

'Maria, I think you are very beautiful and very desirable. If it were not for another woman, I would take you with great pleasure, but I love that other woman.'

'But she is not here now – tonight we just have fun together. Do not think about her and she will not exist.' She could feel the panic building inside her as she thought of the Corsican.

'No. It's not possible.'

'Then just lie with me. We can lie in each other's arms – there is no need for sex. We will just enjoy being close to each other – you will see.' She took his hand and pulled gently towards the bed.

Nick was tempted, very tempted, but he also knew that if he lay on the bed he would succumb to her attractions and all his good intentions would be as nothing. He carefully broke her grip on his hand and moved away. 'No, Maria, it cannot be.'

She tried again to reach for him but he took her wrists and pressed her back to sit on the bunk. Then he turned away to leave the cabin. At last the truth sank in and she realized that she had lost him. She realized too that she must face the anger of the Corsican and she shuddered with terror. Something inside her snapped and she was filled with fury towards the man who had done this to her. She sprang at him and clawed at his back. He turned and held her away and saw that her beautiful face had turned ugly with a fierce anger. As he held her at arm's length she twisted and struggled. Her husky voice turned harsh as she cursed him violently in her native patois. She spat in his face and he felt the spittle run down his cheek. He was stunned – was this the girl who only minutes ago had been so beautiful, so desirable? Her fury astonished him. Of course he had heard the old adage – 'Hell have no fury like a woman scorned' – but he wasn't prepared for what had happened. He thrust her away from him onto the bunk and, as she started to rise, slapped her face sharply. He did so again, hating himself for doing it – hitting girls was not his style, but he could think of no other way of calming her, no other way to stop the awful fit of temper.

She sank back, buried her face in her hands and sobbed. Her shoulders shook and he let her sit alone for a short time, half afraid to touch her in case he sparked off the tirade again. When he was sure that the fury was past, he sat down beside her and put his arm around her shoulders. She didn't push him away, she just continued to sob. He felt that he should say something to comfort her but could think of nothing, so they sat in silence for a while until the sobbing eased. Then he heard her murmur softly, 'Je suis morte ... je suis morte.' Looking up at him she said simply and quietly in her accented English, 'You have killed me.' The fury had gone from her voice, to be replaced by a strange resignation.

Nick couldn't understand what was happening. He stood up and looked down at the girl. She must be mentally deranged, he thought. 'Come on, Maria, get dressed. I'll go and make some coffee then I'll take you home.' He waited for some reply but there was none, so he went up into the cockpit and down into the forward cabin. As he set about making the coffee, he heard her in the cockpit and felt the boat move slightly. He went up on deck in time to see her run away across the waterfront. He called after her, but she ignored him and ran on until she disappeared into the night.

Nick sat in the cockpit thinking about the events of the evening. He was worried about the girl and disgusted with himself. Although an easygoing sort of guy, he was ashamed of his behaviour. The sooner he could find the Australian and sail away from this island and its memories the better.

As he sat he sipped at the glass of wine in front of him, but he was sober and staying that way. He didn't really notice the time passing and the first streaks of dawn were in the sky before he became aware of it. He shook himself and stretched. He'd go into the town and find some bread or croissants for breakfast, then look for the Aussie and get the hell out of Corsica.

In the car parked on the other side of the waterfront, the Corsican and his two Arabs sat waiting as they had been all the night. They had watched Nick and the girl go on board the boat and the Corsican had grunted with satisfaction. A short time later they had watched the girl run ashore and make off while Nick had called after her. This time the Corsican had cursed. 'That useless slut has cocked it up. God help her when I catch up with her.'

One of the Arabs spoke. 'What do we do now? Do we just go on board and take him?'

'We can't risk that. He's a powerful guy. If he knows how to look after himself, and he probably does, all hell will break loose. We want to do this without attracting too much attention. Don't forget we want him alive – that's essential. If he dies like the last one, the boss will tear us apart.'

They sat and waited in the car while Nick sat in the cockpit. The Corsican angled back his seat. 'I'm going to get some sleep. Call me if he makes a move to come ashore – maybe we can ambush him in one of the alleys. Keep a proper watch and don't sleep, or you too will taste my anger.'

It was actually hours, but it seemed only minutes, later that the Arab shook him. 'He's making some kind of move. He's either going to bed or else he's going to come ashore.'

The Corsican shrugged. 'It doesn't matter either way. Anything is better than his sitting in the damned cockpit ... Look out! He's coming ashore. Keep your heads down. When he's passed by, Ahmed, you go quickly round to meet him at the other end of the alley. He's walking slowly, so you should do it easily. We'll come up behind him – take him in the alley. Have your knives on show but for God's sake don't stick him.'

Nick strolled casually across the waterfront, enjoying the fresh, early-morning air and trying to think of anything except Maria. He spotted the car parked away to his left and, guessing that it belonged to one of the yachtsmen, didn't give it another thought. He headed towards the mouth of a narrow alley leading to the town. After the brilliant sunshine the alley was dark, but he quickly became accustomed to the gloom and soon he could see sets of steps leading upwards, separated by stretches of rough stone track. He started forward, concentrating on his footing on the uneven surface, and was surprised when he looked up to see someone blocking his way. The man was quite big and clearly of Arab extraction. Nick was about to offer a greeting when he saw the glint of the knife, held low in an experienced manner. Oh God, he thought, not a mugger – that really finishes the day. The man was crouched forward slightly, standing very still, except for the gentle side-to-side waving of the knife.

He weighed up his chances and decided that fast retreat was the order of the day. As he turned he saw that two other men – another Arab, also armed with a knife, and, worse, a thickset man with a large handgun – blocked his way. Nick was scared. This was no ordinary hold-up; he could see that. He was unprepared for this kind of thing. He backed slowly to the wall, his gaze switching from one side to the other. The first Arab had come quite close now and he could feel the other's eyes boring into him, watching his every move. That was probably why he didn't notice the silent approach of a fourth man, who seemed to glide up behind the thickset one. Nick watched fascinated as the newcomer closed on the gunman and chopped hard against the side of the throat with the edge of his hand. The man dropped as if pole-axed, his gun clattering across the rough stones as he fell. As he lay there, twitching slightly, his partner swung round and looked at him in disbelief. He had always viewed the Corsican as indestructible. In his bewilderment he wasted valuable seconds and was thus unprepared for the newcomer's next assault, and for the blow to his solar plexus delivered expertly with the extended knuckles of the right hand. He reeled back against the building that sided the alley, bending forward and clutching his middle, the knife falling to the ground. His unknown assailant gave him no time to recover. He danced forward lightly on bare feet and, grabbing the long hair with a hand either side of the man's head, pulled it sharply down while at the same time smartly raising his knee for the impact. The Arab, his face already a bloody mess, collapsed alongside the Corsican, both moaning slightly while the newcomer hopped about on his left foot rubbing his right knee in pain.

The remaining Arab recovered his senses quickly. His first thoughts were to turn and run but he still had his knife and knew that he must not leave his Chief. He lunged forward in an attempt to wound Nick, but was hampered by the memory of the Corsican's warning not to kill. Nick sidestepped the lunge and grabbed at the other man's knife-hand, but he was too slow. As they closed the Arab crashed his head into Nick's nose and the blood spurted freely. His opponent followed up quickly, too quickly in fact. His carelessness allowed Nick to grab his wrist and, although dazed, to hang on grimly. Eventually, Nick's greater strength proved too much and he forced the man back against the side of the alley; there he banged the knife-hand repeatedly against the rough brickwork while crushing his right forearm across his assailant's throat. The man struggled fiercely and used his left hand to grab a handful of Nick's hair. He jerked it hard, but Nick held on. He felt the man release his hair and try for his eyes instead. The other's fetid breath, strong with garlic, was hot in his face. As the knife dropped to the ground, he crashed his knee into the other man's crutch. He heard a groan and brought his knee up a second time. His time he felt the struggle weaken but he kept the pressure on for a while, then stepped back and released him. Dazed and in pain, the man started to pitch forward. It was then that Nick hit him with a full-blooded punch to the chin. The Arab collapsed and lay still, while Nick shook his hand in pain.

The fight had taken place in silence and seemed somehow unreal. However, the three unconscious figures were very real indeed. Nick was temporarily stunned by what had happened and blood still poured from his nose, but the newcomer beckoned to him. 'Let's get to hell out of here.' Many questions shot through his mind but he wasted no time asking them. He spotted the Corsican's gun lying beside him and, although he didn't want it himself, felt he should deprive the opposition of it. Holding a handkerchief to his nose, he bent down and scooped it up, then stood looking down at the fallen bodies. The first Arab wasn't moving. Nick checked he was still breathing and found with relief that he was. The other was moaning and the Corsican was beginning to move.

'For Christ's sake hurry, mate – let's get back to the boat before he wakes up.'

'Surely we should call the police.'

'Like hell. Forget the bloody police. Just get your bloody legs moving.'

Nick hesitated for a second, then turned and followed the other as he raced barefooted across the waterfront and onto the yacht.

His rescuer was obviously well acquainted with the boat and he was able to produce a key to start the boat's engine without hesitation. As he ran aft to remove the gangplank he shouted orders to Nick. 'Let go the aft mooring lines and go up to the bows to take in the anchor as I go ahead.' Nick didn't argue. The stranger edged the boat forward as Nick worked the winch to haul up the anchor. After a few minutes he called that the cable was 'up and down', meaning that the anchor was clear of the bottom, and the man at the wheel increased the engine speed. In no time they were slipping out of the moorings and heading for the open sea.

Nick secured the anchor and went below to tend to his nose. The bleeding had almost stopped but it felt painful and bruised. He splashed water on it freely before returning to the cockpit. For the first time he was able to study his companion properly. He had already guessed the man's identity from his strong Australian accent. Now he could see that Steve was of medium height and well-built, with a boyish mop of fair wavy hair and bright blue eyes shining out from a very tanned face. He wore a tatty blue denim shirt with the sleeves torn out and equally tatty shorts of the same material. Nick guessed he was older than he at first appeared, probably around thirty. He grinned broadly under Nick's inspection.

'Well, mate, I hope you don't object to me taking over your boat, but I feel we ought to put a bit of water between them and us, even if we have got their artillery.' He nodded to the gun that Nick had dropped on the cockpit cushion. Nick reached forward and picked it up, weighed it in his hand for a moment, then tossed it over the side. He heard Steve draw in his breath sharply.

'I don't like guns,' he explained.

'Neither do I, but you should have hung on to that one. It might have come in handy.'

Nick was silent for a while considering what had happened. While it was obvious the young Australian was on his side what he needed to know was who was on the other side. He also had a deep suspicion that Harlow was up to his tricks again and that Steve was involved.

'Too bad, maybe if I knew what was going on I would have kept it. You are obviously Steve. Now I want a few answers. Grateful as I am for the rescue act, if you don't tell me what's happening and what Harlow is up to, I'm going to throw you in after the bloody gun. Now start talking.'

'Hey, come off it, mate,' protested the younger man. 'I don't know much more than you and I certainly don't know anyone called Harlow.'

Nick ignored the plea of ignorance. 'Let's hear what you do know. Don't mess about because the further out we get the further you'll have to swim back if I'm not satisfied.'

'Some bloody way to show gratitude that is. In case you've forgotten, I'm the one who's just saved your bloody arse. You're a typical pommie bastard.' However, the twinkle didn't leave his eye or the smile his lips. 'Okay, it goes like this. I knew you were coming of course, but I had to go to Ajaccio yesterday so I wasn't around when you arrived. It was late when I got back and you were in the bar talking to that delightful little bitch, Maria, and I didn't like to interrupt. Now, strangely enough, the night before Beardsley went missing, he brought Maria back to the boat with him. I went ashore and left him to it.'

'Hold it. You say he went missing. I understood he went back to England.'

Steve shrugged. 'Could be, but I doubt it. When I came back on board the next day there was no sign of him or Maria. He'd just gone – and without any of his belongings. I reckon it's odds on that he's dead. Anyway, because of that, last night I thought I'd keep an eye open to see what happened.'

'Why didn't you come on board and speak to me then?'

'Ah, come on, mate. You were alone on the boat with the delightful Maria. I'm sure that you'd have welcomed me with open arms.'

In spite of his sore nose, Nick grinned. 'Point taken, carry on.'

'There's not much more to tell. I hid on a nearby boat I knew was empty and kept watch – bloody cold I got too. I saw Maria run away – what the hell did you do to her?'

'Nothing – that was the trouble.'

Steve grinned licentiously. 'I'll have to take your word for that.'

'I don't give a damn whether you take my word or not.'

'Anyway, I decided to wait on. I saw you leave the boat and walk ashore and I saw the others get out of the car and follow, so I joined in. There you have it.'

'I'm sure there's more. I have a distinct feeling you know who the muggers were.'

'Hell, yes. They were no ordinary muggers – that's why we had to get out fast, and that's why I think Beardsley is dead.'

'Who the hell are they? And how do you know them? Don't keep me in suspense.'

'Most people living on the island know Pierre Ricard and his two henchmen. He's the chief hit man for the Union Corse.'

'And who the hell are they? Could they be protecting Maria?'

'I doubt it. That bastard would as soon kill her as look at her. She works for him. Sleeps with friends and seduces people generally. She's well equipped for that kind of work, as you've no doubt noticed. I quite like the little bitch really. I feel sorry for her, being controlled by that animal, Ricard.'

'Now tell me about this Union Corse. I suppose they're some kind of secret society.'

'Sort of. All the militant separatist groups originally worked together as the Corsican Liberation Front, but that broke into several splinter groups that are always at each other's throats. Like most of these so-called revolutionary groups the world over they're more interested in power and what they can get for themselves than in separation from France. The Union Front of Corsica is the biggest of these. It has outstripped the others and it's become a kind of Mafia. Drugs, prostitution, murder – you name it and they've got their dirty fingers in it. The Union may not be as famous as the Mafia, but, God knows, they are just as vile, if not more so.' Steve's voice had become bitter as he spoke and the laughter in it had turned to hatred.

'You sound like you've got a personal thing about them.'

'Oh, yes I have. I've come to love Corsica. It really is the Isle of Beauty, but these bastards are ruining it and terrorizing the ordinary people who just want to live in peace.'

'Why hasn't something been done about them? Hell, man, this is France, not some third world country.'

'Too true. But this is also Corsica and, along with its beauty, it's got a history of bandits and violence. Unfortunately, most of the police and the judiciary are under their thumb – either by blackmail, bribery or threat – and no one knows who to trust. To take action in court you need witnesses, and they are in short supply – too many of them die early.'

'You seem to be remarkably well informed. Do you know who the leader is?'

'I made it my business to be well informed. A guy tends to live longer if he knows who not to cross. That was my philosophy, but I had to go and meet up with you – now I've blown it. The leader is a sadistic bastard called Debert. He looks like an office clerk – but I'm told that Himmler did too. You want to hope you never meet up with him – he makes Ricard look like an angel.'

'It's all too far-fetched. If what you say is true, Maria obviously went to the bar with the intention of picking me up. But why? That's what I'd like to know. Were the American's involved?'

'I'd guess not. At least, the skipper is unlikely to have been. He's quite well-known and respected. Maybe the youngster was, but it's doubtful.'

Nick was silent for a while, thinking. 'It's that bugger Harlow. That's it. It has to be Harlow. Christ, I should have known better.'

'Who's this guy Harlow you keep on about?'

Nick looked at his companion with narrowed eyes. 'I wish I could believe you're as innocent as you make out. If I ever find out different, I'll wring your bloody neck. For now, just take it that he's a man I know who has a nasty habit of getting me into tight spots. He works for a government Department which doesn't seem to exist – at least, no one will admit to knowing it.'

'Sounds like you mix with strange people. Maybe it's a good thing we're out of Corsica. Pity one way, though. I was just beginning to have fun with this little sheila in Ajaccio. Hey, Nick, you should have seen her – like Venus with arms she is. Now if I'd only . . .'

'I'm sorry to interrupt a report of your love life, but we have a more immediate problem on our hands. Where the hell do we go now? We can't go on moving around in circles.'

'Good point. Let's hoist the sails and sail off west into the sunset.'

'Except that the sun has only just risen, it seems better than nothing.'

Steve continued. 'Then we'll alter course to the south-west as soon as we're clear of land. If Ricard is determined to get to you

– and if he wasn't before, he sure as hell is now – he'll assume that we're headed for Gibraltar and home. If what I've heard about him is right, he'll take steps to intercept us on the way.'

'God, you really are comforting, aren't you? Okay, what do we do? You tell me.'

'We head out south-west until we're out of sight then we double back and go to the one place the Union is reluctant to operate – the home of the Mafia: Sicily. We lie low there until you've contacted your mate, Harlow, and everything has quietened down. Then you go back to England and I'll see what the sheilas are like in Sicily. I always fancied the dark Latin types and I'm dead keen on spaghetti.'

'Harlow is not my mate and I couldn't give a damn about your bloody sheilas, but otherwise I agree. The way things are going, we'll probably end up tangling with the Mafia too. Maybe I should try to call up Harlow with the radio.'

Steve shook his head. 'Sorry, no go. The thing's buggered. Beardsley had it in pieces trying to get it to work a couple of days before he disappeared, but he gave it up. Apparently, you can receive on it but there's no way you can transmit.'

'Well, maybe it's for the best. Too many people could listen in. Let's head for Sicily.'

4

Nick felt much better now that he had some sort of plan to work to and, at the wheel with the boat creaming along, sails stretched taut by the fresh, northerly wind, he was able to think more constructively. The only noise was the water rushing past the hull and the slight creaking of the rigging.

They had already decided that they should sail back to Sicily by way of the Straits of Bonifacio which separate Corsica and Sardinia. Although there was a slight risk of being spotted from the shore, it was very unlikely and to go round either island would add considerably to the journey. The only real problem was deciding how far to go on their present south-westerly course. If they held it too long they stood a chance of being overhauled by some sort of power-boat, but if they turned back too soon they increased the chance of being seen from the shore. Nick judged that Ricard would refer to his boss before putting to sea in pursuit and that they probably had a few hours start. He therefore planned to turn onto a more southerly course in another two hours. At the speed they were sailing that would keep them more than ten miles away from the coast. When they sailed through the straits it would probably be early in the morning and, anyway, they would keep to the Sardinian side, well away from any prying eyes on the cliffs at Bonifacio.

Ricard was furious. His neck and head ached horribly and he had lost face in front of his men. Perhaps the worst thing of all was that, as Nick had surmised, he had to go back and report failure to his boss – Jean Debert. Of deceptively mild appearance,

Debert was known for cruelty, not tolerance, and he was the one man Ricard really feared. Now he stood before him – and, as he faced the scholarly-looking man with thinning grey hair and steel-rimmed glasses, he knew that his position, indeed his life, hung in the balance. In the Union Corse you did not hand in your resignation, nor were you given formal notice – departure tended to be permanent.

'Monsieur Debert, that's the full story. I've hidden nothing.' Ricard always called him Monsieur Debert. 'If it had not been for the intervention of that bloody Australian we would have Byers here now. That slut, Maria, is to blame and I will deal with her. She will never fail again. You can be sure of that.'

'You will do nothing of the kind.' Debert's voice was as deceptive as his appearance. He was softly spoken, but those who knew him could detect the menace just below the surface. He stood up and turned his back on Ricard to gaze out of the window. The view across the rocky terrain and down to the blue sea was wonderful, but he did not notice it. He was too concerned about the danger they were in owing to Ricard's failure. 'You are to blame personally, Ricard. Do not try to pass your failure on to others. You know the importance of this operation. You have failed me twice. With Beardsley you were foolish enough to use your gun instead of your head; now you have let Byers slip through your fingers.'

'But ...' Ricard tried to interrupt but Debert waved him to silence.

'As you know, I do not tolerate failure at any time but this time it is vital that you do not fail again. Which way did they head when they got out to sea? They have two choices. Either they head for the French mainland or south-west for Gibraltar and home.'

'I kept a watcher on the coast and he has reported they are heading south-west, so it seems likely they are making for Gibraltar. Since they left in a hurry they will probably stop off in the Balearics for more provisions.'

'Place agents there and at Gibraltar. Also alert our men in Marseille, in case they alter course. Where is the big power-boat?'

'Unfortunately, it is in Bastia for a refit at the moment. It will take at least four or five hours to get round and in pursuit.'

'What else do we have on this side of the island?'

'Nothing that could mount a suitable chase. They are so far away now that radar will be required. We can easily take over one of the boats in Calvi. None of the owners would dare to object.'

Debert swung round and spoke sharply. 'Fool! The last thing we must do is to attract attention to ourselves in this. No, send a couple of small boats – maybe they will be lucky. Get the big boat around as a matter of urgency. Tell the skipper there will be a large reward if he finds them.'

'Yes, Monsieur Debert. Have no fear, I will get it back for you.'

'You are the one who should fear, Ricard. You have failed twice and, as I said, I do not like failure. To fail a third time would be totally unacceptable. Now go.'

The room in the old part of Calvi was small but clean and tidy. Efforts had obviously been made to make it a home. Cheap pictures adorned the walls and worn, cuddly toys were arranged on top of the chest of drawers. A crucifix hung on the wall above her bed where Maria sat hunched, pressed into the corner of the room. She had her knees drawn up to her chin and was sobbing uncontrollably. She knew that Ricard would come for her, and was terrified of what he might do. Her beautiful hair hung down untidily across her tear-streaked face. She was still dressed in the skirt and blouse she had worn the previous evening. The hands holding the tumbler of wine were shaking and, as she tried to drink, it splashed onto the bedding – but she was oblivious to it.

She didn't hear the footsteps on the stairs but when the door burst open her fear turned to horror. Ricard stood there, hands on hips, glaring. She shrank even further into the corner of the room.

'You failed me. You let me down, so I am in trouble with the boss. Now I will make you pay, as I promised.' His voice was cold. Slowly, he moved towards her, the menace clear in every step.

She put out a hand in a futile attempt to fend him off. He laughed and knocked it aside. Then he grasped the front of the blouse with one hand and lifted her until her face was only inches from his. She could smell his fetid breath as he leered at her.

'Now I'm going to teach you a little lesson,' he grated. He held her away from him and crashed his right hand across her face. First the palm to the left side, then the back of his hand to the other. He hit her slowly, time and time again, relishing the small cries of pain which were forced from her. The large rings on his fingers cut into her soft flesh until the blood flowed freely. When the cries stopped he threw her back onto the bed, where she lay whimpering, her face already swollen and covered with blood. He reached down to her again but this time when he grasped her blouse it was with two hands and he tore it from her, revealing her small, firm breasts. Then he reached for the skirt and tore that away as well, leaving her naked on the bed, her body shuddering with pain and fear. He dropped his trousers and pushed her legs apart. She made only the slightest groan as he forced himself roughly into her.

When he had finished he stood back and hauled up his trousers. 'That's a little taste of what you've got to come. I haven't got time to waste on you now but I'll be back. You're lucky I promised the boss not to kill you, but if you ever fail me again I certainly will.' She didn't hear him, for she had fortunately passed into unconsciousness. He looked down at her again and spat on her body before crashing from the room.

In the ground floor flat her landlady had listened to her cries. Even though she knew the girl's background, she liked young

Maria, but there was no way she would interfere. She knew Ricard and, like everyone else, was terrified of him. However, after the footsteps had thundered back down the bare wooden stairs, she made her way upstairs and knocked quietly on the door, calling softly, 'Maria, Maria. Are you all right?'

When there was no reply, she tried the door and found it unlocked. She slowly pushed it open and peered anxiously into the small room. Seeing the girl lying still on the bed she crossed tentatively towards her and looked down at her battered face. At first she thought that Maria was dead, but the girl made a slight murmur. The older woman reached out and touched her tenderly. She felt anger and hatred towards the evil man who had done this terrible thing. Forgetting her own fear in compassion for the injured girl she hurried down to the telephone and called the hospital.

As dusk closed in on them, Nick decided they had given any pursuers the slip, so he sailed closer to land. The occasional lights gave him some indication of their position, especially when they passed the mass of light that was Ajaccio, the capital of the island. He backed this up with constant reference to the electronic navigation system.

As he became used to the boat so his confidence increased and he began to enjoy the present, while putting the past in proper perspective. He pondered over the previous night and the events of the morning. Had he really been frightened about very little? What proof had he that he had fallen foul of the Union? Only the word of the young Australian, who was probably exaggerating the whole thing. Oh, sure, Nick thought, he wasn't intentionally lying – just making the most of a good story. It was far more likely that the gunman in the alley was a relation of Maria's and had decided to teach a lecherous foreigner a lesson. Yes, he could almost hear her relating to the man how she had been lured on board and assaulted. Of course – that was what had happened. Probably the same kind of thing had befallen Beardsley and he had taken fright in the same way and scuttled back to England.

The more he thought about it the more he became certain that he had found the truth. All the pieces fitted and he felt a lot happier. There would be no pursuit by vicious, gun-toting bandits, out for his blood; he was running away from an avenging relation who would certainly let the matter rest now that he had left Corsica. At first, he was tempted to call in at Bonifacio and put Steve ashore before heading for home, but he decided to stick to their agreed plan. There was no denying that the young Aussie had made himself unpopular in Corsica, whoever the attackers were. Anyway, it would be a nice sail down to Sicily and it would give him a chance to get to know the boat while he had Steve to help sail it. When he got to Sicily he would ring Sarah again and ask her to join him there – tactfully, of course.

While exercising care about Steve's imagination, Nick had no doubts about his seamanship. In consequence, he was able to leave him to keep watch by himself while he caught up on lost sleep. It had been a long day.

It was just dawn when they entered the Straits and, although they kept to the Sardinian side, Bonifacio seemed very close on that beautifully clear morning. Above them the taut white sails were silhouetted against the lightening sky as the boat surged along. They were making good speed now with the big genoa again forcing them on. They had hoisted the working jib instead during the night to give more control in case of an emergency in the dark.

They sailed uneventfully through the following day and night with Nick keeping a dead-reckoning chart – more for his own amusement than from necessity, since they had only to press a button to get an up-to-date position from their electronic equipment.

On the evening of the second day, they were out of sight of all land and experiencing the peace which all sailors feel when they are alone on a friendly sea. Nick decided that he would go below to his chart table and work out an estimated time of arrival at Palermo. In the Mediterranean this is a relatively simple thing to do because of the absence of major tides, but it still gave Nick a bit of mental exercise.

As he worked at the chart table, memories of Ricard faded to be replaced by pleasanter ones of Sarah. How he missed her and what a bloody fool he'd been. He completed plotting the course and collected a couple of cans of Fosters from the locker.

As he climbed into the cockpit he handed Steve one of the cans. 'There you go, digger. Have a tube.'

Steve pulled the tab off the can and took a long swig. 'You're obviously very pleased with yourself.'

Nick screwed up his face in concentration. 'I reckon that, give or take the odd few seconds, we'll be in Palermo at twenty-one hundred tomorrow evening.'

Steve shook his head slowly. 'Not a chance.'

'Well, I may have been a bit rash about the seconds – how about minutes?'

'No, I didn't mean that. I meant not a chance of getting there tomorrow, or possibly even the next day.'

'Come off it, my navigation isn't that bad.'

'Now don't get all hurt. It's just that I reckon we're in for one hell of a blow.'

Nick stuck out his jaw and looked around the horizon. There was a bit of high cloud forming but otherwise it was a fine evening. 'And what, may I ask, makes you think that? I'm beginning to believe you like bringing bad tidings. A right little Jeremiah, in fact.'

'I honestly don't know. It's just a feeling I get and it's not usually wrong.'

'You should rent yourself out to the met. office. In the meantime, go down and make some supper while we can still eat it. I'll take the wheel.'

Steve started down to the forward cabin and called over his shoulder, 'There's no need to be sarcastic. Just wait and see.'

Although he had taken the mickey out of Steve, Nick was disturbed by the forecast he had been given. He had heard of other people able to forecast bad weather without knowing why. The last thing he needed at that moment was a full-blooded gale. Although the boat looked in good nick generally, he hadn't had a chance to go over it in detail. He would have to take a few precautions.

When Steve came back to the cockpit, he was bearing steaming mugs of coffee, large hunks of bread and a slab of the strong local cheese. Nick grinned at him. 'Okay, you prophet of doom. At the first sign of the wind strengthening, we change to the storm jib and reef the main and the mizzen. How does that suit you?'

Steve nodded. 'I don't think you'll regret it.'

'Hang on. I'm not convinced of your forecast yet. However, in the unlikely event that it does blow hard, we'll take down the main and heave to on mizzen and jib. We've got plenty of sea room to play with.'

'Sounds good to me.'

By eight that evening the wind had freshened considerably. Nick shrugged his shoulders. 'Okay. You win. I'll reef the mizzen. Then you can go forward and change the jibs. And clip on a bloody life line. I don't fancy hunting around for you in the dark.'

Steve grinned and tugged at his forelock. 'Aye, aye, cap'n sir.'

Steve got more and more on edge as the wind strengthened during the evening. By ten o'clock it was blowing near gale force. Together they backed the jib and hauled down the mainsail. Then they tightened in the mizzen sheets and lashed down the helm. The boat was now hove to, lying almost across the wind and making very little headway. Nick knew they would get blown to leeward – maybe up to three knots, depending on the gale – but there was plenty of room before they got into danger.

Having stowed away all loose gear and lashed down the spinnaker pole, they took a final look round the horizon to check for lights before going below and shutting the hatches.

Gina Scarfiotti stormed out of the house. She had had enough. She loved her father and knew that he tried to keep her out of the business, but she was involved whether he liked it or not. What she saw was only a fraction of what actually happened, but even that was too much for her to stomach. She prayed that her father would give up the whole thing, but knew in her heart that it was impossible. It was a way of life into which he had been born, handed down from generation to generation. Now, however, it was coming to an end, for he had no son to carry on and times were changing.

Not only was Gina disgusted by the Organisation's activities but, more and more, it was affecting her personally. Every time she made a friend things went well until they learned who she was – then it was all over. The weak excuses just made it worse. She would go away to some place where no one knew her, a place where she could start afresh. She would get into her small cruising yacht and just sail away, never to return.

The wheels of the Alfa Romeo spun on the gravel as she accelerated and headed towards the harbour in a cloud of dust. Her driving was always inconsiderate, if not downright dangerous. Why did the police never stop her for speeding? It didn't occur to her that her father's position might have something to do with it.

The car skidded to a halt alongside a pontoon to which was moored to a tidy little seven-metre sloop. She didn't bother to check on provisions and fuel because it was always well stocked. Anyway, she had played out this very scene several times before, only to return after a few hours. This time, however, she meant to carry it through. She would sail up to the French Riviera, assume a false name and just get lost. She didn't have to worry about money; in fact, unlike most runaways, that was the least of her worries. Her bank account in Switzerland was more than just healthy.

It was that creep, Vincente, who had been the final straw. He had promised her eternal love – and she had believed him. He would never neglect her – that was until he learned who she really was. Then he remembered the dear old feeble mother whom he could never desert. He had had to send her a letter to tell her about it. He was sure she would understand. Sure, she understood: the cowardly creep didn't have the guts to say it to her face.

She hoisted the sails, cast off from the pontoon and headed out of the harbour; this time she would leave Palermo for good. She would keep in touch with her father but would not let him know where she had gone. Even though the wind was fresh she had hoisted the genoa, for she sailed in the same way as she drove a car. She sat at the helm and, as the wind ruffled her short, black hair and the boat heeled, dipping the lee gunwale, she calmed down – but she was still determined. Her black eyes flashed from her deeply tanned face – a face not beautiful, but very attractive. The mouth was a little too big and the nose a little too short but that simply added to the charm. She was of average height, and the T shirt and shorts just exaggerated her fine figure and lovely legs.

She sailed on through the day and as Sicily fell away astern she realized that she had never gone this far before. This was it. She sailed on a long starboard tack for most of the day before going about onto the port tack during the night. She didn't bother to lower the genoa during the dark neither did she bother with sleep. She made herself coffee at odd intervals and ate biscuits.

The next day was a repeat of the previous one, although she did manage to grab a few minutes sleep. Towards evening she felt the temperature drop and changed into jeans and a thick sweater, but thought no more about it. The Mediterranean seemed nearly empty of other shipping and she was still sailing under genoa and unreefed main when night fell. She was now so tired that she failed to notice the wind strengthening, until it was blowing half a gale. She donned a lifejacket and made her way forward to reduce sail. The genoa's halyards had jammed tight and, after fighting with them for what seemed ages, she realized that she would have to cut them. Had she been wide awake she would have taken in the mainsail, but tiredness had marred her judgement and she worked her way back to the cockpit to get a knife. It was then that a particularly vicious gust hit the boat and the boom crashed over. If Gina had been conscious when she splashed into the water she would have known she had committed another cardinal sin – she had not tied herself on. As she floated, semi-conscious, the small sloop ploughed on, shipping water fast through the open hatches.

Nick and Steve were warm and relatively dry, if not comfortable. Although the jib and the mizzen cut down the roll they tended to lay the boat almost on its beam ends. To make matters worse it was being tossed around like a cork in the ever-strengthening storm. The noise of the storm was as frightening as the actual movement. The wind roared through the rigging and waves crashed against the boat's sides. As the planks of timber creaked and groaned it seemed that they would be smashed to pieces, but the boat withstood all that nature threw at it. There were a couple of minor leaks from the hatches and the cabin lights but nothing serious. Nick's admiration and affection for the boat grew more and more with each minute that passed.

There was no hope of sleep and they just had to hang on. There was one almighty crash as a locker burst open and crockery was spread over the deck.

From time to time they took turns to stick their heads out into the cockpit, but most of the time was spent wedged in the leeward saloon bunk. When they did look out there was really very little to see except masses of white water. The short sea was vicious and hammered the boat in quick time; hardly had one wave crashed against the side before the next one followed it. It seemed that the wind was so strong that it was actually blowing the tops off the waves and reducing them in size, but it also cut down visibility to a few yards.

Shortly after midnight Steve attempted to climb the companionway ladder just as a particularly violent wave picked up the boat and threw it sideways. The Aussie was hurled onto the top of the port pilot berth landing in an uncomfortable heap, bruising his ribs and banging his head.

'Bugger this,' he said when he had extracted himself and got back to the saloon berth. 'That's the last bloody time I try to go up top.'

The storm raged on through the night, but during the forenoon the wind dropped to a stiff breeze, and the short, vicious sea began settling back. Nick made his way to the cockpit. The sun was shining brightly and being reflected by the wet decks.

Nick leaned into the cabin. 'Come on, you lazy sod, the danger's over. Climb out of your cotton wool and come up to see the world. The sun is burning your eyeballs out. It's time we got this boat under way.'

Steve's head appeared at the hatchway. 'Have some patience, anyone would think you were in a hurry to get somewhere.'

'I am in a hurry – to get the sails up so that you can make some breakfast; I'm starving. We'll leave the storm jib up and hoist a reefed main. We'll take it easy until everything calms down properly.'

'Okay, I may as well humour you.' He hooked on a safety line and climbed out onto the side deck. There he stopped and stared down to the south.

'What's wrong with you now? Have I got to do it myself?'

'I thought I saw something in the water.'

'What sort of something? Another boat?'

'No. It was more like an orange buoy, or a lifejacket or something. It's difficult to see properly looking into the sun.'

Nick climbed up beside him and together they scanned the sea to the south. Suddenly, Nick pointed. 'There! I see it too. Come on, let's get the engine started and find out what it is. I'll take control while you act as look out.'

Gradually they approached the object.

'It's a man in a lifejacket,' Steve shouted.

'Right, you take the helm and I'll see if I can pull him out.'

As Steve lay the boat skilfully alongside the man in the water, it was obvious that he was either unconscious or worse, so Nick took the end of the main sheet and hung over the side. He made the sheet secure under the lifejacket and between them they tried to lift him on board by his arms, but he was too heavy.

'Steve, get the diving ladder and fit it this side. I'll hang onto him, but for God's sake hurry.'

With the ladder in place Nick lashed himself to the boat and climbed down so that he was able to get his shoulder under the man. Together they were able to lift him slowly onto the side deck. 'Let's get him into the cockpit. We don't want to lose him now. I'm buggered – I couldn't get him out again.'

Before they moved him, Steve checked that his mouth was clear, then gave him two or three breaths with the kiss of life. In the cockpit he carried on with the resuscitation, while Nick fetched a blanket to throw over the sodden figure.

Suddenly, Steve yelled. 'Nick, he's alive. He's breathing and there's a pulse. He's only a youngster though. Can't be more than sixteen. Poor little bugger.'

'Let's get him into the after cabin and take these clothes off. He's probably suffering from hypothermia so the quicker we get him wrapped up in dry blankets the better.'

Now that he was out of the water, the youngster was quite light, in spite of the sodden clothes, and, between them, they had no trouble carrying him into the after cabin. They laid him on the port berth, after first covering it with a waterproof sheet. 'No point in getting him dry, then letting him lie in a soggy bunk. You go back to the cockpit, Steve, I'll manage from here.'

Okay, boss, but should I have a search around in case there are others? He's a bit young to be out by himself.'

'Good idea. I'll get this lad wrapped up warm, then come up to join you.' While they were talking, Nick had eased the sodden sweater and T-shirt gently over the lad's head. 'Bloody hell, have we ever made a mistake.'

Steve swung round and looked at the figure lying half naked on the bunk. 'Jesus! Two mistakes – age and sex. Shall I stay while you take the wheel, captain?'

'Get lost. I'll be with you shortly.'

Nick turned his attention back to the figure on the bunk. Their survivor was a well-developed girl, probably in her mid-twenties. He pulled off the wet jeans and the flimsy panties and threw them on the deck. Having towelled her as dry as possible he covered her with a thick blanket. Finally, he unzipped one of the sleeping bags and eased her inside, complete with the blanket. He checked she was breathing properly. Only then did he strip off his own clammy clothes and put on dry ones.

'How's our prize catch?' Steve greeted him as he climbed into the cockpit.

'I reckon she'll live, thanks to you. If you hadn't seen her she wouldn't have stood a snowball's hope in hell of surviving. There's no other shipping around, is there?'

'Not a thing. I've started a sort of box search in case there are others in the water. There's no sign of anything yet. No wreckage – nothing.'

'Well done. We'll complete your search pattern. If there's still nothing we'll think again. In the meantime, I'll check that she is alive every fifteen minutes.'

'I don't mind helping with that.'

'I'm sure you don't, you randy bugger, but I'll manage somehow. I need your eagle eyes up here.'

It was on the second visit below that Nick noticed a change in the girl. Her breathing was stronger and some colour had returned to her face. He bent over and laid his hand on her forehead to find that it was quite warm. As he did so her eyes flickered open. They steadied as she gazed up at him in silence.

'Don't be frightened. You're quite safe now.' He spoke soothingly in English, not thinking that she might not understand.

She tried to speak but only a croak came.

'Take your time. You'll be all right.'

The girl tried again. 'Who are you? Where am I?' She spoke in English but it was quite strongly accented.

'My name is Nick Byers, and this is my boat, *White Albatross*. You joined us the difficult way – we fished you out of the sea after the storm. Now, since you can talk all right, we need to know if you were alone or whether we should carry on looking for more survivors.'

'I was alone. I was sailing in my boat and I tried to take in some sails when the storm began. I don't remember what happened, but I must have been knocked overboard.' Nick found her accent surprisingly attractive.

'Okay, girl. I won't be a second.' He turned to the bottom of the ladder and called up. 'The girl's awake. She was alone, so we can quit searching. Get some sails up and stop the engine. Set a course due south and I'll be with you soon to work out a proper one.'

Turning back he spoke softly. 'Now, young lady, tell me about yourself and where you were heading.'

She looked at him with her big black eyes and after a moment's hesitation said, 'My name is Gina – Gina Scarfiotti.' She stared at him as if expecting some sort of recognition. When she saw none she continued more confidently, 'I live in Palermo and I was sailing alone in my boat to visit France, but the storm caught me unprepared. I think my boat must have sunk, because the sails were still up and the hatches were open. Don't look at me like that. I know I made mistakes, but I was tired.'

Nick smiled at her. 'I'm not condemning you, Gina. I'm just

happy that we were around to pull you out. We are heading for Palermo so we'll be able to see you safe home. Now if you'd care to wriggle out of the blanket and pass it to me you'll be more comfortable in just the sleeping bag until I can find some dry clothes.'

Gina did as she was told, then she peeped inside the sleeping bag before looking at Nick with a wry smile. 'You…?' she queried.

Nick nodded with a grin. 'Yes, but don't be embarrassed. You have nothing to be ashamed of.'

Gina chuckled. 'You are not alone?'

'No, I have an Australian guy, called Steve, crewing for me. He's the one who spotted you in the sea. I'm going up to relieve him now so he can come down to meet you and make you a hot drink. He's probably got some clothes that will be nearer to your size than mine are.' He turned to go.

'Nick.' She smiled up at him and reached out her hand; as he took it she said simply, 'Thank you.'

As he climbed up to the cockpit he found that the wind had dropped right away and the sea was calm and clear of white horses. With the sun shining brightly, it was like another world, the previous night's storm just a bad dream. But, like all sailors who weather a severe storm, he had a wonderful sense of satisfaction mixed with relief. 'Right, Steve, I'll take over now and you can go and make your number with the lovely lass below. It's a new world up here, isn't it?'

'It certainly is. That's one thing about the Med. – the weather changes so quickly and, being a short sea, it reacts quickly too. Now tell me about the girl. What's her name?'

'Gina Scarfiotti. It's a funny thing, but I got a feeling that she expected me to know it.'

'Scarfiotti,' repeated Steve. 'You know, I think I've heard it before but I'm damned if I know where. Maybe it will come to me after I've talked to her.'

'While you're down there I'll try to plot our course to Palermo, which, incidentally, is her home. It would seem that she was heading for France all by herself. I know lots of people go in for lone sailing, but I get a feeling there's something not quite right here.'

'Leave it to me, mate, I'll find out everything. Girls crumble in front of me. I don't know whether it's my good looks or my charm.'

Nick grinned. 'Get lost, you conceived little bugger.'

When Steve had left the cockpit Nick considered the navigation. He would have liked to fix his position manually with the sextant he had seen below, but he opted instead for the GPS method. Although not as satisfying, he had to admit that it was more convenient and probably more accurate. He was quite surprised to see that they hadn't drifted far during the night. He plotted the position on the chart and laid off a course for Palermo, making a small allowance for leeway since the wind had veered slightly and was now coming onto the port beam, giving them a broad reach – a true soldier's wind.

Down in the after cabin Steve and Gina were getting along well and he succeeded in making her laugh freely for, in spite of his facetiousness, Steve did indeed possess considerable charm. However, he found himself quite unable to prise out any information of value about her background by indirect questioning. Eventually, he gave up trying. 'How would you like some coffee? I can't supply espresso but at least it won't be instant.'

'It sounds great. I'm very hungry as well if you can manage something to eat. I can't remember when I ate last.'

'I'll cook it myself. Would you like eggs, bacon and the rest – the whole works?'

She laughed. 'Oh, no, no. Just some toast, if you have some.'

'We have some. Is there anything else you would like?'

'If you could find me some clothes, I could get up. I feel well enough to sit in the sunshine and I want to see the rest of the boat.'

He bent down to the drawers under the bunk and, after fishing around, produced some jeans, a T-shirt and a sweater. 'These belonged to the previous skipper. He was quite small so they should fit you, with a few tucks here and there. Your own clothes are flying from the guard rails and should be dry soon. I'll leave you to change and you can go up top when you're ready.'

They were all settled around the cockpit, relaxing in the early afternoon sun. Nick and Steve had stripped to the waist and Gina, demonstrating amazing powers of recovery, was stretched out on the cushion wearing the baggy T-shirt. Nick felt that this was the time to probe a little more into the girl's background.

'I hesitate to forecast a time of arrival after my last little effort, but I reckon that we'll be in Palermo early tomorrow afternoon. I'm sorry, Gina, but we have no radio so I can't call ahead to tell people you're safe. Will your family be worried about you?'

'No, I think not. There is only my father and he will not know that the boat sank.'

'But surely he'll know about the storm and you sailing alone. If I had a daughter I'd be worried stiff.'

'He didn't know I was sailing alone. He was away on a business trip when I left.'

'You mean to say that you sailed away to France, a couple of hundred miles, without telling him you were going?'

'He's a very busy man and we had quarrelled. I would have called him from France to make it better.' Yes, she thought, and by now he'd be busy turning Sicily inside out looking for her.

Nick had a feeling she was beginning to get a little touchy but he ploughed on. 'What does your father do for a living?'

'He's a business man.'

'What business?'

'He buys and sells things. Now, I'm tired so, if you'll excuse me, I'll go below for sleep.'

'Use the after cabin. I'll sleep in the pilot's berth and Steve has got the pipe-cot in the bows. I'm sorry if I upset you with my questions.'

'It's all right. I'm not upset,' she lied as she made for the companionway. 'Thank you for being so kind.' She had left quickly, but not before Nick had noticed the tears in her eyes.

'Hell, Steve, I didn't mean to upset her, but there's something very strange about the whole thing. People don't just sail away without a word to their family and friends, unless they're running away. What's more, from her actions in the storm it's clear that she was unprepared. She probably left in a hurry.'

'Maybe you're right, but I don't think she's on the run from the law. I would know – I'm sure I would.'

'I hope your masculine intuition is right. Anyway, we'll leave it for now – all will be revealed tomorrow. I think we ought to keep a close eye on her tonight, just in case. When you're on watch don't leave her alone on deck.'

'Don't worry, mate. I'll watch her all the time – with great pleasure.'

Down in the after cabin the girl lay on the bunk and sobbed quietly. She just couldn't get away. Everywhere she went it followed her. Those two nice guys up on deck had saved her life and she couldn't be honest with them, even though they clearly suspected something was amiss.

They sailed on through the afternoon and an uneventful night. Gina had recovered her composure and made a point of keeping them both company for a spell during the watches. She kept them supplied with coffee, and informed about Sicily in general, but nothing about her personal life.

During the forenoon the next day they spotted land. It appeared first as a hazy shadow on the horizon, but as they drew closer it took a more distinct form.

Nick couldn't make out any landmarks and he passed the binoculars to Gina. 'Can you recognize anything, Gina? We should be bang on course.'

Gina quietly swept the land ahead, before handing them back. 'It's Sicily.'

'Hell, girl, I know it's Sicily. Tell me how we get in to Palermo. That must be Capo Gallo right ahead.'

'Sorry, Nick, you're miles off course. That cape away to starboard is Capo St Vito and it's about fifty kilometres west of Gallo with the Gulf of Castellammare between them.'

'It can't be. You must be mistaken. We couldn't possibly have steered such a bad course and there are virtually no tides to worry about. Have another look.'

'I don't need another look. I've sailed these waters often and I know just where we are. If you don't believe me go and check it on your GPS.'

'I'll do just that.' He swung himself down into the cabin. Only minutes later he reappeared and the look on his face was enough to show what he had found. 'I'm sorry for doubting you, Gina. Steve, come round to port as close to the wind as you can get. Fortunately, it has backed a little so we may make Capo Gallo on one tack. Keep an eye on that damned compass though – it must be all to cock. It must have been the storm. It must have moved the magnets or something. It looks as if it will be early evening when we get there. So much for my forecasts.

They rounded Capo Gallo with plenty of sea room to spare. When they had passed the headland and turned south into the Gulf of Palermo, Nick took the opportunity to check the compass by steering along some transits he had taken from the charts. He discovered it to be more than ten degrees out and decided that it would be wise to spend a little time correcting it. With Steve at the helm steering carefully along the transit, Nick was able to alter the adjustment magnets to bring it back into alignment.

'That's the best I can do for the time being, but I'd like to do it properly when we have more time to spare.'

'Well, there you have it, sir. It would seem there was some sort of disturbance ashore and Byers sailed the boat away in a hurry. That's all we really know, except that the following day a storm blew up out of nowhere and nothing has been heard of it since.

Byers wasn't used to the boat so it's possible that it sank.' Harlow sat still, waiting for some kind of reaction from the Chief.

'John, I can't help feeling that it's the best thing for all concerned.'

'Except Byers,' muttered Harlow.

'Of course I feel sorry about Byers, but sacrifices have to be made. Now, I think you forgot to tell me about the back-up agent out there.'

Hell, thought Harlow. You couldn't get anything past this man. 'Yes, sir, I did place a man out there some time ago. He was more or less on a training mission until this thing with Beardsley blew up. It's all been cleared with French Intelligence. Unfortunately, I've heard nothing from him since before the boat sailed.'

'Okay, John, recall him and wrap the case up. If Byers has sunk then it's all over, if he turns up we'll have to think again. In the meantime, let's try to get everyone and everything out of Corsica.'

'As soon as I can, sir.'

But Harlow had already decided it would be a while before he actioned it. He had a feeling Byers would turn up somewhere and that the operation was still running.

Ricard stood in front of Debert's desk. This time he wasn't exactly reporting failure; it was more lack of success. 'That's it, M. Debert. There's not a sign of them anywhere and we are of the opinion that the boat has sunk and the disc with it. So, really, we have succeeded in our efforts.'

'We have not succeeded, Ricard. We do not know for sure that it was on board. It may be lodged ashore somewhere and the boat was a diversion. What's more, we do not *know* that the boat has sunk. Just pray that it survived so we can make sure. Now keep up the surveillance in Marseilles, the Balearics and Gibraltar.'

* * *

'What do we do now, James?' The Englishman's voice trembled. 'If the boat's lost in the storm, we've lost everything. I knew we should have got it off the night Byers arrived.'

'Don't be stupid, Harold. How could we? Beardsley didn't tell us where he was hiding it. Anyway, you saw that he took that slut, Maria, back to the boat with him. I'm sure he'd have been only too pleased to talk business with us,' he finished sarcastically.

'So, what do we do now?' repeated Harold.

'We wait and watch for a couple of days, and if there's no news we get the hell out of Corsica and try hard to cover our trail.'

'That means losing everything.'

'But we'll still be alive – hopefully.'

After the boat had rounded Capo Gallo, Nick was able to get a first sight of Palermo. It was much bigger than he had anticipated. Gina directed them towards the harbour, but she was obviously disturbed.

'Do you have to report to the *carabinieri* when you arrive?'

'I think it's wise, even if we *are* all in the European Union. Officials like using their rubber stamps and it will save a lot of hassle later on. We told you something of our problems on the way over, so you can see that we can't afford trouble here. Why do you ask?'

'It's just that I'd rather you didn't say I am on board.'

Nick frowned. 'Come on, Gina. Are you on the run from the law?'

She shook her head. 'No, Nick. I promise you on the Blessed Virgin that I am not.'

'Okay. You point out where we tie up, then go below. If no one asks I will say nothing but I will not lie. That's the best I can do.'

Nick brought the *White Albatross* into the harbour under engine with Steve standing on the side deck ready to jump ashore with the mooring lines, an act which proved unnecessary since the quay was lined with quite a crowd of people, many of whom proved very willing to help. Gina had remained below as agreed and was therefore out of the view of the *carabiniere* officer, who stood out from the rest in his highly decorated uniform. He came to attention as the boat was made fast, saluted Nick smartly and spoke in excellent English.

'Phillipo Fiore at your service, Signor. I am pleased to welcome you to Palermo and hope that you have had a good voyage.'

'Other than getting caught in a severe storm, a good voyage. Now that we are all in the European Union, do we still have to fill in a lot of papers?'

'No, it will not be necessary. I'll just make a record of your names and your last port of call. That should be sufficient.'

Fiore took notes with his gold pen as Nick provided the information, but they reached a stumbling block when it emerged that Steve was Australian. However, as soon as he produced his passport everything was fine.

'Signor, I must ask if you are the only people on board.'

Nick hesitated for a second, then decided that they couldn't possibly afford to take chances. 'No. There is a young lady below, but she is Sicilian.'

'I see. What is her name?'

'Gina Scarfiotti.'

Nick certainly didn't expect the reaction this information produced. Fiore's mouth dropped open and his gold pen and note pad fell into the sea. 'G-Gina S-Scarfiotti?' he stammered.

'That's right. Shall I fetch her?'

Fiore nodded silently and Nick swung down the companionway. 'Sorry, Gina, but I had to tell him. Do you know Fiore?' She shook her head. 'Well, he sure as hell knows you. He almost had apoplexy when I mentioned your name. Now I think you should let me in on the secret, before we go up top to see him, don't you?'

'Yes, Nick. I'm sorry. I should have told you before, but I just couldn't. I am the daughter of Giuseppe Scarfiotti, who is the head of the Palermo Cosa Nostra – the Mafia to you.'

Now it was Nick's turn to stare open-mouthed. 'Oh, shit. First the Union Corse and now the Mafia – and I'm trying to keep a low profile.'

'At least you haven't upset the Mafia. Quite the reverse – you are returning Papa's daughter to him.' Then, for the first time, her mouth widened into a grin. 'Of course, I shall have to tell him that you stripped all my clothes off.'

He thumped his forehead theatrically. 'Oh, no. Not that. Will he kill me?'

'Of course, and very slowly. Maybe you will be made to marry me instead.' She stood up and put her arms round him and kissed him. 'Thank you again, Nick. I owe you my life and Papa will be truly grateful. My mother is dead and I am his only child. Now let's go and face the law.'

On the quay Fiore had recovered some of his composure and he greeted Gina with respect but, in obvious deference to Nick and Steve, continued to use English. 'Signorina Scarfiotti, I am delighted to see you. Your father has been most worried for you and there is an alert all over the island. When your boat was missing we feared you might be lost in the storm.'

'I would have been if it had not been for these two gentlemen, who pulled me from the sea. The boat has gone.'

Fiore nodded to the other two. 'In that case, you are doubly welcome to our city. Signorina, I have taken the liberty of sending a messenger to inform your father of your presence and I'm sure he'll be here shortly.'

'I'm sure he will. Let's wait for him on board the boat. Nick can open another bottle of his wine.'

5

The large black Mercedes drove slowly along the quayside, which had emptied as if by magic once the word had got around. The highly polished bodywork of the car gleamed in the bright sunshine. As it drew to a halt alongside the boat the front-seat passenger leapt out and, after a good look round, opened the rear door. A large man climbed out and also took a quick look round. Satisfied with what he saw, he bent down and spoke to somebody in the car. Nick watched, fascinated. He had tried to imagine the kind of man Gina's father would be and he felt something of an anticlimax as the very ordinary looking businessman emerged. He was short but well-built. His well-groomed, black hair was beginning to grey at the temples and recede from the sun-tanned forehead. He was dressed soberly in a dark-grey suit with a white shirt and blue necktie. Nick thought he looked like many people's idea of a prospective Tory candidate and placed him in his late fifties.

Gina jumped up onto the quay and threw her arms round her father while the others followed more slowly. Nick saw Gina stand back while still holding her father's hands and he could hear her talking quietly in Italian. He saw Scarfiotti nod at intervals and glance in his direction a couple of times as they all stood, awaiting an audience. All the time, the passengers from the car were keeping a careful watch on them and the surrounding area. They were dressed in dark suits like their boss, but in their case the jackets were pulled out of shape slightly by the shoulder holsters. The driver had now left the car and was carefully polishing the bonnet to remove the dust which had dared to settle there.

After a while Gina stopped talking and led her father across to them. Fiore sprang to attention and saluted smartly. Scarfiotti acknowledged the salute with a brief nod and spoke quickly to him, both thanking and dismissing him. Fiore saluted again, almost clicking his heels, and marched off towards his car which was parked nearby. Nick was quite disgusted at this display of subservience by a law officer to a gangster.

Scarfiotti turned to the others and held out his hand to Nick. 'I understand from my daughter that I have you to thank both for saving her from an almost certain death and returning her to me. I am, of course, truly thankful and am in your debt. If I can be of any service to you please tell me, for it is a debt I will never be able to repay fully.'

His English was excellent and there was no doubting the sincerity of his words. As he spoke, his eyes seemed to look deep inside them, as if searching for their innermost thoughts. Nick revised his opinion – this was no ordinary businessman.

'Think nothing of it,' replied Nick with a dismissive wave of the hand. 'We are only too pleased that we were in the right place at the right time.'

'Maybe, but I understand that you have been told my position. Many men would have taken advantage of my daughter's plight to get to me. I am truly grateful that she fell into the hands of honourable men. Now I insist that you come to my house for dinner this evening. I will send a car for you at eight o'clock and the dress will, of course, be casual. I am aware that yachting people do not carry a full wardrobe around with them.' He thanked them again and guided Gina to the car.

As they drove away Steve wiped his hand across his forehead. 'Phew! I'm glad that one is on our side.'

'Me too. I don't suppose he's any better than the bossman of the Union Corse and I'm reluctant to accept help from him, but with things as they are it may be essential. In fact I wouldn't turn away the devil himself if he wanted to help. Now I've just got time to make that telephone call I spoke about earlier.'

He had already found out the whereabouts of the nearest phone and blessed this age when it was possible to use plastic cards for everything, including telephone calls. Maybe, he thought, there was some point to monetary union.

Sarah was worried. It was days since she had spoken to Nick and he had made no attempt to call her again. That was unlike him. He could be very unreasonable at times but he didn't sulk. She had tried calling Harlow on their special contact number but was told he was out of the office for several days. How true that was she had no way of telling.

She was getting quite desperate when the receptionist called her room as she was dressing for dinner. 'There's a Nick Byers calling you from Palermo, Miss Drew.'

'Palermo! Okay, put him through.'

'Nick, where the devil have you been and what are you doing in Sicily? That's not on the way home. I thought you could navigate. Oh, Nick, I've been worried stiff. Why didn't you call me?'

'I'm sorry. I couldn't call you earlier – I was at sea. It's a long story and I'll tell you all about it if you fly out here to join me – please.' He emphasized the last word.

'Well, it's a better approach, Nick. I'll give you that. Now tell me why I should.'

'Mainly because I need you. Oh, Sarah, you're so important to me. I have a beautiful boat here, the weather is wonderful and I've got a great young Aussie crewing for me. All I need is you – please come.'

'Hang on a minute. Is the Aussie male or female?'

'Male, of course. Steve is a young guy and you'll like him when you meet him. If you come, that is.'

'Oh, Nick, for a grown man you can be incredibly stupid at times, but I guess I was no better. I'll come. I'll have to, because you can't be trusted to look after yourself. I'll check on flights and ring you back. What number can I get you on?'

'Sorry, I haven't got a number here – this is a public phone. I'm going out to dinner tonight but I'll ring you first thing tomorrow to find out what you've been able to arrange.'

'And who might you be going out to dinner with in a strange place?'

'The boss man of the Mafia,' Nick replied truthfully.

'I see that you haven't lost your warped sense of humour,' Sarah said with a laugh.

The car that arrived to collect Nick and Steve was the same Mercedes they had seen earlier. This time the rear-seat bodyguard was driving and he was alone. As he greeted them with a firm handshake, Nick realized for the first time just how big the man was.

'I'm Paolo. Signor Scarfiotti asked me to collect you.' As he spoke, he smiled and his whole face lit up in an expression of friendship. He was unusually fair for an Italian and his eyes were blue. Nick had a hard job to see him as the Mafioso and killer he undoubtedly was.

'Hello, Paolo. I'm Nick and this is Steve.'

The giant grinned. 'We have heard how you saved Signorina Gina and everyone is very grateful to you. We all love her very much – she is a fine young lady.'

The car swept them through the city centre and out into the wooded countryside. Nick quickly became aware of the fact that other traffic gave way to them, even in a country noted for its aggressive drivers. It was only a short time before they swung into a driveway and approached some huge wrought-iron gates. On either side of the gates a high wall stretched away. The area outside the wall had been cleared of all vegetation for several metres back. They waited for a short time while video cameras mounted on either side scrutinized them. Then the gates slowly swung open. Paolo stopped the car just inside and another big man approached and looked around inside the car while a third kept close watch from the lodge – he held a machine pistol. The first man nodded to Paolo and he unlatched the car boot. The man glanced quickly inside, then slammed the lid down. Coming back to the site he muttered, 'Okay, Paolo.' and raised his hand as the big Italian pulled slowly away.

'I'm sorry about that, but it is necessary to be careful. Signor Scarfiotti has many enemies.'

'Hardly surprising,' muttered Nick, almost inaudibly.

The driveway curved through extensive grounds almost all of which were laid in well-kept lawns. Here and there was an odd mature tree but none were close to the wall or the house, which was large and elegant.

Gina met them at the door and kissed them on both cheeks. She was wearing a plain red dress with a full skirt and short sleeves. The only jewellery she wore was a silver locket on a chain round her neck. She looked quite stunning.

Steve whistled softly through his teeth. 'Is this the same woman that we pulled out of the sea?'

She laughed. 'It sure is, and she's delighted to see you again. Come inside and meet Papa properly and you'll see that he is no ogre.'

Scarfiotti was waiting for them in a beautiful reception room. The wood-panelled walls were hung with traditional paintings and the mosaic floor shone like a mirror. Having shaken them by the hand, he offered them glasses of sparkling wine.

'This is not champagne. Foreigners think we make only Chianti and Lambrusco in Italy, but we have our own excellent wines.' He raised his glass. 'To your health.'

Nick sipped the cold dry wine and nodded his appreciation. 'I must make a point of learning more about them.'

In the course of a delightful evening they found that their host made them very welcome and seemed interested in all their activities, especially Nick's diving adventures. He talked at length about Sicily, its history and its problems. They were careful not to ask about his affairs, even though it was difficult to imagine that this friendly, amusing man was head of one of the deadliest and most vicious societies in the world.

The evening passed quickly. Dinner was excellent and the wine good. All conversation was in English. Afterwards, as they sat in deep armchairs, Scarfiotti spoke to his daughter. 'Gina, why not show Steve around the house and the grounds. It's a beautiful night.'

As they left he turned to Nick. 'Gina said you experienced a little trouble in Corsica. Tell me all about it.'

Nick did as he was told without question. He finished up, 'Steve thinks the gunman was a guy called Ricard who's in the Union Corse, but I'm not so sure. I think he was probably connected to Maria in some way.'

Scarfiotti sat silently for a while. 'I hope that you are right and the man is not Ricard, for he is a very evil and dangerous man. As Steve said, he is the chief hit man in the Union and, like so many of his kind, he takes pleasure in his work. He is a sadist.'

Nick said nothing but could not help thinking that the man in front of him should be the last person to describe another like that.

Scarfiotti gazed at him with a rather sad smile. 'I can guess you are thinking this is a case of the pot calling the kettle black – I think that is how you say it?'

Nick nodded.

'Sadly it is partially true, but you should know something of the history of our organization before you condemn us totally. To put it very simply, we were formed in the nineteenth century to help protect the peasants and common people from exploitation by the wicked landowners. As with all groups which hold power it was abused in many ways. However, until recently, the old families limited their activities and concentrated mainly on illegal building speculation, bribery and so on. Prostitution, narcotics and their likes were against our beliefs. Unfortunately, offshoots had spread to the States and, during prohibition, these became strong and totally unscrupulous. When prohibition ended they turned their attentions to anything that would make money and increase their power. Some of these people saw an opportunity to return to Sicily and oppose the old families. They do not follow the codes and nothing is too bad for them. Extortion, narcotics, prostitution, murder: you name it, they do it. At present there is almost an open war between the old and the new – which is why I'm so well guarded.'

Nick had listened with fascination. Now he asked, 'And who is winning?'

'Unfortunately the newcomers have almost wiped out the old families,' replied Scarfiotti. 'Our days are numbered; then, God help the people of Sicily.'

He shrugged suddenly. 'Enough of that, back to your problem. I will make some enquiries and see if I can clarify the situation. You should be safe at the moment because, even if it is Ricard, he doesn't know you are in Palermo. If he finds out he would be unlikely to take any action against you while you are under my protection, and since there is no love lost between the Union Corse and the new people here he cannot enlist their help. I should know something by midday tomorrow.'

On the way back to the boat, Steve asked what Scarfiotti had said.

'Not a lot,' replied Nick. 'Mostly he was trying to justify his way of life and, what's more, he was very convincing. Maybe I just wanted to believe all he said, not only for our sakes but for Gina too. It's very difficult to rub shoulders with evil without some of it rubbing off on you. Anyway, at the moment I'm prepared to accept help from anyone and he said he'd try to find out what's happening in Corsica, so I guess he's got spies everywhere. He agrees we should be safe since no one knows where we are. So I'm going back to get a good night's sleep.'

He awoke early the next day and waited impatiently for the time difference to permit his calling Sarah at a reasonable hour. At eleven o'clock he decided that it was late enough and made his way to the phone. To his delight he found that Sarah had booked a flight to Palermo from Heathrow and was leaving the hotel directly. She should arrive in Sicily early the next day. Nick asked why she didn't fly direct from Glasgow, and was told that the clothes required for the Med. were somewhat different from those one wore in Scotland.

He made his way jubilantly back to the boat and found Steve lying back in the cockpit nursing a cup of coffee. He broke the news of Sarah's imminent arrival and was surprised to see that the younger man looked unusually solemn.

'I'm pleased for you Nick. I guess you won't be needing me any more, so I'll start looking for somewhere to stay.'

'Oh, come on, Steve. Don't be so bloody stupid. I want you to help with the running of the boat. You're welcome to stay for as long as you like – all the way back to UK if you wish.'

Steve's face brightened. 'You mean that? Are you sure I won't be in the way?'

'God, no. The boat's big enough for us not to get under each other's feet and I'm sure you and Sarah will get along fine.'

Steve sat up cheerfully. 'I think I'll take a stroll into town to get some provisions – if you've got some money, that is.'

Nick passed across a bundle of Euros he'd picked up when he'd gone to phone. 'Take this, but don't spend it all.' He grinned as Steve went away whistling happily.

Steve wasn't as happy when he returned to the boat a short time later – in fact he looked decidedly grim.

'And what the hell is the matter now?' asked Nick. 'You look as if you've dropped a pound and found a penny.'

Steve threw a copy of a local newspaper onto the cushion. 'Take a quick gander at that and you'll see. All the papers – Italian, French and English – seem to have got the story, although I must admit that this one has the best picture. Ricard has probably choked over his cornflakes.'

Nick picked up the paper and there, on the front page, was a picture of them in the cockpit. Even though it was written in Italian there was no mistaking the caption: 'British Yachtsmen Save Scarfiotti's Daughter'.

He leaned back and sighed. 'Bloody hell! Won't anything go right? It's too late to stop Sarah coming out, so we're stuck here until tomorrow morning – and what the hell do we do then? I only hope Scarfiotti turns up some good news.'

It was at that moment that Gina's Alfa Romeo appeared at the end of the quay and raced along towards them, coming to a stop with screeching brakes in a cloud of dust. She stepped aboard the boat and kissed them both, before saying, 'Nick, I'm afraid the news from Papa is not good. It would seem that the whole of the Union Corse has been alerted to watch out for you both and to report back if you are found. The boat is also regarded as important. We have been unable to find out what is behind all this, except that you have something belonging to them. We don't know what it is. Father thinks you'll be safe while you stay here but the problem will come when you leave.'

'Sicily may be a great place, but I don't intend to stay here all my bloody life and, with due respect to your Dad, I don't fancy becoming too involved with the Mafia. The trouble is that, even if we leave the boat here and fly out, we don't know whether they'll let us go. That bastard, Harlow, will pay for this. In the meantime, what do we do? Any ideas?'

It was Steve who answered. 'First of all, we search this boat from stem to stern, inside and out – then we do it again. If we find whatever it is they want, we give it to them. If we don't, we wait for Sarah and then make a run for it.' In reply to Gina's questioning eyebrow he added, 'Nick's girlfriend – she's arriving tomorrow morning.'

'At last someone is thinking straight. You start at the bows and I'll begin aft. The only snag I see is that we don't know what we're looking for.'

* * *

In an apartment overlooking Ajaccio harbour, James looked across at his companion who was sitting by the open window. Harold suffered from the heat and was sweating profusely. As he mopped his forehead repeatedly with the large white handkerchief, James felt a wave of disgust pass over him. How had he got himself mixed up with such a fellow, when there were so many presentable men around who would be far more suited to him? He carefully placed the newspaper on the table with the photograph of *White Albatross* showing.

'The gods have smiled on us and given us a way out of our dilemma.'

'What are we going to do now, James?'

'Go to Sicily, of course, and collect what is rightfully ours.'

'But what if Byers won't give it to us? Don't forget, he's friends with the Mafia now.'

'Have faith in me. I'll find a way. Now I will book a flight to Palermo.' He picked up the telephone and spoke to the airport. He had no trouble in arranging flights. 'Okay. We arrive in Palermo at eight-fifteen tomorrow morning. Now we'll speak to our friends there and get them to take a few simple precautions.'

Ricard looked at the newspaper which Debert had placed before him and cringed inwardly as the other man spoke. 'So the newspapers are doing your job for you, Ricard. Maybe you will now be able to take over from them and recover our belongings.'

'It will not be easy. They are under Scarfiotti's protection now.'

'Scarfiotti is a has-been.'

Ricard dared to argue with his boss. 'Not yet – he still has a lot of power and influence. He has a small army of men loyal to him. First of all, it will be necessary to have the boat watched carefully.'

'I'm sure you will find a way of recovering our belongings, Ricard; else I will be forced to replace you with someone who can – and I feel that you are much too young to go into retirement.'

In the office in London, Harlow sat with a pile of papers in front of him. He had read them all several times and still couldn't understand why there was no word from his cover agent. He didn't like working only with information from the press to go on. He was thankful the Chief was away for the day so that he had a bit of time to sort things out, and the only way of doing that was to speak to Byers – but how? He had no telephone number to call and he certainly couldn't go through 'official channels', so he could only sit and wait. He had a feeling that it wouldn't be long before an irate Byers was burning the lines to him, but he knew that he must appear innocent.

He picked up the telephone and spoke to the exchange. 'I'm expecting a call from Sicily from a guy called Nick Byers. When it comes I want you to give him the usual run-around, then let me know.'

On board the boat, the atmosphere was grim. Their searches had revealed nothing. It was Steve who suggested ringing Harlow. 'Do you have his number?'

'Oh, yes,' replied Nick. 'The main problem is to get him to accept the call. Still, it's definitely worth a try.'

Gina stood up. 'I'll drive you to the telephone.'

'No, I'd rather walk. It will give me time to think. Anyway, I saw the way you arrived here and I'm in quite enough danger, thank you.'

Nick dialled the number he had from his previous encounters with Harlow, crossing fingers that they hadn't changed it. He was in luck. An efficient sounding female voice came back to him.

'This is European Commercial Insurance – Sonia speaking. How can I help you?'

'You can put me through to John Harlow.'

'I'm sorry, sir, we have no one of that name in the company. Do you have an extension number?'

'Look, lass, I'm in no mood to play your bloody games. I'll ring off and call back in ten minutes time. Tell him that if he doesn't take the call, I'll sink his bloody boat in the deepest bit of sea that I can find.'

When he called back the call was answered by the same receptionist.

'Okay, Sonia, let's speak to the bastard.'

'There's no need to be like that, sir. I'm new to the job and didn't know the name.'

'Balls. Now put me through to him.'

Harlow's voice came on the line, the soft Welsh accent easy to spot. Byers had a feeling that he had been listening in. 'Come, come, Nick. What's the problem? You mustn't go upsetting our girls like that. They'll complain about sexual harassment, and then where would we be?'

'I know where you'll be if you don't sort out this blasted mess we're in.'

'What mess? As far as I was aware you were having a nice holiday in the Med. – except that you've gone a bit off course and ended up in Sicily.'

'Don't mess with me, Harlow. What the hell does the Union Corse want with the boat? Because, whatever it is, they were quite happy to kill Beardsley – and now I'm next in line for the chop. That's bad enough, but Sarah joins us tomorrow and I don't want her in danger too.'

'I'm sorry, Nick, but this is all news to me,' Harlow persisted. 'Beardsley is safe in a nursing home here. He had a heart attack when he came back to England on business.'

'I don't believe a word you say. I want you out here, pronto.'

'Nick, I'd love to come out and share your holiday, but I'm a busy man. I do promise that I'll see my Chief and ask his permission. Do you have a number we can call you on?'

'No. I'll ring you tomorrow and you'd better have decided to come out or I promise I'll sink the bloody boat.' He hung up the telephone with a crash and returned to the vessel.

They hung about for the rest of the day, with Nick behaving like a bear with a sore head. Steve tried to be cheerful, and pointed out that, while in Palermo, they were quite safe and by tomorrow it could all be sorted out.

The next day Gina arrived early and offered to take them to the airport to meet Sarah. Nick couldn't think of a good reason for refusing. At the airport they learned that there was a hold-up on Sarah's flight, so they sat in the lounge with coffees and waited. That was when Nick spotted the two Englishmen walk past. He sank in his seat and felt sure he had not been noticed. When they'd passed he drew Gina's attention to them.

'Those two men are English. I saw them in the Bar des Sports in Calvi. It's a hell of a coincidence them turning up here.'

'I agree,' said Gina, rising quickly from her seat. She hurried out of the room and followed them. They went straight to a rather battered local car which pulled away slowly with a fair amount of smoke. Gina spoke to one of the waiting taxi drivers who nodded and set off in pursuit.

Back with the others, she said, 'They got into a car and made off. I've told a taxi driver to follow them and find out who they are.'

'Will he do that?' asked Steve.

'He recognized me. Yes, he will do it,' replied Gina simply.

They didn't have to wait long for Sarah to arrive. As she approached them she looked quite beautiful: her hair shone black and purple in the airport lights and her body seemed to flow gracefully as she walked. Steve whistled softly. 'Hey, Nick that's some sheila you've got there.'

Nick grinned. 'She is that.'

Nick introduced them all. Sarah looked at Steve and took his hand. 'I've heard about you. I hope you've been looking after him.'

Then she looked at Gina for a while before she smiled. It was a genuine smile that lit up her eyes. 'It would seem I should have arrived earlier; your picture in the paper doesn't do you justice. You are much too attractive for Nick to be left alone with.' She held out her hand. 'I'm sure that we will be great friends.'

Gina smiled back. 'I'm sure we will too.'

Back on the boat, Sarah looked at Nick as the other two went down into the saloon. 'Okay, Nick, out with it. What the hell is going on? You could never keep a secret from me. Now I want the full story. It's that bastard Harlow, isn't it?'

Nick decided that honesty was the best policy and told her everything – or almost everything. He did edit the episode with Maria somewhat. She had already read about Gina and the rest didn't take long. She sat in silence for a while, considering what she had been told. 'You just can't be trusted to keep out of trouble. It's a good thing I came out to be with you. I'm not going to say "I told you so". One thing does concern me very much however. Gina seems to be charming, but how do you feel about being protected by the Mafia?'

'Sarah, I wouldn't mind if it was the devil himself if he could get us out of this mess. Now I'll give you a quick tour of the boat, produce a glass of wine and let you freshen up. We'll be using the after cabin, with Steve as far away as possible – up in the bows.'

The tour of the boat didn't take long and it was only minutes later that he left her in the after cabin and went to the saloon to join the others. Steve was sitting on the port seat, nursing a glass of wine. One look at him and Nick knew that something was amiss. 'Come on, out with it. What's wrong?'

'I waited till Sarah was away. I didn't want to alarm her as soon as she arrived. Nick, we've had visitors. Someone searched the boat while we were away. They obviously picked the locks on the companionway doors – you can see the scratches. Down below several things have been moved and not put back in quite the same place. It looks as if they've moved fast.'

'Hang on. Don't let's jump to conclusions. It could just have been a local petty thief.'

'In that case, why didn't they take anything? There are loads of valuables down there. Anyway, I bet it's common knowledge by now that we are in the Mafia's good books. We could leave the bloody boat unlocked and no petty thief would touch it.'

'I see your point. We'd better tell the others, then do another search of the boat. If nothing has been taken, maybe something unpleasant has been left, so we'd better not hang around.'

Once more the search revealed nothing and the four of them sat in the cockpit and held a council of war. Nick began. 'It's obvious that the Union Corse not only knows where we are but are prepared to act, if only in a limited way. When they get organized we could be in a lot of trouble, so what do we do now?'

'Couldn't we go to the police?' asked Sarah.

'What do we tell them? They're hardly likely to give us protection twenty-four hours a day on the strength of one break-in when nothing was taken. On the other hand, we can't just wait until something does happen.'

'I think we must rely for the present on the protection being given by Gina's father,' said Steve. 'Then, if we could find some way of disappearing again while still keeping that protection – just in case – maybe they'd give up.'

'You mean, abandon the boat?'

'Possibly, or else find somewhere to hide it.'

'That's a bit of a tall order and, strangely enough, I'm getting attached to this beauty,' replied Nick, patting the decking beside him. 'What's more, I think the answer to our dilemma is aboard this boat somewhere, if we could only find it.'

Gina spoke at last. 'I think I might know just the place to hide out and still be within my father's territory. It's a group of islands up to the north of Sicily – the Aeolian Islands. Lipari is the biggest, but there are several smaller ones.'

'Sounds good to me. Anyway, it's better than just sitting here. We've probably got charts of them but if you've got any more suggestions before we leave, I'd be grateful, Gina.'

'Just what gives you the idea you are leaving me behind, Nick Byers? I am going with you.'

'We can't take you into danger unnecessarily. I only wish we hadn't got Sarah involved too.'

'Aside from my wanting to go, you need me. I'm sorry to disappoint your male ego, but I carry more weight around here than you do.'

'And stop being a male chauvinist, Nick. We little women can look after ourselves,' added Sarah.

'Okay, okay.' Nick crossed his arms in front of his face. 'I give in. Point taken, Gina. When do we leave?'

Gina grinned. 'That's better. I'll go home and see what I can find out about the two Englishmen and collect a few sailing things. I'll return this evening and we can slide quietly out at about one o'clock in the morning and I'll get some of my father's men to check we're not being watched.'

The two Englishmen in question were at that moment sitting in a small, rather dirty house on the outskirts of Palermo with a swarthy Italian, dressed in a rather grubby T-shirt and jeans. James looked at him distastefully.

'You obviously got our message about the *White Albatross*. Did you do as I instructed?'

'But of course. I went on board while they were away and searched it as well as I could, but I was short of time so I found nothing. I did, however, leave a transmitter under the cockpit coaming. They will never find it – and they spend a lot of time in the cockpit in this hot weather.'

'Good. Where is the receiver? Can we listen from here?'

'Regretfully, no. The only transmitter I could get was an old style one with a very limited range. My brother is listening down in the docks and will telephone here if there is anything of importance. He is very reliable.'

'He'd better be. I suppose that's the best we can do for the time being.'

'You mean that we've got to sit and wait in this hole?' grumbled Harold, wiping the sweat from his red brow.

Before James could reply, the telephone rang, startlingly loud, in the corner of the room. The Italian went across and answered it. 'Si... si... si...' He spoke for a while in Italian, which the other two could not understand, then rang off and turned to face them, a look of triumph on his face. 'My little bug works. We can hear everything they say and find out where they are going. It was a very clever idea of mine, wasn't it?'

'Okay, okay, so you're a clever bugger,' said James impatiently. 'Just tell us what your little bug said.'

'They are leaving Palermo at one o'clock in the morning. They are going to sail the boat to the Lipari Islands which are...'

James waved his hand. 'I know where they are. Now isn't that just perfect. Not too far away, but far enough for us to act without having to look over our shoulder for Scarfiotti's men. They're keeping an eye on us at the moment, so we'll have to give them the slip. That's not going to be easy, but I'll think of a way.'

'His daughter is going with them.'

'We'll have to take care not to harm the Scarfiotti girl in any way. I don't want her old man after my blood. Byers and his woman are a different matter. If we have to dispose of them, we've only got the law to worry about – and that's no problem.'

The night was very dark and still when Gina arrived back at the boat on foot. 'Papa's car dropped me at the gate of the docks. Are you ready to go?'

'Yes,' replied Nick, 'but we'll have to use the engine. There's no wind at all.'

'It is unfortunate, but the engine is quite quiet and we'll just have to keep the power down.'

'I hope you know the way out, because the lights seem few and far between.'

'It's okay,' laughed Gina. 'I told you that you would need me.' She was still chuckling as the boat slid gently away from the quay, displaying no navigation lights.

As they sailed clear of the harbour, Gina told them what she had discovered about the two Englishmen. 'The taxi driver followed them to a house on the outskirts of Palermo and reported back to my father, who made more enquiries about them. It would seem that they are quite well known in the criminal circles. The smaller man is called James Dawson and the other one Harold Nixon. Both of them are believed to be drug smugglers and small-time crooks, but nothing has been proved. The house they are in belongs to an Italian called Guido. He is also involved with drugs.'

'That's all we need – to get mixed up with a pair of drug peddlers,' sighed Sarah. 'I wonder if they are tied up with Ricard.'

'It seems a bit too much of a coincidence to be any other way,' replied Nick. 'Is your father keeping an eye on them, Gina?'

'Yes. They will be kept under observation but, of course, we must take no chances.'

They sailed well out to the north before turning eastward and heading for the Aeolian Islands. Daybreak found them alone on a calm blue sea with only the gentlest of breezes filling the large genoa and easing them along, well out of sight of land and with no other shipping visible. Everything was calm and peaceful.

Away in Corsica, everything was far from calm and peaceful.

'What do you mean, *they've gone*?' Ricard thundered into the telephone. 'Where have they gone? They can't have just disappeared. Why weren't you watching?'

His agent in Sicily explained that Mafiosi had been all over the area throughout the night making surveillance impossible.

Ricard slammed the phone down and, with trembling hands, called his boss. To his surprise Debert listened quietly before saying simply, 'Find them – and when you do, take action, regardless of Scarfiotti. This is too important to play about. We will have to take risks.'

In the house in Palermo, Dawson sat in silence as he heard the latest report from Guido's brother. The attention of the Mafia was the last thing he needed. The fact that Byers knew about them, even their names, disturbed him considerably, but he hid his doubts from the others.

'What do we do now?' asked Nixon, on the verge of panic. 'We'll have to get away and hide, won't we?'

'Calm down,' replied Dawson, disgust plain in his voice. 'We have the advantage of being warned and they don't know that. We can also keep a check on the boat. Yes, now we must disappear from Palermo and go into hiding but, while we do, I'm sure one of Guido's friends can go to Lipari and keep watch. Then, when the time is right, we must act swiftly and decisively, but without harming the Scarfiotti girl.'

Guido nodded his head firmly. 'I have some friends in another Mafia family who do not like Scarfiotti. They will help us.'

As they sailed peacefully towards the Aeolian Islands it was difficult to remember that they were involved in such drama, or even to think seriously about it. However, Nick eventually made a big effort.

'We've searched the boat several times and found nothing, but we haven't looked at the outside of the hull and that's something we must do,' he declared.

Steve nodded. 'We've got all the necessary equipment aboard and I can dive, so why not?'

'Sarah and I can dive as well. What about you, Gina?'

'I've dived since I was a small girl and I love it.'

'We seem to have no shortage of equipment or talent, so let's get the gear together. Then we'll heave to and search. We only need one diver and since I thought of it I guess that I get to go.' Nick was looking forward to his first dive in the clear water and made his way below to change into the shorty wetsuit he had brought along.

He checked the scuba gear thoroughly while the others looked on. He fitted one of the demand valves onto a scuba set and turned on the air-bottle. A check of the contents gauge showed the bottle to be full. Sucking on the mouthpiece, he breathed from the set for a couple of minutes. 'The air tastes all right, let's hope it is.'

'I can't be sure when they were charged,' said Steve, 'but Beardsley struck me as being pretty meticulous where that kind of thing was concerned. Anyway, if he'd got exhaust fumes in the bottles you should be able to taste it. We'll keep you on a rope, just in case. There's no point in taking unnecessary chances.'

'I couldn't agree more. A rope will be no handicap on a job like this. Just how deep is the water around here anyway?'

'If you're really interested I could go and check the chart, but I'd guess that it's several hundred metres. A little bit deeper than you plan to go.'

Nick laughed. 'I bloody well hope so. No, don't bother to check. I'm not sure I really want to know.'

Having checked all the equipment thoroughly, he wriggled into the straps of the scuba set, then he picked up the quick release weight belt. 'It's a long time since I dived without a proper suit on, so I'm not really sure how much weight I'll need. I'll take a couple of kilo weights first and see what it's like.'

'I'll be hanging on to the rope so you won't sink too far.' Steve grinned.

They lowered all the sails and the boat lay still on the calm sea, the breeze too light to move her under bare poles. Nick jumped over the side and was surprised at the sharp chill of the water but it didn't take him long to become accustomed to his environment. The water was crystal clear and as he looked down it seemed that he could see a hundred metres into the blue-grey void. Rays of bright sunlight struck through the water, picking out the few tiny particles which were held in suspension – like minute stars in an infinite background.

Nick felt at ease with the world and checked his buoyancy by holding his breath and floating upright in the water with just his eyes clear. As he breathed out so he sank slowly. Just right. Breathing normally, but in a controlled manner, he kept steady and began the search of the boat's hull.

He was pleased to see that the anti-fouling was in good condition. Not only did it help the sailing, it also made the search easier. He started at the bows and worked his way slowly aft along the port side until he could check out the propeller and rudder, then forward up the starboard side. He surfaced, pulled off his fins, weightbelt and scuba set and passed them to Steve before climbing up the ladder onto the deck.

As he towelled himself down he felt a sense of disappointment that he had found nothing. He was sure that the answer lay under the water. Furthermore, if they could find the secret of the boat, they would know what action to take. He thought again about Harlow. The man had many faults and was as devious as hell, but Nick was dead certain that he wouldn't condone drug-smuggling, so the chances were that they were not looking for a package of drugs – it would be something smaller. The presence of Dawson and Nixon had to be a coincidence.

They hoisted sails and cruised slowly on. Nick had already checked with the chart and decided that, at the leisurely pace they were going, it would probably be well into the following morning before they reached Filicudi, the island which Gina had suggested would be the most suitable. He wasn't worried about how long it took them. While at sea he felt secure. They were way out of sight of land and had seen very little shipping, certainly none close enough to identify them.

He wasn't far out with his estimation and it was just after dawn that they spotted the island of Alcudi, fine on the starboard bow. This small island lay some ten miles to the west of their destination, Filicudi and it was a further two hours before that island became clear ahead of them. As the outline hardened, Nick noticed with surprise how green it was and remarked on it to Gina.

'Yes. Some years ago it was covered in grass and had only a tiny population. The only shop doubled as store and post office, not to mention café. Now tourism has struck and there are hotels and the like. It's a pity, but the local people need the income. You can see that it's really two hills joined by a low neck of land. There's a reasonable anchorage on the other side of that neck.'

Nick took Gina's advice and they dropped anchor quite close to the shore on the east side of the island. After making sure they were securely anchored, they inflated the dinghy and fitted the small outboard motor. Sarah, Gina and Nick went ashore to buy provisions while Steve charged the air-bottle that Nick had used on his short dive. When he connected the bottle to the compressor and read off the contents from the gauge he was surprised to see that Nick had used a remarkable amount of air. He shrugged his shoulders, thinking that maybe Nick was a bit out of practice, or else he just wasn't bothered about controlling his rate of breathing on such a short dive. He gave it no more thought.

They sat around, generally relaxing, until Nick felt they should occupy themselves a bit more fully and asked Gina, 'Do you know any good diving around here? The water is so clear it must be great down below.'

'It certainly is. The scenery is magnificent and there are lots of fish. If you're very lucky you might find spiny lobster for supper.'

'What about old wreck sites? Are there any of those?' queried

Steve. 'You know – with amphora and everything.'

'There's a reef off the south-east end of the island and at the bottom of it there's the site of a Phoenician boat which has been dated four hundred BC.'

'Is there anything to see?'

There are a number of amphora scattered around but most of them are broken. If you dig around you may find some of their black pottery. I must warn you that it's against the law to lift any of it – or anything else for that matter.'

'Are we allowed to dive on it, then?'

'This particular wreck has been heavily worked for many years, so no one is likely to object. Unfortunately, it's deep.'

'What do you call "deep"?'

'Forty to forty-five metres, but the water is clear so it doesn't seem deep and you can come up the side of the reef to decompress. We used to do two stops on ledges where we could sit and watch the fish. On the second one, which is about three to four metres down, you can just sit until you run out of air. If we keep the dive short we should have no problems. Ten minutes on the bottom and we'll be very safe.'

'It sounds reasonable,' agreed Nick. 'Of late, we've been using dive computers to work out decompression, but I seem to recall that the no-stop time for forty-two metres is nine minutes, so what you are suggesting sounds about right. With these fifteen-litre bottles we should have loads of air.'

They all agreed that that would be the thing to do, but Nick was firm. 'No staying down too long, and no bringing up souvenirs. We can't afford to have anything go wrong.'

Sarah was all in favour. 'It's still early – let's go now.'

Nick was more cautious. 'No. I think you should all have a shallow dive first to get used to everything. I know you haven't dived for several months, Sarah. How about you, Gina?'

'The same for me. I agree with you, Nick. You went down yesterday so you could keep watch while we play about in the shallows.'

Steve nodded. 'I've been diving a lot recently but I don't mind coming along with two lovely ladies.'

Sarah sighed and said to Gina, 'Sounds like we've graduated – we're not sheilas any more.' Turning to Steve she said, 'Come along, Steve, the ladies will look after you.'

Nick was happy to keep watch while the others enjoyed themselves in the shallow water. In spite of the dangers which surrounded them he was delighted to have Sarah back with him. The company of Steve and Gina made the whole thing seem a bit like a holiday.

The day passed pleasantly and the following morning they had a light breakfast early and prepared for the dive on the wreck site. It was decided that Steve and Gina would dive first; Sarah and Nick would go later. It was a bit of a squeeze in the inflatable for four, especially when two of them were dressed for diving. Gina and Steve had their own wet-suits, which was fortunate, for they guessed that the water at depth would be cold.

Gina directed them to the top of the reef with no trouble and they were able to look down and see the weed and rock below. They dropped a small anchor and the two divers wasted no time in rolling gently backward into the water and continuing down with no flapping of fins.

As they glided down Gina led the way, stopping on top of the reef to check all was well. Looking up she could see the rippled surface of the water sparkling in the bright sunlight. Shafts of light lit up the top of the reef, exposing the colours of the rocks and the life which dwelt there. She looked down to where the cliff disappeared into a blue-grey mist many metres below, and began the descent. The rocky side of the reef was steep but not quite vertical and Gina finned strongly to make her way down. Her time on the dive was limited and she couldn't afford to dally. Just behind her, and slightly to one side, Steve followed, impressed with her positive approach. At about five metres Gina held her nose and blew in order to equalize the pressure on her eardrums. Steve, who had had more recent diving time, cleared his easily by just swallowing. The effect was the same in both cases: they felt the familiar pop of the ears clearing, accompanied by a sense of well-being.

At ten metres down the colours began to fade as the water, clear though it was, began to filter them out. First the reds disappeared, followed by the other colours, until, at thirty metres, all that was left was the blue-grey which they knew so well. The vegetation had also thinned out and the rocks were covered in a thin layer of silt which billowed up in clouds with the movement of their fins. As the bottom began to level out they stopped swimming and sank slowly through the water. Around them Steve could see the remains of amphora scattered out across the seabed, some intact but most broken. He couldn't help wondering what had happened to cause this wreck over two thousand years ago. There must have been a storm – how else could the ship have hit such a reef? He saw Gina sink gently to the bottom and lift something from the silt. She handed him the small bowl she had found. It was black, with lighter figures marked on it – a very good example of Phoenician black pottery.

Steve looked around, vainly hoping to find more, and was surprised when Gina touched his shoulder and pointed to her watch. It was time already to begin the ascent. They swam slowly upwards, keeping just clear of the reef. They did not hurry but maintained a steady speed, watching the bubbles from their exhaled breath climb away above them. Gradually, the colours returned and, looking up, they could see the dinghy on the surface with the bubbles bursting around it. At about eight metres from the surface, Gina settled upon a ledge and beckoned to Steve to join her. As they sat side by side he could see the excitement in her eyes and knew that his reflected it. They breathed slowly, conserving their air and, after ten minutes, Gina signalled for them to move up to the top of the reef, where once again she settled down. This time she took out her knife, cut open a sea urchin and placed it on the reef beside her. Before long, several small fish gathered for the feast. Then Steve realized that other, larger fish were gathering, until they were the centre of a circling wheel of colourful fish of all descriptions. He watched in fascination until he felt his demand valve tighten as the air ran out. He signalled to Gina who nodded back and they both rose to the surface.

There they shrugged out of their diving gear and passed it, together with the Phoenician dish, into the boat. Nick raised an eyebrow at the dish, but Gina laughed. 'I brought it up so that you could see it in daylight. When you dive you can return it to its resting place – it's a pity though. It is so beautiful.'

Rather than try to climb into the inflatable, they clung to the side as Nick towed them back to the yacht. Then it was his and Sarah's turn to dive. Theirs was almost a repeat of the first dive.

As they rolled backward into the water Nick felt satisfaction and pleasure. He was at ease with his environment. The thought of the dive ahead in the company of Sarah thrilled him and he forgot his problems. They swam down the reef, following the same course as Gina and Steve, until they settled gently on the bottom where Nick replaced the small dish.

They looked around in the clear water, Nick deciding which way to go, when, to his surprise, he felt his demand valve tighten. The flow of air was cut off and he could not breathe. He didn't panic; all his training had prepared him for this. With lungs aching he grabbed Sarah's arm, pulled her round to face him and pointed to his valve in the universal emergency signal. He could feel dizziness beginning owing to the lack of oxygen. The build up of carbon dioxide in his body was forcing him to breathe, but there was nothing to breathe except water. Sarah looked at his eyes through the face mask, saw the agony and responded immediately. She took a deep breath, removed her own mouthpiece and handed it to Nick, who took a couple of breaths before handing it back. As the new air entered his lungs he felt the pain ease and his vision cleared. Then they started the well-rehearsed buddy-breathing technique that all experienced divers know so well. With each taking a couple of breaths in turn, they passed the mouthpiece backward and forward as they rose slowly to the surface in a controlled ascent, taking care to observe they rose more slowly than the bubbles they were exhaling. They hadn't spent long on the bottom, so a decompression stop was unnecessary. Nevertheless they rested on the top of the reef and emptied Sarah's air-bottle before surfacing.

Steve received their gear in the dinghy. 'Hey, mate, that was quick. What happened?'

'What happened? I'll tell you what happened. I ran out of bloody air on the bottom. God knows why. I checked that bloody tank was full and I'm not that much out of practice. Hell, I was controlling my breathing as normal.'

Steve replied thoughtfully, 'When I charged your set after you searched the bottom of the boat, I was surprised to see how much air you had used.'

'Was it the same bottle?'

'Yes, I'm sure it was. I noticed this mark on it. Let's face it, with bottles as big as these it should be possible to make that dive twice over.'

'Don't I know it. There must be something wrong with that bloody bottle. Did it charge normally?'

'I didn't really notice, but it was full when you started so there's nothing wrong with your contents valve.'

'Let's get back to the boat and get to the bottom of this.'

In the confined space of the forward, and with Steve looking on, Nick set to work on the air-bottle. The forward hatch was open to let in fresh air but it also provided royal circle seats for the two girls to see what was going on, as they stretched out on the deck.

Nick managed to fit the bottle into the vice on the work-bench. Then, having checked that the bottle was absolutely empty, he fitted a spanner to the pillar valve and tried to remove it. The valve was screwed into the bottle on a twenty-four centimetre thread and sealed with an O-ring so it should have unscrewed easily, but this one had been deliberately over-tightened and it required all Nick's strength to move it. With Steve holding the bench steady, it eventually gave and he was able to remove it from the air-bottle, leaving a hole about an inch in diameter.

Having checked that the valve itself was clear, he turned his attention to the bottle. Even with the help of a torch he couldn't see inside, so he searched around until he found a length of stiff wire and probed the interior with it. He wasn't surprised to find that he could only get it about a third of the way in.

'To hell with whoever owns the bottle, I intend to find out what's in it.' He picked up a hacksaw and set about sawing through the bottle just below the shoulder. The blade was good and cut quickly through the metal. At last, he was able to see the obstruction. The bottom two-thirds of the bottle was filled with a thin, plastic-coated sausage. The sausage was held in place by some sort of wax. It was thin enough to have been passed in through the neck of the bottle and pliable enough to bed down easily. The molten wax had obviously been poured in later.

Nick cut open one end of the sausage and saw that it was filled with a white powder. Looking up at Gina, he asked, 'What is it? Some sort of drug?'

'Why ask me?' she replied indignantly. 'I wouldn't know heroin from sugar.'

Steve leaned across and touched the powder with his finger. 'I can't be sure, but I think it's heroin.'

Nick pulled the remaining sausage clear and emptied into a bucket. Having done so he picked it up and said, 'Whatever it is, I know what I'm going to do.' Climbing through the fore hatch, past the girls, he threw the whole lot over the side. They watched, fascinated, as the white powder dispersed through the clear seawater.

'That should give the local fish one hell of a high.' Steve had followed him onto the deck. 'There were three or four kilos there. You know you've just thrown away a small fortune?'

'I couldn't give a damn. I despise people who deal in the stuff.'

'I wasn't thinking about selling it. It's too late now, but it would have been a good bargaining point to get these people off our backs. This was clearly what Ricard was after.'

'I'm not so sure,' said Gina. 'I agree that stuff was worth a lot of money to a small dealer but it would be very little to the Union Corse. Certainly not enough for them to risk a confrontation with the Cosa Nostra.'

'I see your point,' agreed Nick. 'I think our next move is to go to Lipari and contact Harlow again. I can't honestly see him as a drug-dealer, so what the hell is happening?'

In the half-derelict farm in the mountainous area of the north-eastern part of Sicily, the two Englishmen waited impatiently. The actual buildings were bad enough, with the dirt, dust and flies, but even worse was the lack of contact with the outside world. They didn't even have a telephone. They had to rely on Guido to keep them briefed on what was happening. Nixon was no help. Since the news that the Mafia had them spotted he had become nothing more than a quivering heap. Dawson wriggled his nose in distaste at his surroundings and brushed the dust from his previously spotless white shirt. He looked at his watch again. Guido was late, as usual.

At that moment a car drew up in the courtyard amidst a cloud of dust and Guido stepped out. He made his way to the farmhouse, coughing, and beating the dust from his clothes.

As soon as he entered he broke the news to the Englishmen, forestalling any complaints about his tardiness. 'We think they've found the drugs.'

'What do you mean "think"?'

'They went diving on the Phoenician wreck and returned to the boat complaining about one of the air-bottles. On board they took it forward to investigate, so we could only get bits of their conversation. What's more the transmitter is beginning to break down. I warned you, it was an old one but it was all we could get in the time. Anyway, we heard them mention drugs and they talked about going to Lipari to contact some guy called Harlow. Do you know him?'

Dawson shook his head and thought for several minutes before speaking. 'We don't need to worry too much about the bug – it's done its job. Here's what we do . . .'

6

The town of Lipari was much bigger than Nick had expected and the small harbour was bustling with all kinds of boats. There were two main quays, one of which was obviously reserved for the ferry which operates from Milazzo, on the mainland of Sicily. He had towed the inflatable dinghy behind the yacht on the journey from Filicudi, so now he decided to anchor the boat out in the harbour to provide a certain amount of privacy.

As soon as they were securely anchored, Nick announced that he would go ashore to telephone Harlow.

'That's good. I'll go ashore with you and telephone my father to see if there is any more information.' Gina was already pulling the dinghy alongside as she spoke.

In his office in London, Harlow was getting more and more frustrated. Everything seemed to be backfiring on him. His agent in Corsica had gone missing and now Byers and the bloody yacht had disappeared from Palermo. The telephone on the desk rang and he picked it up. 'Yes?' he barked into the mouthpiece.

'I have Mr Byers on the line from Lipari. Will you take the call?'

'Too bloody right I will. And where the hell is Lipari, anyway?'

'It's a small island to the north of Sicily. I spent a holiday there once. It's very beautiful and...'

'All right, all right. I don't want a bloody travelogue. Put Byers on.'

The operator put the call through and raised her eyebrows at the other girl in the office. Mr Harlow must be very upset to behave in that manner.

'What the hell are you playing at, Byers?'

'What am I playing at?' echoed Nick. 'Let's get this straight. I'm trying to get out of the mess you landed us in. What the hell is it about this boat that interests the Union Corse so much?'

'I don't know what you're talking about. As far as I know there's nothing unusual on board.'

'In that case, you won't mind that I threw the four kilos of heroin overboard.'

'You threw what overboard?' asked Harlow in amazement.

'The heroin I found hidden in one of the diving bottles.'

After a few moments silence Harlow said, 'Nick, I tell you truthfully, I had no idea it was on board.' That bastard, Beardsley, was obviously doing a bit of private trading. 'I think you did the right thing.'

Nick thought he was probably telling the truth. 'Okay, Harlow, I'll accept that, but what else is there?'

'There's nothing, I tell you.' He sighed loudly. 'You obviously don't believe me so, busy as I am, I'll come out to Lipari to see you. I can't afford to have you whining over the telephone at me every five minutes. Call back in half an hour and I'll tell you when I can get there. In the meantime, don't go missing again.'

Outside the phone kiosk Gina was already waiting; her father had no further news about the Union Corse. They had agreed to pick up some fresh provisions for their evening meal while they were ashore and decided to do just that while Nick was waiting to call Harlow again. They wandered round the shops, taking their time and strolling along like a couple of tourists. Through lack of attention Nick was almost flattened by a small ambulance which raced past down the narrow streets, but Gina quickly pulled him out of the way.

'You've got to be careful of vehicles over here. Italian drivers are a law unto themselves. That was probably some poor devil on his way to the mainland for major surgery,' she said. 'It's heading for the quay.'

When Nick called London again he learned that Harlow had already left the office and was due to arrive in Lipari on the hydrofoil at eleven the following morning. He returned to the boat feeling somewhat easier. For all his faults, Harlow's imminent arrival gave him some confidence.

They made their way leisurely to the dinghy and rowed out to the yacht.

The small, middle-aged man in the grey suit had watched Nick and Gina come ashore. As soon as they had landed he looked down at the youngster in the boat tied up alongside the quay. 'How much to take me out to that yacht, lad?'

The youngster eyed the man speculatively. 'I should be going home now, so it will cost you five Euros.'

The man in grey chuckled. 'Good try, son. However, since it's only spitting distance away I'll give you two. I'm not going to argue. If you don't want it someone else will.'

The youngster considered the offer carefully. This man was carrying a briefcase and wearing a suit. He was obviously an official of some kind. He'd better be careful. 'Okay, boss. You win. I'll pick you up at the steps.'

Sarah and Steve watched them draw close and went to the side of the cockpit to meet them. The man in grey introduced himself formally while standing in the small boat.

'My name is Ballastreno and I am the personal representative of the professor in charge of the museum.'

'I'm Sarah Drew and this is Steve. Won't you come aboard?'

'Thank you but I regret that I am in a great hurry. I have to catch the ferry to Milazzo. However, I should tell you that the professor has learned that you have been diving on the Phoenician wreck off Filicudi and that is a restricted wreck site. I must ask, did you raise any artefacts from it?'

'No, not a thing. We had been warned that taking things is prohibited, but we didn't know the site was restricted.'

'In that case, if the captain would care to come ashore with me and make a declaration to the professor, that will suffice. We try not to be unreasonable.'

'I'm sure you do but, unfortunately, the captain is ashore at the moment. If you'd care to wait on board you are welcome. We have a nice bottle of wine just waiting to be sampled.'

'That's a very attractive invitation, but, as I said, I am in a great hurry. Is it possible that you can speak for him?'

'Well, yes, I suppose so. If that's all that's required I guess I could do it. What do you reckon, Steve?'

'I don't see why not. If Signor Ballastreno is happy, I'm sure Nick won't argue.'

'Okay, I'll go, signor. Give me a hand down.'

As she swung over the side the young boatman was mesmerized by the long shapely legs. In an island known for its pretty girls, this one was streets ahead of the rest. He wished that the trip to the shore was ten times as long. He was aroused from his reverie by the man in grey.

'Come on lad, wake up. I haven't got all day.'

'Where's Sarah?' asked Nick.

'I thought you'd probably see her. Just after you left she went ashore with the man from the museum.'

'Which man from the museum?' asked Gina with a frown.

'A man came and said that he represented the professor in charge of the museum. They had been told we'd been diving on the Phoenician wreck and, apparently, it's a prohibited site. He wanted someone to go ashore to the museum and sign a declaration that nothing had been raised. He couldn't wait for you to come back because he's going away to the mainland today, so Sarah said she would go. That's all. I thought she would have been back by now.'

Gina asked, 'What did this man look like? Did he give a name?'

Nick could see that she was getting agitated and cold fingers began crawling up his spine.

Steve was also getting uneasy. 'He was small and neat. About fifty, with thinning grey hair and rimless spectacles. He spoke excellent English with only the slightest accent. He wore a lightweight grey suit and a tie. He said his name was Signor Ballastreno, or something like that. He came out on one of those small boats – that one I think.' He pointed to a small red boat lying, unattended, at the quay.

'Nick, I'm worried.' Gina's concern showed in her face. 'I know of no one like that at the museum and that wreck site is not restricted. If it were they would require more than a statement – they would search the boat. I think we should go to the museum to check.'

'Oh God, not Sarah,' whispered Nick. 'Let's go now.'

Gina and Nick piled into the dinghy and he rowed strongly to the quay. Once ashore Gina took his hand and half pulled him along the narrow streets to a small doorway. She knocked and went straight inside. The room they entered was cluttered with pieces of amphora and other relics and in one corner an elderly man sat at a large desk. He was in his late sixties and totally bald; a pair of half-glasses perched on the end of his nose. He looked up from the paper he was studying and, when he saw Gina, his eyes sparkled. He rose to his feet, throwing down his spectacles. He welcomed her with both hands and kissed her cheeks. She didn't introduce Nick but spoke quickly in Italian. Nick couldn't understand a word, but from the way the man kept glancing at him he knew roughly what was being said.

Finally, the man looked at him sadly and spoke in English. 'I'm sorry, Signor, but I gave no instructions and we have no such man working for us. I suggest you contact the police.'

Dizziness swept over Nick. He couldn't speak; he just staggered to the doorway and leant against the wall outside. He sucked in the warm air in deep gulps, trying desperately to gather his wits. He felt someone shaking his arm viciously and heard Gina's voice as she shouted at him. 'Nick, Nick. Speak to me, Nick. Come to your senses, Nick. For Sarah's sake listen to me.'

Eventually, her words sank into his muddled brain and he looked down at her. 'Oh, Gina, what shall we do?'

'We look at this thing calmly and work out what has happened to her and what we do to get her back safely.'

Sarah followed the dapper man as he walked quickly off the quay into the narrow streets of the town. He seemed nervous now and, for the first time, she felt she had made a mistake in not waiting for Nick and Gina. No – this little man looked so innocent; surely there was nothing to be scared of.

His short legs moved even faster. He was almost running and she had to stride out in order to keep up with him. 'Hey, signor, what's the hurry?'

'I'm sorry, Signorina, but I must catch the ferry. Please, we are almost there and I will leave you with the professor to sign the papers. He'll arrange an escort back to your boat.'

A short distance later he stopped in front of a low doorway in an old stone building. 'Here we are, this is it.'

Sarah looked at the building and, once again, suspicion grew in her. 'This is a strange place for a museum.'

The Italian laughed. 'That's because it's the back entrance. It saves us walking a long way round to get to the front door. Just follow me and keep quite close because it's rather dim inside after the bright sunshine.'

As he pushed open the door she noticed a small ambulance pull up onto the pathway further along the narrow street. 'It looks like somebody has got a problem. I hope it's not serious.'

He nodded his agreement and stepped through into a big store-room with amphora stacked along the wall. Sarah followed him closely in the dim light and was reassured by the sight of the amphora – all this must be genuine. Just as she breathed a sign of relief and relaxed, she felt herself grabbed from behind and a soft pad was pressed over her mouth and nose. The smell of ether was strong. She struggled violently and kicked back with her heel. She heard a grunt of pain and an obvious curse which she couldn't understand, but the grip on her did not slacken. She tried not to breathe, but it was impossible. Dizziness swept over her and she sank into unconsciousness. As her body went limp her assailant hung onto her for a short time longer, then lowered her to the ground.

Guido spoke in Italian to the dapper man. 'She's a right little vixen, that one, but she certainly is a good-looker.' He bent down, ripped open her shirt-front and savagely tore away her bra to reveal the small, firm breasts and, running his fingers over them, he chuckled. 'I'm going to enjoy this one before this thing is through. I certainly won't get competition from the Englishmen. They don't know a good thing when they see it. Don't just stand there – go and call the ambulance while I give her a little jab with a needle to keep her sleeping peacefully.'

The other man looked at him with a mixture of fear and disgust. He started to speak but thought better of it and went outside to signal the ambulance, which moved slowly down the street to stop outside the door with light flashing. The driver, a big, dark-skinned man with a mop of curly black hair, got out and, together, he and Guido lifted Sarah onto a stretcher and carried her to the vehicle. The driver spoke sharply to Guido. 'Get in the back and hold tight because this is an emergency and we've got to get her onto the ferry and to the hospital in Messina.' He laughed cruelly. 'Or maybe to a dirty old place in the mountains – I wouldn't mind operating on that one myself.'

He slammed the ambulance into gear. As it rushed towards the quay, with siren blaring and lights flashing, it brushed past a large foreigner who was pulled to safety by the girl with him.

It was Gina who broke the silence. 'There is little to do before we hear from the kidnappers. They are sure to contact us with their demands and, in the meantime, they will keep Sarah safe. We are fairly sure that one of the things they want is the package of drugs – and that's one thing we can't give them. So we must stall and I will arrange with my father to have them investigated. We must remain calm.'

Nick was sullen. 'That's easy to say, Gina, but I feel so useless. I love her and she is in dire trouble because of my stupidity. I should never have become involved with Harlow in the first place.'

Gina was about to reply when, looking over his shoulder, she noticed a small dinghy heading their way. 'Nick, I've a feeling things are happening.' She stood up and leant on the guard rails. The occupant of the boat was a young boy, not yet in his teens. He looked up at Gina and spoke in Italian. 'I have a message for Signor Byers.'

Gina answered in the same language. 'This is Signor Byers. Give me the message.'

The boy handed over a crumpled piece of paper, which she glanced at and passed over to Nick, who seized it eagerly.

'Who gave it to you?' asked Gina.

'It was a stranger. I have never seen him before.'

'Where is he now? Where did he go?'

'I don't know. He gave it to me an hour ago and told me to deliver it at eight o'clock. He gave me five Euros.'

Gina told Nick what the boy had said. He took out a banknote. 'Give him this and tell him to come back to us if he sees the man again.'

When the boy had departed Nick read aloud the contents of the note. *'You have something belonging to us and we have something you want. If you want to see the girl alive again do exactly as you are instructed and tell no one. Go to Milazzo on the midday boat tomorrow and go into the Bar Napoli at three o'clock in the afternoon. If you don't turn up alone, the girl will die.'*

He started to crumple the note slowly in his hands, but Gina stopped him. 'Don't. It may be important.' She prised it from between his fingers. 'Now think, Nick. Is there anything about the note which will help us?'

He shook his head dejectedly. She smoothed the paper out in front of him. 'Look at it again. If you really love her look at it and think.'

Her words stung him from his apathy and he examined it again. He started to shake his head once more, then braced back his shoulders sharply. 'God, yes, Gina. This note was written by an Englishman. I'm certain of it. There are little things. Foreigners wouldn't have said "turn up alone". They'd have said 'come alone' or something like that. But how does it help us, Gina?'

It was Steve who, at long last, broke his silence and answered. 'It means that in all probability Sarah is not a prisoner of the Union Corse, but of those two Englishmen in Palermo. What are they called? Dawson and Nixon, isn't it? They are into drugs and they probably want the ones you ditched.'

'I think you may be right, but how does it help us? She's still in danger. They are just as likely to kill her as Ricard is.'

Gina spoke softly but firmly. 'I don't think so. They haven't got the resources to try something else. What's more they haven't got the resources to keep a complete watch over their operation. Nick, her greatest danger is if they find out the drugs no longer exist. It's important that I contact my father and tell him everything and ask for his help.'

'No, they said to tell no one. We can't risk telling him.'

'We can't risk not telling him, Nick. We need his help. It's a must.' Steve's reply was curt and to the point. Nick was forced to consider the pros and cons. He had to agree. The others were right, of course.

'Okay, Gina, go ahead but please tell him to be careful.'

'There's no need to tell him that, Nick; his men are experts at what they do. Although we all hate it, they are true professionals. I'll go ashore now and call him. I'll take the dinghy and go by myself. I can visit an old friend of mine – an elderly lady – and phone from there, so no one will know.'

'Thank you, Gina – and be careful yourself.'

'Don't worry, no one will harm me.'

While she was away the two men talked over the situation again and again, but it always came back to the same thing. They were green at this business and would have to rely on Scarfiotti – and, of course, Harlow, who was due the following morning. Nick wondered what he would think of the Mafia running the show. Too bad – it was his own fault.

In a small hut near the quay, Guido's brother had sat with earphones on trying to pick up the transmissions from the bug in the yacht's cockpit. He was receiving about one word in twenty and eventually tossed the head-set down in disgust and went away to get himself a meal.

When Gina returned she wasted no time in telling them that Paolo would be coming the following day and would arrive on the early boat.

'It should be interesting to see how he and your mate, Harlow, get along together.' Steve spoke lightheartedly and even Nick managed a smile.

'To be honest, Steve, I don't give a damn,' he replied.

The following day dawned with the sun climbing into a clear blue sky. The little harbour bustled with activity. The fishing boats were landing their catch and the tripper boats were preparing for their daily round of the islands. Already, cargo and passengers were assembling for the trip to mainland Sicily. On the quay a group of seamen laughed loudly at some unheard, and probably unrepeatable, joke.

In the yacht, Nick felt a sense of grievance that others could laugh while he was in torment. He knew he was being unreasonable and tried to shake himself out of it. He'd had a sleepless night with his mind in turmoil and that wasn't helping.

Just at that moment Gina appeared on deck with an understanding smile and two cups of coffee. His first reaction was to shake his head in refusal, but she forestalled him. 'Come on, Nick. Try not to give way to depression. If you are going to help Sarah you will need to be at your best.'

He knew she was right. He returned the smile weakly and took the coffee, cradling the warm cup in his hands. 'My head is in a whirl. I keep wondering if she is somewhere close by, or whether she has been taken to the mainland, and if so, how? She must have been tied up and gagged – or drugged.'

'That's it!' Gina snapped her fingers. 'It has to be the ambulance – the one which nearly hit you last evening. The perfect way to carry her and no one would think to check on it. I've got to meet Paolo shortly and we will make enquiries. There's not much you can do at the moment. You've got to meet this man, Harlow, at eleven and then catch the midday boat, so I suggest you wait on board for now. There may be some more messages from the kidnappers.'

He rowed her ashore and took the dinghy back to the yacht. It was quieter than ever without her. Steve had gone ashore much earlier, ostensibly to shop, but Nick wondered if he might have other plans as well. He couldn't rid himself of the idea that there was a connection between the younger man and Harlow. He was certainly taking his time about buying a bit of food for breakfast. He shrugged. Maybe he was misjudging the lad. There was a lot to see ashore and there was no hurry.

It was a few minutes before eleven when he saw the hydrofoil approaching the harbour. It had slowed down and was riding on its main hull. He quickly rowed ashore and walked round to the far quay to meet Harlow.

The hydrofoil had already docked when he arrived and the passengers were streaming off. He saw Harlow standing on the quay looking around. He was dressed in an open-necked, white shirt and light-grey slacks. A lightweight jacket was slung over one arm and he stood near the wall with a green hold-all at his feet. When he saw Nick he raised a hand in salute and, picking up the case, advanced to meet him, smiling broadly.

'Well now, boyo, I was beginning to think that you had gone missing again. You've had me very worried – and all you were meant to do was enjoy yourself.'

'Cut the crap, Harlow. Sarah's been kidnapped and I don't feel like playing silly buggers. I want her back and I'm willing to do anything to get her – yes, anything.'

The smile left Harlow's face and he said seriously, 'Are you sure about this? There can be no mistake?'

Nick nodded glumly.

'Do you know who holds her? Have they contacted you?'

Nick nodded again and explained briefly what had happened. Harlow listened closely. 'This girl, Gina – you are sure that she is innocent? After all, she is tied up with the Mafia and they're no angels.'

'She's the only person in this whole bloody mess that I'm sure about. I'd stake my life that she is straight.'

'And Sarah's?'

Nick spoke firmly. 'Yes. And Sarah's.'

'What about the young fellow, Steve – are you as sure about him?'

Nick hesitated. 'I don't think that he's bent, but I've a feeling he's got ties with your nasty little organization.'

'None whatsoever.'

'You're bound to say that. It means nothing.'

Harlow shrugged his shoulders. 'If that's the way you feel, too bad. Nothing I say will change your mind.'

Nick was no longer listening, his eyes were fixed on the tall figure walking towards them. It was Peter Cassells, the writer from Calvi. 'Now this is taking coincidence a bit too far,' said Nick. 'I don't believe that guy is for real.'

Cassells approached and greeted them with a diffident smile. 'Hello, I hope I'm not barging in.'

'What the hell are you doing on Lipari – writing about tourism here too? I don't believe it.'

Cassells coloured and stammered his reply. 'I – I – I saw the report about you in the paper and thought it would make a good story, so I followed it up. I hope you're not offended.'

'The reports said we were in Palermo. How the hell did you find us here?'

Cassells began to speak but Harlow waved him to silence. 'All right, Nick. Peter is one of my men, working undercover in this part of the Med. I asked him to keep an eye on you. For your own good, of course.'

'He didn't do much of a job, did he? Anyway why did I need a back-up?'

'We didn't know where you'd gone to, so you can't blame him for Sarah's disappearance. And the reason we kept watch was because I did suspect that Beardsley had been doing a bit of smuggling on the side, but I didn't think it was serious. I'm sorry.'

'It's too bloody late to be sorry. Let's get back to the boat and see whether Gina's doing a better job than you.'

'I'll come with you. You, Peter, ferret around and see if anyone knows anything. Keep it close and don't let anything slip out.'

'Okay, boss, I get the word.' He grinned and made off, dropping his shy manner for just a moment.

'He's some actor, isn't he?'

'Yes, Nick, and he's a damned fine agent, whose life is in danger if the word gets out. So keep it to yourself. Not a word to your Mafia friends.'

'Get this – they are not friends. They are helping me as a return favour, and I'll accept their help along with that of anyone else who offers.'

Back at the boat Gina and Paolo had already returned and

were watching out for them. Gina rowed in to collect them and on the way back she said briefly, 'When you get on board, don't speak until Paolo does.'

Mystified, Nick nodded.

Paolo was waiting in the cockpit and when they arrived he beckoned them to the port side. He reached under the coaming and, with a quick jerk, produced a small black box about half the size of a match box. He showed it to them and Harlow nodded; then he threw it over the side.

'Now that's gone we can speak. I think it was probably worn out, but there was no point in taking chances. That's how they knew your plans to come to the islands.'

Nick said, 'I haven't got long. I have to catch the boat to Milazzo, but was that likely to have been planted by the Union Corse.'

Paolo shook his head, but it was Harlow who replied. 'Unlikely. It was a very old model and not very efficient. I'm sure that they have much better equipment.' Paolo nodded agreement and Harlow continued. 'You seem to be obsessed with the Union Corse. I think you'll find that it was all a big mistake and you'll hear no more from them.'

Paolo raised an eyebrow. 'I wish, Signor, that I could be as certain.'

Gina went on to explain that the ambulance had been stolen the previous afternoon and found abandoned that morning in Palermo. There was little doubt that it had been used to take Sarah across to Milazzo. The owner of the ambulance was in the clear: he had been beaten and tied up. No one had noticed until this morning because the previous day had been the driver's day off. It was also fairly obvious that the whole thing had been the work of Dawson and Nixon, with the help of Guido. Gina's father had alerted all his men to find out where the Englishmen were hiding.

'All this is fine,' said Nick, 'but I don't want any interference while I'm in Milazzo. I'll have enough trouble bargaining, since the drugs no longer exist.'

'That's the final thing which I have to report,' Gina replied. 'As a very last resort, my father will acquire the necessary quantity of drugs to make a transfer possible.'

'That's a comfort in one way, but I can't stand the thought of them getting onto the streets once Sarah is free.'

'Let's hope it doesn't prove necessary to trade them, but, if it does, I think the drugs will probably be recovered and destroyed long before they get on to the streets.'

'What about the two Englishmen and Guido?'

'You should not worry about their future,' replied Paulo.

'At the moment I really couldn't care less about their fate. They've taken Sarah and, somehow, I can't find it in me to forgive and forget.'

Ricard spoke on the telephone to Debert. 'We've found them. They are in Lipari. That's a small island...'

'I know where Lipari is. What are your plans?'

'It appears they've got mixed up with those two clowns, Nixon and Dawson. They think that Byers has some stuff belonging to them, so they've taken his woman in order to trade. We know where they are holding her, so we'll step in and borrow her. We can use the same idea. That way we don't fall foul of Scarfiotti. By the time he finds out we'll be back in Corsica. He's unlikely to follow up because he couldn't give a damn about Dawson and Nixon and that crowd of cheap crooks.'

'Okay, Ricard. Go ahead, but watch your step. Don't get us into a war with Scarfiotti. We have enough problems without that.'

Milazzo is quite an attractive town, which falls into two distinct areas – the old town on the hill, enclosed by sixteenth-century walls, and the modern part surrounding a busy port. Long beaches stretch away on either side of the port. However, Nick was impervious to all this. He found the Bar Napoli in the new part of town with no difficulty. He glanced at his watch as he walked past the front. It was now half past two – half an hour to go. He had decided to stick to the instructions to the letter, to avoid any misunderstanding. So he walked back towards the harbour for ten minutes and then returned slowly.

The bar was not as he had imagined. It was a newish building with lots of glass and mirrors. Inside everything was spotlessly clean and the glass-topped tables were polished brightly. There was only one other person, sitting at a table at the far side enjoying a glass of wine and the air conditioning. The waiter was young and smartly dressed. This seemed a very unlikely place to hold talks about ransoming a kidnapped victim. It was, he thought, the kind of place frequented by Dawson and Nixon. They themselves would probably not appear, and the chances were that this was merely the first stop of a roundabout journey.

Nick sat at a table with a view of the door and ordered an espresso coffee. He paid at once in order to be free to leave quickly. He waited for ten minutes but nobody appeared; then, as he was getting anxious, an elderly man came into the bar and moved towards him. Nick started to rise but the other walked straight past him to a table a few metres away. Nick sank back into his seat in disappointment and waited on.

Five minutes later, an elderly woman dressed in black came through the door and headed for the newly arrived man. She spoke to him softly for a short time, then turned back towards the door. As she passed Nick's table she dropped her shopping bag and the contents spilled on the floor. Nick immediately dropped to his knees to help her recover them while she muttered her thanks. She had left before he realized there was a piece of paper under his cup. He grabbed the paper and ran to the door but there was no sign of the woman. Returning to the bar he discovered that the man had also disappeared.

Sitting down, he opened the paper and read: *'You should now go out and walk down the street towards the harbour. If you are alone you will be contacted.'*

Nick did as instructed. As he walked slowly down the road a small boy running from the other direction cannoned into him and, without stopping, forced something into his hand. The boy ran between a couple of burly men and disappeared into a narrow alley. By the time Nick had pushed past them, the boy had vanished.

The object in his hand was a key – a car key, in all probability – and it was wrapped in another note. *'This key fits the red Fiat Bravo parked across the road from where you stand now. Take it and drive out to meet the Messina to Palermo main road. NOT THE MOTORWAY. Drive towards Messina.'*

Nick looked across the road and, sure enough, there was a red Fiat parked as described. Since it was a 'no waiting' area it probably had not been there long. He hurried over and unlocked the car. He noticed at once that the rear-view mirrors had been broken off, so he would be unable to watch out for followers.

The roads were well signposted. He found the main Messina road after three or four kilometres, turned along it and headed east. It was very quiet; all the traffic was using the motorway which ran alongside. After a couple of kilometres a Mercedes saloon overtook him. A card in the rear window instructed him to follow. The leading car continued along the main road for another kilometre before turning off to the right, crossing over the motorway and heading up into the Peloritani Mountains.

These barren mountains form most of the north-eastern corner of Sicily. The many stream-beds are dry most of the time. What little rainfall there is runs off the soft, crystalline rock, leaving nothing but dust and gravel. There are few roads and those that there are peter out into dusty tracks after a short distance, usually ending in deserted, derelict farmhouses – monuments to those men who strove hard but lost the battle against the elements.

The road the Mercedes followed had already turned into a track, bounded by huge boulders as big as houses, and the clouds of dust which billowed up forced Nick to drop well back in order to see clearly. He rounded a sharp bend to find that the road had widened into a small plateau and the other car had parked facing back the way they had come. The dust cloud still hung around it. On all sides giant boulders were piled high.

He halted and remained inside, waiting for the other man to make the next move – but it was not to be. After a few minutes he realized that it was up to him to trigger further action. He got warily out of the Fiat and, keeping a good look out, crossed slowly to the other car. The Mercedes was fitted with darkened side windows and he couldn't be sure without opening the door that the driver was inside. He reached out and touched the handle, then withdrew it sharply as if it had burned him. What if it was booby-trapped? He'd witnessed the results of a car bomb before and didn't want an action replay with himself as the star performer. He was considering his next move when he felt the muzzle of a handgun pressed against the back of his neck.

'Move to the car and put your hands on the roof – then spread yourself, like they do in the American movies.' The English was good, but heavily accented.

He did as he was told and felt himself being expertly frisked.

'Okay, Byers. I hope you have brought the drugs.'

'I hope you have brought the girl.'

'I would not be stupid enough to do that until I was sure you are ready to trade. When you give us the drugs you'll get the girl back.'

'No drugs until I see she is all right. Do you take me for a fool?'

The other man considered the impasse and realized he would have to make a concession. 'Meet me here tomorrow at nine in the morning and have the stuff with you. Come alone and we will exchange the girl. Try anything and she will die. You will be watched all the way so do not try to be clever. Now go back to your car and wait until I've departed.'

Nick sat in his car wondering if there was some move he could make, when the Mercedes moved away, passing close to him. The driver leaned out of the open window with the gun in his hand. Nick's reaction was to duck low, but the shots were not intended for him – both went into his rear tyre. By the time Nick realized what had happened the other car had disappeared in a cloud of dust. He stood, hands on hips, and looked at the flat tyre.

'Shit!' he said, and set about changing the wheel.

Ricard watched the Mercedes approach the dilapidated farmhouse and drive straight into the broken down barn. From where they were positioned in the rocks on the hillside they had a clear view of Guido as he walked from the car and entered the house.

'It's time to go,' he said to his two Arab sidekicks. 'You know what to do. We work our way round and approach the house via the barn. I'll lead the way. When we get there, you follow me in through the door, Ahmed, while Hassan goes to the window. Wait for me to go in before you open fire. Remember – don't harm the woman; but I want all the others dead.'

The other two nodded and they set off in single file to work their way slowly round to the back of the barn. Once there they found a hole large enough for them to crawl through. They eased past the Mercedes, feeling its warmth and smelling the hot oil. There was only one stretch of open ground to cover, and this they did as quickly as possible, before crawling along the front of the veranda and taking up their positions by the door and window.

Guido parked the Mercedes in the broken-down barn and walked across the dusty yard. He pushed open the door of the ramshackle farmhouse and went inside. Dawson, who had been watching from the window, turned round as he entered.

'So you haven't got it?'

'I didn't expect to get it this time. Byers is no fool. He wants to see the girl before he exchanges, so I've set another meeting at the same place for nine o'clock tomorrow morning. We can have my brother in the rocks with a rifle and he can kill them both when we have the stuff. It's a pity about the girl. I'll have to have fun tonight instead. We can let her come round from the drug a bit so that she can enjoy it too. I will teach her some new tricks.'

'You are disgusting, Guido. You can do what you like, as long as she is alive and conscious tomorrow. I'll go and check her now. And close that bloody door – I don't know what's worse in this dump, the heat or the flies.' He went through a doorway to the other room of the house and there he looked down at Sarah as she lay unconscious on a dirty mattress and an old iron bedstead. Her hands were tied to the bed-head and her ankles to the foot. He grinned maliciously and prodded her hard with stiff fingers to check that she was still out. He couldn't understand what Guido saw in her. She was not his cup of tea at all. He'd tried a woman once – it had left him cold and rather revolted. Still, each to his own. He turned to rejoin the others when he heard the outside door burst open and a shout, followed quickly by the roar of a shotgun, the sharper crack of a handgun and, another roar of shotgun fire. It had happened, his worst nightmare – they had been discovered by the Mafia.

As Ricard burst through the door shouting for them to back up, Guido and Nixon were stunned in amazement. Guido was the first to recover and made a dive for his rifle which was propped up in the corner. He hadn't a chance. Hassan fired through the window and his face took the full blast. Nixon made a dash for the table to hide himself but Ricard's handgun roared in the confined space and the slug took him in the stomach, knocking him back against the wall. A split second later Ahmed's shotgun tore away his chest. Ricard signalled to Ahmed to go through into the bedroom, while he stood back covering him.

Filled with a terrible fear, Dawson backed to the far corner of the room and drew his own revolver. His hands were shaking as he aimed for the doorway. The figure which filled it was carrying a gun at the ready but Dawson managed to get the first shot. The figure swung away with a gasp, but the drug-dealer failed to follow up with more shots. Instead, he looked around in panic for some hiding place. There was none. There was no way out. When the Arab made an effort and brought the shotgun back to bear he could do nothing to protect himself. All his plans were for nothing. His dreams of riches were blown away as the blast of shot caught him in the chest and smashed him against the wall, sending his revolver spinning away under the bedstead. Ahmed staggered out clutching at his right shoulder, the blood oozing through his fingers. He stopped at the outside door and leant against the lintel until Hassan came to support him.

Ricard emerged from the building and looked at Ahmed with disgust. 'You must be getting too old. You, with a shotgun and surprise on your side – you let yourself get hit by a cream-puff with a handgun. Get him back to the car, Hassan. I guess we'll have to find a doctor before we fly home.'

He went back into the building and through to the bedroom. He barely glanced at the blood-covered body of Dawson. He stood for a short time, looking down at the girl on the bed. Her torn and dishevelled clothing revealed her bare breasts, but he didn't bother to cover them; instead he checked the pulse in her neck and lifted one eyelid. He grunted with satisfaction and, taking out a large knife, quickly slashed through the ropes binding her to the bed. With ease he lifted her unconscious body and hoisted it over a shoulder. After a quick glance round the building he followed the others to the car.

Nick, having changed the wheel, drove back into Milazzo and abandoned the car in a side road. He had no doubt it was stolen and felt that the quicker he rid himself of it the better. He walked down to the harbour and a telephone he had seen earlier. As pre-arranged, he put in a call to a hotel in Lipari and asked for Harlow. In seconds he was on the line.

'How did it go?'

'As we expected, there's another meeting tomorrow.' He went on to explain what had happened. Then he said, 'We'll have to take up Scarfiotti's offer to provide some more heroin. It's the only way. We need something to bargain with.'

'I'm not sure that I can go along with that.'

'Come off it, Harlow. This is chicken-feed compared to some of the things you do. Sarah's life is at stake, so stop buggering about and organize it for me.'

'I'm staying well out of that part. You seem to forget that I'm a government employee, and the one thing which is definitely frowned upon is the handling of drugs. I'll pass your request to Paolo and let him deal with it – that's the best I can do.'

'Okay, okay – you clear your yard-arm, but I want the bloody drugs. In the meantime, it's pointless having the boat in Lipari now. Tell Steve to sail it over here. With Gina to help he should have no problems.'

'The boat's ready to go. They had already decided to do just that as soon as they heard from you. Steve thought that it would take about four hours, so we should be with you early evening.'

Harlow was disturbed. The more he heard about Dawson and Nixon the more he suspected that they had no intention of releasing Sarah. As soon as they got what they wanted they would use her and kill her, and probably Nick as well.

Paolo was on the boat and Harlow told him what had happened, and also voiced his suspicions. The big Mafioso nodded his agreement. 'Yes, you are right. We will provide the drugs, but we will also take other action. We must withhold this from Byers, though.'

Nick stood on the quayside and watched the yacht glide gently into the harbour. Even with his worries about Sarah he appreciated the beauty of the boat and felt a strange affection for it. Steve handled it skilfully and brought it alongside the quay without the slightest bump. Nick took the mooring lines, which Gina handed him and, having made it fast, went on board. Steve greeted him with a wave of the hand and Gina with a kiss on each cheek.

'Are you alone? Where's Harlow?'

'He and Paolo came across earlier on the hydrofoil. He said he had things to do and would see us later,' replied Steve.

'I bet he has, the devious bastard.' He went on to tell them what had happened at the meeting.

Steve listened intently before asking, 'Where do we go from here?'

'There's nothing we can do except wait and hope. I'll keep the rendezvous at nine tomorrow and, if I get Sarah back safely, I'm going to catch the first flight to England and to hell with Harlow. He can clear up his own bloody mess.'

Steve went below to the saloon and came back with a bottle of wine and some glasses. 'If we've got to wait around doing nothing, we may as well do it in comfort.' He filled the glasses and swung his feet up onto the cockpit seating.

In spite of his worries, Nick couldn't help but smile. 'Steve, I think you're very good for me.' He picked up another of the glasses and spread himself out opposite.

'If you two gentlemen would make enough space I could be comfortable too.' Gina stood, hands on hips, looking down at them with a mock scowl.

'You can come and be comfortable with me anytime, Gina.' Steve moved up and patted the cushion next to him.

Gina sniffed theatrically. 'I think I can manage by myself.'

Nick listened to the banter with a certain amusement, but he had already sensed a closeness between Steve and Gina. He hoped the young man knew what he was doing. To fool around with that particular young lady could be madness – and fatal madness at that.

7

Harlow and Paolo returned to the boat quite late in the evening. They arrived together and Nick had the feeling they had spent much of the afternoon together – so much for Harlow's sense of propriety.

After the usual exchange of greetings, Nick asked outright, 'Well, do I get it?'

'If course. Signor Scarfiotti is a man of his word. I will have it here at eight o'clock tomorrow morning. After the signorina is free we will recover it again.' Paolo spoke in a matter-of-fact way but there was a menace in his words. Nick thought they probably spelt out the exit for Messrs. Dawson and Nixon.

Paolo was speaking again. 'The man in the Mercedes is called Guido. He is the accomplice of the two Englishmen. His uncle owned a farm in the Peloritani Mountain area. It's derelict now, but we think that it would make a good hideout for them and is probably where they are holding the girl.'

Nick was furious. 'How the hell do you know about the Mercedes and who was in it. You were supposed to stay well clear. You may have endangered Sarah with your stupid meddling. What if they've spotted you?'

'Calm down, Nick. They weren't spotted. These people are experts.' Surprisingly, it was Harlow who spoke on Paolo's behalf. 'If some of my men were half as good I'd be happy. For instance, did you notice that you were shadowed all day?'

Nick shook his head slowly. 'I only hope you are right.'

Harlow replied with conviction. 'Oh, I'm right. Nevertheless, we'll try to get Sarah back by bargaining first. If that fails we'll move in on the farm. There's no sign of life there at the moment but the Mercedes is parked in the barn at the side. The only other choice you have is to call in the police and I fear that could be the end for Sarah. So stop whinging and accept expert help when it's available.'

Nick realized the sense in Harlow's argument but it didn't stop him being uneasy. He had the feeling he had lost control of things and was now little more than a puppet. The feeling increased when, having stated that he wanted to hire a car, he was told that Paolo had organized one for him already. He shrugged his shoulders and decided that he would accept it until Sarah was safe; then they would push off together and to hell with the lot of them.

The following morning he was awake and ready to go, with lots of time to spare. He was impatient to be away and, as a result, became touchy and irritable. The car that Paolo had provided was a Fiat similar to the one he had used before. Before leaving he stressed that no one was to follow him, however professional they might be. 'If I spot a tail, I'll break his bloody neck.'

The trip to the clearing was uneventful and, having parked the car, he walked over to a boulder and sat in the early morning sunshine. He watched a small lizard as it wriggled its way among the rocks in search of insects. There was little evidence of other life in that barren place, except for the perpetual buzzing of flies. He tried to relax and wait patiently, but it was difficult. All he wanted was to hold Sarah in his arms again.

As it neared nine o'clock he began to get nervous and his impatience grew. Nine came and went, without anybody arriving. By half past nine he was distinctly worried, and half an hour later he felt certain that something was wrong – badly wrong. He would wait another half hour and then give up.

His first thoughts were to blame Paolo. He was seething with anger and disappointment. He never doubted that he would get her back eventually, but this latest delay meant that she would have to spend even more time as a prisoner. Obviously, Guido had spotted the watchers on the previous day and decided not to keep the appointment. As he waited, however, his thinking became more rational. If they had spotted Paolo's men the previous day, surely they wouldn't have kept the first appointment. No – there must be more to it than that.

The drive back to the yacht was a nightmare. He couldn't concentrate and, with having to drive on the 'wrong' side of the road, there were several near misses. In a country where everybody tends to drive on their horns, he really brought out the worst in the other drivers – the resultant sound was impressive. At the yacht he vented his anger on Harlow, who listened in silence until Nick dried up.

Harlow was worried, but he endeavoured to hide it. He had far more experience than Nick in dealing with exchanges of that sort and a failure to keep to the timetable usually spelt disaster. He said quietly, 'Having got that off your chest, I suggest you pay attention and I'll tell you about plan B. Paolo and I discussed what to do in the event of there being a slip-up in the exchange. In order to be prepared, his men are stationed about a mile away from the farm – far enough away not to endanger your rendezvous, but close enough to take fast and decisive action should it prove necessary. In my opinion, it is now necessary.' He held up a hand to stop Nick's attempted interruption. 'No, please listen. It is obvious that something has gone wrong and I'm sure you wouldn't want to leave Sarah's fate in the hands of a group of seedy crooks. Guido, certainly, has been known to kill before. She has become an embarrassment to them and there's no telling what they might do. Paolo has already gone to join his men. I'll go out there with them and give the go-ahead. We'll have Sarah back to you in no time.'

'You don't honestly think that I'm going to sit here and wait patiently, do you? I'm going with you, and that's final.'

'You'll get in the way, Nick, and that could endanger Sarah. You're not trained for this kind of thing.'

'I won't get in the way. I'll keep well back and do as I'm told, but I'm not staying here.'

'Okay. But remember what you've just said.'

The journey out to the assembly point did not take long. When they arrived there were half a dozen men sitting in the shade of a cliff, smoking and chatting among themselves. A couple of cars were parked nearby. The men were all armed with automatic rifles and looked as if they knew how to use them. Paolo rose to meet them as they drove up. When he saw Nick he raised an eyebrow at Harlow, who merely shrugged.

'I've sent a scout out to have a look at the farm. He should be back any minute now; then we'll decide how we set about it. I've got far more men than I need but I wanted to play safe. I think this is going to be a job where stealth is more important than strength. At the moment, my plan is to surround the place secretly, then two of my best men will go down and take the place through the front door.'

Just then, a young man, slim and swarthy, seemed to materialize from nowhere. He spoke to Paolo in Italian, his report accompanied by much gesturing of the arms. Eventually, Paolo turned to them and spoke in English. 'Vincente says there is still no sign of life at the farm. The Mercedes is still in the barn and the front door of the house is still closed. The windows are open and everything is just as it was yesterday evening. It's all very odd. If they'd made an escape, surely they would have used the car. It's the only way they have and I can't see those two fancy Englishmen walking through this desert. Let's go and find out. Nick, please stay well back – for your own sake and that of your woman. We go on foot from here.'

Vincente led the way, with Paolo second and the rest following in single file and Nick bringing up the rear. The going was rough and, although it was only a mile, Nick was quite pleased when Paolo turned and signalled them to keep down and spread out. They dropped to their hands and knees and crawled forward with the Mafiosi fanning out to right and left. Nick followed close to Harlow who waved him down beside him. As they lay side by side in the dust, Harlow spoke softly. 'Ease yourself forward on your belly and look between those two rocks over there – but peep. Keep your bloody head down and, whatever happens, don't interfere. Okay?'

Nick nodded and eased his way forward to the gap Harlow had indicated. He lifted his head slowly and saw the farmhouse for the first time. It was far more ramshackle than he had imagined and was situated in the middle of an area of flat ground. On the far side of the house stood a dilapidated barn. Nick could see the bonnet of the Mercedes just inside the doorway. The door itself had long since fallen off and was lying in the dust.

Nick waited impatiently for something to happen but he knew that this was an operation that couldn't be hurried. He wondered how the two Mafiosi would approach the place unseen. Then he spotted Vincente and the other man working their way forward on the far side of the barn, invisible from the house. They disappeared from view, then reappeared next to the house. They crawled along the front of the broken-down veranda and stationed themselves, one either side of the door. They produced handguns and held them ready while they waited, obviously listening. Nick held his breath. This was it. Suddenly, Vincente moved. In one movement he kicked open the door and they were through into the house and out of sight. Nick waited for gun fire, but there was none. He started to breathe normally. The figure of Vincente appeared in the doorway and waved his arms for them to join him. Nick could hardly contain himself. Was Sarah inside? If so, was she alive? He leapt to his feet and charged forward, stumbling over he boulder-strewn ground. More than once he found himself spread-eagled in the dust. Harlow, on the other hand, moved like a young gazelle, covering the ground in half the time. He went into the house and stopped in horror. To Vincente he said briefly, 'The girl?'

The Italian simply shook his head and Harlow breathed a sigh of relief. He turned to the door and was just in time to stop Nick entering. 'Please don't go in there, Nick. Sarah's not inside.'

'Get out of the way, Harlow. I want to see.'

Harlow shrugged and moved to one side, letting the other man through. 'If you must, but I've warned you.'

Nick entered the farmhouse. At first he could see very little but he was aware of an unpleasant smell and a strange buzzing noise. Then he saw the two bodies. One, Nixon, was sitting on the floor and leaning against the wall. His chest had been completely pulverized. It was now a mass of bloody flesh and the multitude of flies formed a black, seething crust. The other body stretched out on the floor was probably Guido, but he couldn't be sure for the face no longer existed – just pulp and more flies. As Nick moved the insects rose from the bodies in a mass and the buzzing increased. He felt the nausea rising, but he had to know. He stumbled to the door on the far side of the room and leant against it while he peered in. There was Dawson against the wall, his chest torn to pieces and covered in more of those loathsome flies. The eyes were wide open and staring, but they too had become covered with the creatures.

Nick tore his eyes away and looked around the room. To his relief, it was empty. At least Sarah hadn't perished in that hell-hole. Sick to the pit of his stomach, he staggered out onto the veranda, where he vomited violently. Leaning back against the outside of the building he stared in fascination at the two splashes of blood on the floor at his feet. He had never seen as much blood as there was in that building. It had splattered the walls and formed pools on the floor – and everywhere there were flies. He shuddered again.

'I tried to stop you, but you had to go in. Still, I suppose it was necessary.' Harlow's voice held a certain sympathy. 'Now we know the kind of people we are up against, and we can be pretty certain that Sarah is alive. You can surely see now that the police are out of the question.'

'But we can't just leave those bodies to rot there.'

'Paolo's men will dispose of them. They will just disappear.'

Paolo had approached them quietly. 'Yes, I will take my men away and arrange with some "undertakers" to come and collect the bodies – they will have a proper burial.'

'Since there's nothing more to do here, I just want to go away – somewhere where I can breathe clean air and listen while you tell me what happens next.'

'Okay,' replied Harlow; but he had an awful feeling that he didn't know what to do next.

Gina and Steve greeted the news with horror, and there was no doubting the sincerity of their expressions of sympathy. Harlow acknowledged that he was uncertain about their next move.

'Quite frankly, I don't know that we can do anything yet. Unless Paolo has some bright idea, all we can do is to wait until someone contacts us with some kind of ransom demand.'

When Paolo arrived he freely admitted that he had no better idea. When they discussed who might be responsible for the shootings, he was no wiser.

'Could it have been some other branch of the Mafia?' asked Harlow. 'After all, those shootings were done with a shotgun and that's the Mafia's weapon.'

'Other people use them too and, what's more, they could have used a shotgun to mislead us. Besides, we've been keeping a close watch on the others and they've not shown any interest in this venture. I think we will just have to wait.'

That night Nick couldn't sleep. While it wasn't surprising after the horrors of the day, there was something else bothering him, but he couldn't work out what it was. Something he had seen out at the farm was not right, but what was it? At dawn, he got up and dressed, went up on deck and started ashore.

'And where might you be going?' The voice stopped him in his tracks and he turned round to see Harlow sitting on the cabin-top with his back against the mast and his knees up under his chin.

'I can't sit around here doing nothing, just waiting, so I thought I would take a drive to try and stop my mind whirling. What are you sitting there for?'

'Let's just say I couldn't sleep either. I'd go with you, but one of us should remain here.'

'I agree. Cheers.' Nick made his way ashore and drove off in the Fiat. He followed the road they took the previous day – the road to the old farm. He was determined to find out what it was that was niggling away at him. He hoped the bodies had been removed. He didn't think he could face them again, especially since another day had elapsed.

He stopped short of the farm and pulled the car off the track. Making his way on foot, he approached the barn first. The Mercedes was still parked there as before. Other than a few old, broken farm utensils the place was empty. The barn obviously hadn't been used for years and the sun shone through the gaps in the roof. He made his way reluctantly towards the house. The door was open and he peered in. He breathed a sigh of relief when he saw that the bodies had gone. The place still smelled of death and the flies were there in abundance. He looked around the living room but could see nothing out of place, so he went through to the bedroom. There he took note of the cut bonds which had clearly secured Sarah to the bed – evidence that she was still alive: they would hardly have taken one dead body and left three others. Other than the bed, the room was empty of furniture. He bent down and looked under it. Against the back wall a handgun lay in the dust. He reached over and recovered it. The safety catch was off so he put that right, then lifted the muzzle to his nose. He thought he could smell cordite, but he wasn't sure. He wasn't experienced in that kind of thing. He put the gun in his pocket and, after another look around, made his way outside onto the veranda.

He looked down at where he had vomited and felt unreasonably ashamed. Then he looked at the blood splashes. That was when he realized what had been bugging him. The splashes outside must have been from another casualty and not from one of the three inside. His first thought was for Sarah, then he noticed that they formed a trail back into the house. He followed it to the bedroom door and there it stopped. There was no blood by the bed but there was a smear on the wall, quite high up – much too high to have been from Sarah.

Feeling relief coupled with a sense of achievement, he went back outside and stood on the veranda once more. He took a last look at the place where he had vomited, wrinkled his nose in disgust and started away. It was then he noticed that someone else had been sick close by. Since it was hardly likely to have been Harlow, or the Mafiosi, or the killers, someone else must have been there as well. He looked uneasily at the surrounding rocks and when he saw the flash of the sun on some bright object up there the back of his neck really started tingling.

Pretending that he hadn't noticed he walked slowly back to the car and climbed into the driving seat. Carefully, he turned the car and drove back down the track, watching out for other vehicles on the way. At last he came to the stop. The place was just what he needed: a sharp blind corner followed by a narrow neck of road with boulders close on either side. He drove round the corner and stopped, swinging the car broadside across the track, blocking it completely.

Getting out quickly, he knelt behind the bonnet and, holding the handgun in a two-handed grip, he rested it on the car and waited. He had realized it was unlikely that the other person had walked out into the desert and must, therefore, have hidden a vehicle somewhere, so that he – or she – would have to come out along the track. He waited for several minutes, the excitement rising in him, before he heard the approaching motorcycle confirming his assumption. The engine sounded like a small two-stroke, possibly a scooter, and it was going quite fast. Nick hoped he had parked far enough from the corner to give the rider time to stop, but it was too late to worry about it.

As the scooter rounded the corner Nick had a glimpse of the

rider wearing T-shirt and jeans. A scarf covered the face and there was no crash helmet, only a mass of long dark hair. He was unsure about what happened next because everything was obscured in a cloud of dust. The only thing he knew for certain was that the riderless scooter careered forward and slammed into the side of the car. He waited in the silence that followed with the gun steady, alert for any movement. Then, as the dust cleared, he saw the figure some twenty feet away on hands and knees, head hanging, clearly dazed.

Nick called out in English, 'Stay on your knees and put your hands behind your head.'

The face was still hidden by the scarf, but from the general shape he guessed that it was a woman – and this was confirmed by the cursing that came to him in a feminine voice. He cut it short with a sharp 'Shut it.'

'You are mad. You could have killed me.' She was clearly Italian and the English was heavily accented. 'I cannot stay like this. Let me get up.'

He thought it unlikely that the girl was armed but he'd seen enough in the past twenty-four hours to take no chances. 'Okay, get to your feet but stay where you are.'

She did as he told her.

'Now, take off your jeans.'

She was furious. 'I will not undress for your amusement.' She tore away the scarf and stood with hands on hips glaring at him. She was deeply tanned with dark eyes; her long black hair was a mess. She was not pretty but he found her strangely attractive.

'I'm the one who has the gun and you *will* undress, but not for my amusement. Now I will count to three; then I will start shooting.' He hoped she wouldn't call his bluff, because one thing was certain – he could never shoot her.

'You dirty Mafioso,' she hissed at him, but she kicked off her sandals and dropped her jeans, revealing a minute pair of scarlet panties.

'Take off your shirt and then turn round.' She scowled at him and hatred shone from her black eyes, but she pulled off the shirt. She wore no bra and her sun-tanned body showed no light patch over her full breasts which she thrust out with a sneer. She certainly was not armed in any way.

'Okay, get dressed again.'

She was surprised; she had expected him to take her. 'Are you not going to rape me, like the murdering coward that you are?'

'I am not going to rape you and I've never murdered anyone in my life. The reason I wanted you undressed was to be sure you have no weapons. Too many people have died recently and I didn't want to be another one. Now, when you are dressed, come over to the car slowly and introduce yourself.'

She hurriedly dressed and dusted herself down with her hands. Then she took an elastic band from her pocket, shook her hair, and tied it back in a pony-tail. Having had a few seconds to compose herself, she approached the car, prepared for anything. 'I'm Claudia Bugiatti, but you probably knew that – most Mafiosi do.' She clearly expected some reaction to her name and was oddly disappointed when there was none.

'I've never heard of you and, furthermore, I'm not a Mafioso. My name is Nick Byers. I am an English yachtsman who has got out of his depth. Why are you here? You were obviously following me.'

'Just as I followed you all yesterday when you killed the men at the barn. I know. I saw them after you left.'

'If you saw them you should know that they were dead long before we got there. If you followed us you would know that no shots were fired in the farmhouse, so how could we have killed them? Do you think we tore out their chests with our bare hands? Try not to be stupid. Those men were killed with shotguns, and I've never heard of a silenced shotgun – have you? What's more, you should have noticed that the men with me were armed only with automatic rifles.'

'But shotguns are the weapons of the Mafia, almost their trademark.'

'Not on this occasion, and you know it.'

His arguments were getting to her and she was now uncertain about what had happened. Certainly there had been no shots fired and the bodies had looked as if they had been there for some time. She shuddered as she remembered those awful flies. Some of the anger had gone from her face and doubt had replaced it. 'But you are still a friend of the Mafia.'

'Oh, no. Far from it. I hate all they stand for. I unwittingly did them a big favour and they are repaying it. With the situation I'm in, I'd accept help from anyone.' He decided to take a chance. 'Your scooter is a write-off, so come with me in the car and we'll find a little café, where we can have breakfast. I'll tell you the full story. Here, you can take the gun – I hate them anyway.' He slid the gun across the bonnet to her.

She picked it up and weighed it in her hand, uncertainty written all over her face. Then she made a decision. 'Okay. But the story had better be good or I go to the police and take you with me.'

Nick grinned for the first time in days. 'It's a deal.' He held the passenger door open for her and she murmured her thanks. When he went round to the driver's side he could see that it was badly buckled around the rear door and the bodywork was pressing against the wheel. He bent down and gripped the wheel arch with both hands; it needed all his strength to pull it clear. The tyre seemed to be undamaged. He shoved the scooter off the road, climbed into the driving seat and started off down the track.

The café was very basic – bare walls and wooden tables. However, the coffee was welcome and the pastries were very good. They sat opposite each other. Although the drive had been in near silence, she now felt sufficiently at ease with him to have left the gun in the car. 'In spite of what you thought earlier, I can't conceal it in these clothes and I can hardly put it on the table while we eat.'

Nick grinned. 'I told you I couldn't take chances. Anyway

looking back, it was an excellent idea.'

'You have a dirty mind.'

'No, I just appreciate fine things.'

She couldn't repress a cheeky smile. 'You were going to tell me the whole story, so let us concentrate on that and forget my body, shall we?'

'I'm not sure that I can do that, but I will tell you the story from the very beginning.' He did just that, starting at Harlow's request to ferry the yacht back to England. As he spoke she listened intently without interruption, her face showing clearly that she believed what she was being told. 'That is the full story. I gave it in rather an abridged form, because I must get back to Harlow and tell him about the blood on the veranda. It could be important. But why did you follow us out to the farm? Why are you so interested?'

'Let's go out to the car and I'll tell you on the way to the harbour. I think your bloodstains may be more important than you think, and the quicker your friend starts working on it the better.'

In the car Claudia explained that she worked as a freelance journalist. 'I guess I just followed my father. He was a good journalist and he loved Sicily. He realized that we could never take our real place in Europe until we rid ourselves of the Mafia. He ran many stories about the corruption in our society and carried out many investigations, in spite of the dangers. Everybody warned him but he took no notice. Then, one day, they killed him. They shot him with their dreadful shotguns so that we could not recognize him.' There were tears in her eyes as she continued. 'I made a vow that I would take over his work and do my best to expose them for what they are – murdering cowards.'

There was silence in the car for a while and Nick glanced at her – tears were making channels through the dust which still powdered her face. He reached across and squeezed her hand to show his understanding.

'When I saw Paolo Pinetti on your boat I knew that something was about to happen because he never leaves Scarfiotti unless it's important. I hid on the quay and followed him when he went ashore. I'm very good at following people, even if I'm not very good as a reporter. I missed the story about you rescuing Gina Scarfiotti. I should have seen it, but I have been so busy following up my own stories. I am pleased that you saved her life. She is a good woman, and should not be condemned alongside her father.'

'I'm pleased you think that, because I like her. You are living very dangerously. If I spotted you I'm sure that Paolo would catch on to you in seconds. He must have known you were around – I wonder why didn't he do anything about it.'

'You do not believe I am good at tracking, but I am. Now stop here before we get to the harbour, so that Pinetti and his men do not see me.'

Nick shook his head slowly in amazement at the girl. 'If you go on the way you are, you'll end up like your father, and that will help no one.'

'Maybe. But if they kill me many people will sit up and take notice. So it will not have been in vain.' As she swung her legs out of the car, she looked back at him. 'I like you. I hope you find your woman safe and well. If I can help, contact me. I'm sure that Pinetti will know how to find me.'

Nick parked the car and made his way to the boat, his mind in a whirl. Steve was sitting on the cabin-top and greeted him with a wave of the hand. 'How goes it? Have you got any news?'

'I may have. Where's everybody?'

'Gina's gone ashore shopping. Harlow and Paolo are down in the saloon, holding a council of war.'

Nick found the other two sitting either side of the table. They looked up and greeted him with a nod. Harlow said, 'Did you enjoy your drive?'

'Yes, thank you. It was very enlightening.'

Paolo smiled. 'And Signorina Bugiatti is quite charming, isn't she?'

Nick flushed. 'How the hell did you know about that?'

'There is no mystery, Nick. I have had the girl under observation since she joined the party yesterday – partly out of curiosity and partly for her own protection.' He grinned. 'After your rather rough introduction you seemed to get on very well.'

Nick flushed to an even deeper red. 'If you knew she was there, why didn't you do something to stop her?'

'She was doing no harm, and it was better for her to discover the truth than to learn some of the facts and draw the wrong conclusions. She's an interfering young lady, but, strangely enough, I like her; and I feel sad about the way her father was killed.'

'That's great – coming from you.'

'You probably won't believe this, but we had nothing to do with his death. We had warned him that he was on someone's death list, but he took no notice.' He shrugged. 'Enough of that. Did you find anything else at the farm? Anything we missed?'

'As it happens, I did.' He was pleased to see the other two sit up and take notice. 'First of all, I found a handgun under the bed and it had been fired. What's more, there was a trail of blood leading away from the bedroom door and out across the veranda.'

'So what? There was blood everywhere.' Paolo asked.

Harlow was much quicker. 'God, Nick, this is important. It means that one of the attackers was shot. That's the only explanation.'

Now Paolo joined in too. 'Yes, I see it. There are not many places that a man can go with a gunshot wound. The hospitals would report it to the police. Let's hope the shot was not fatal, or that his friends decided not to make it so. I will have a check made around the doctors who would have helped.'

Ricard stood in the surgery, watching the doctor put the final dressing on the Arab's shoulder. The doctor was a small, nervous man with an almost bald head and thick spectacles. He was frightened of the thickset Corsican who had been awake all night sitting by his friend's side. The other Arab had sat with the unconscious girl. The doctor had been forced to keep her comatose and to remove the bullet from the man's shoulder. He had been paid well for his work, but he was longing for them to go. It was soon after dawn and the ambulance was ready outside the door.

Ricard looked questioningly at the Arab. 'Okay?' The other nodded.

Ricard lifted up a bag and turned to the doctor. 'You have been well paid. If you fail to keep your silence I will return and make sure that you never talk again.'

The doctor looked back into those merciless eyes and shuddered. 'I will tell no one, I promise.'

They carried the girl out to the ambulance on the stretcher. The driver had the door open and they slid her inside.

'It's my niece,' explained Ricard to the driver. He indicated the bandaged head. 'She has had a bad blow to the head in a car accident. We have a private aircraft waiting at the airport to fly her home. I fear she may not recover.'

'Poor child. She is so young, too. Was your friend hurt at the same time?'

'Yes. Now we must go.'

Early that evening, Paolo returned to the boat bearing the bad news. 'We have found the doctor who treated a man with a gun shot wound. The man was an Arab and he was accompanied by another Arab and a Frenchman – probably Corsican. They had with them a young woman who was kept sedated.'

He hesitated, but Nick waved his hand impatiently. 'Go on, go on. Where are they now?'

'I'm sorry, Nick. We had to press the doctor but he gave us the name of the ambulance driver who took them to Palermo airport. It would seem that they had a private aircraft awaiting to take them to Corsica.' As Nick sat at the table with his head in his hands, Paolo continued. 'At least you know that the girl is alive and probably unharmed. Unfortunately, we will be unable to help you very much more, since we have no influence there.'

Nick spoke softly. 'That dirty bastard. I will go back to Corsica myself and I swear to God that I will kill him and anyone who stands in my way. I *will* get Sarah back.'

Harlow looked at him sharply. He had never heard such venom in Nick's voice before. 'I think you should wait a bit. Let Peter Cassells go back and make a few enquiries first.'

'Look, Harlow, understand this: I'm not relying on you and your rotten organization any more. Paolo, how can I contact Claudia Bugiatti?'

'She lives in a small apartment in Palermo. I will take you to see her. We can stop on the way and you can telephone to make sure that she is at home. I will give you her number but it will be better if you make the call; if she hears my voice she will probably hang up the receiver.'

The apartment was small but comfortably furnished. The typical Mediterranean tiled floor was spotless and shining brightly; the French windows opened onto a south-facing balcony. The only concession to journalism was the desk in the corner with a personal computer and piles of paper.

She waved her hand to indicate that he should sit in one of the deep rattan chairs, then went to a cabinet and poured a couple of glasses of red wine, handing him one, before sitting in a matching chair. She wore a long white robe, which accentuated her dark complexion and black hair, tied back in a pony-tail.

'How did you get here? Did the Mafioso drive you?'

Nick nodded.

'I hope he is not waiting outside. It would not be good for my reputation.'

Nick smiled. 'No, he's waiting back along the way. Incidentally, he says he likes you.'

Claudia snorted. 'Never believe anything a Mafioso tells you. But enough of this. You have not come to me because of my beautiful body. What is it that you want?'

'We traced the doctor who treated the gunshot wound. There were three men and they had Sarah with them. Apparently, she was sedated on a stretcher, but otherwise unharmed. It must have been Ricard and his men. They had a plane waiting and all flew back to Corsica.'

'So she is with those Corsican bastards. They are even worse than the Mafia. Mind you, they would not have gone to all this trouble for the pleasure of her company; they obviously want something and are prepared to bargain. In that case they will treat her with care. But when they get what they want they will probably kill you both.'

'It's even worse than that. As I told you, I don't know what they want. Even if I did, I don't know where it is. I must go back to Corsica secretly and try to find her and free her.'

'You wish to commit suicide, yes? You must love the girl very much. How can I help you?'

'I need a contact in Corsica. I need someone who can hide me and provide information and, most of all, someone who is not connected with this affair. I will try not to involve them in anything dangerous but I can't promise. I thought you might have journalist connections there.'

'You ask a great deal. However, I will see what I can do. I will contact you at the boat, if I can help. Go now and take that Mafioso away with you.' She escorted him to the door and, as he was about to leave, kissed him very softly on the lips. 'Good luck with your mission.'

She closed the door behind him and leant back against it as his footsteps receded along the passage. 'God help you, you poor romantic fool,' she murmured softly.

As they drove back to Milazzo, Nick explained what he was

intending to do and Paolo listened intently before commenting. 'You intend to fly to Ajaccio and move against Ricard like the charge of the cavalry. You're foolish, and shortly you will be dead and foolish.'

Nick bristled. 'Thank you for your support. I seem to recall you said you couldn't help me, so what am I supposed to do? Wait for Ricard's demands and then end up dead?'

'I didn't say that we couldn't help you. I said that we couldn't help you in Corsica, and that's different. We can help you get to Corsica in secret and we can make sure that you are armed when you are there.' Nick started to interrupt but Paolo stopped him. 'I know that you don't like guns, but this time you will need one. With all the hijacking these days there is no way you can get a gun onto an aircraft. So you must fly to Sardinia, where we can equip you. Then we will arrange a small boat to take you across to Bonifacio. Even then your chances are not good.'

'I know that, but I must try.'

'So be it. Don't scorn the help which Harlow can give you. When you are safely established there, he can be of great assistance. He could make the difference between success and failure.'

'I'll remember what you say.'

Gina had prepared an evening meal for the four of them, Paolo having taken his leave. Despite the delicious food and more than passable wine, the atmosphere was subdued. Eventually, Harlow could stand it no more. 'I know that you don't trust the Department, Nick, but if we're going to get Sarah back, we've got to work together. I don't want to know how you plan to get to Corsica. I just want you to contact me when you get there. If we pool our information we may just pull it off; if you decide to go it alone you haven't a snowball's hope in hell – and neither has Sarah.'

'Sounds like sense to me,' muttered Steve.

'I suppose so,' agreed Nick reluctantly. 'Okay, I'll keep you informed, but I want a promise that you'll keep all information to yourself. No reporting back to base – just the two of us.'

'I agree to that. I'll give you a contact telephone number in Ajaccio. I'll fly there tomorrow and start asking around, but I'll keep our movements to myself. Now we've agreed that, let's do justice to this great meal which Gina has prepared.'

Ricard looked into the cold grey eyes behind the steel-framed spectacles and shuddered slightly. 'I have the girl, Monsieur, in the villa at Favone. It is quite secure and away from prying eyes. When we approach Byers he will give us anything we want to get her back.'

'And how exactly do you intend to approach him?'

'We wait for him to approach us. We have left a trail that even a fool could follow – and he's not a fool.'

'It sounds reasonable,' said Debert grudgingly. 'I am pleased to see that you no longer underestimate him. What happens to them when you get the disc back?'

'I regret they will have a nasty accident – fatal, of course.'

'You will be met in Bonifacio by a man called Jacques Bianchi. He is small, with thick glasses and a large nose – about sixty years old. He will identify himself by asking if you like horse riding. That is the best I can do for you, Nick. He is a very brave and reliable man. Here is a telephone number so that you can let him know your time of arrival.'

'Thank you, Claudia. You have done enough. Does Bianchi know the story?'

'He knows most of it and is happy to take risks if it will harm the Union Corse. He hates them as I hate the Mafia.'

They were standing on the bows of the yacht in the morning sunshine, out of earshot of the others. Nick had called her the previous evening to tell her the route he planned to take and she had organized things accordingly. Now, as they made their farewells and she walked away across the quay with her hips swaying, he hoped they would meet again some day under better circumstances. He watched her as she disappeared down an alleyway, then walked back to the cockpit where Steve sat waiting.

'Nick, there must be something I can do to help. I can't just sit around on my arse.'

'There *is* something, very important. Wait until Harlow has gone, then sail the boat to Sardinia and stay there. Listen out on the radio every six hours, starting at noon. With any luck, you'll get my message. When I'm ready I want you to pick us up from Corsica and we'll make a break for home – hopefully before they know where we are.'

'Sounds good to me. I'll get Gina to crew for me on the way to Sardinia. She can fly home from there and I can manage alone until you join me.'

'Now, there are some things I'd like you to collect from Paolo to bring on the boat with you . . .'

8

The flight from Palermo to Sassari in the north-west of Sardinia was quick and uneventful – a typical commercial flight, with an attractive air stewardess who wore a forced smile when dealing with difficult passengers. As he left the aircraft he wondered how he would recognize his contact. He had been given no name or description. He need not have worried. As he entered the passenger terminal he was approached by a man in a smart grey suit with a gleaming white shirt and dark necktie.

'Mr Byers, I am pleased to meet you. I am Luciano Peretti. I have been asked by mutual friends to look after you during your short stay in Sardinia. I suggest we go straight to the hotel where I have booked you a room. Then you can shower and have an early evening meal. I would suggest that you endeavour to get some sleep because transport has been arranged for you at one o'clock tomorrow morning and I fear that further rest will be unlikely.'

'You seem to have it all organized. Lead on.'

The hotel was outside Sassari, standing in its own grounds. It was very secluded and possessed an air of quality. Peretti left him at the doorway. 'If you require me for anything, please ask reception.'

'I have arranged assistance from a certain Jacques Bianchi in Corsica. If I give you his number can you tell him where and when to meet me?'

'Of course, that will be no problem.'

Nick went in and approached the reception desk. A beautiful young lady greeted him with a smile. 'Good evening, Mr Byers. Welcome to our hotel. You are in room one. I will get a porter to show you.' Her English was faultless. 'If you require anything please call me. You may have dinner any time after seven o'clock.'

'I will be leaving in the early hours of the morning, so can I settle my account this evening?'

The radiant smile again lit up the room. 'There is no account, sir.'

The porter arrived and escorted him up to a luxurious suite of rooms. He showered and stretched out on the huge bed, wishing he had Sarah with him to share all this luxury.

The telephone by the bed woke him. It was dark and the illuminated clock showed it was quarter to one. He picked up the receiver. 'Yes.'

'Luciana Peretti is here to escort you, sir.' The voice was young and feminine and Nick guessed that it belonged to another fabulous beauty.

'I'll be down as soon as I've dressed.'

Peretti was waiting at reception for him, chatting to the beautiful girl behind the desk. Nick smiled to himself. The Italian had changed his suit for a black polo-necked sweater and jeans. On the dusty, bumpy road down to a small cove, Nick understood why.

They clambered onto the power-boat. A grunt was the only greeting from the short, thickset boatman. As he went forward to cast off, they went below to the cabin. Peretti produced a map, covering Corsica and the northern part of Sardinia. He spread it out on the table and stabbed at it with his finger. 'We are there. As you can see, it's only a short distance across to Bonifacio. However, if your friend Ricard is watching out for you, that is certainly one of the places he will cover. We therefore plan to drop you off at Propriano – that's here.' He stabbed the map, indicating a bay about twenty miles up the west coast. 'Jacques Bianchi has been advised of our plans and, hopefully, will be there to meet you.'

As ever, Nick was impressed with the organization. 'Thank you for your efforts. Do you know what this is all about?'

'No, and I have no wish to. I have been told only that you are a special friend of Giuseppe Scarfiotti and you wish to enter Corsica without Pierre Ricard knowing. That is all I need to know. As you will have noticed, the boatman is a man of few words and does as he is told without question. If you require further assistance while in Corsica you have only to telephone and I will help you in any way possible.'

It was about four o'clock in the morning when the boat slipped quietly into the bay at Propriano and moved slowly alongside a small quay. No attempt was made to tie up – Nick simply stepped ashore with his bag and, turning, lifted a hand in farewell. Peretti lifted his in reply, but the boatman ignored him and concentrated only on manoeuvring the boat out to sea.

Nick walked slowly towards the village. There was no sign of life anywhere. All the buildings were in darkness and he was becoming concerned that no one was there to meet him when a small figure detached itself from the shadows.

'Hello, Monsieur Byers. I'm supposed to ask you about horse riding, but it seems stupid at this time of the morning. However, we must humour young Claudia; she does get carried away with the cloak-and-dagger business. Will you just accept that Jacques Bianchi is at your service?'

Nick nodded in the near darkness. 'I think I can do that. Nice to meet you.' He held out his hand and the other man took it. Bianchi's hand was thin and bony, but the grip was firm.

He led the way through the dark streets to an old Renault, climbed into the driving seat and turned the key. The engine started immediately. Bianchi chuckled with satisfaction. 'She may be an old lady, but she still runs well.' He pulled the car out onto the main road and turned in the direction of Ajaccio.

'I've booked you into the Hotel Napoleon, but it would not do to arrive at this hour of the morning. People would start talking. We will go first to my apartment where you can rest and have breakfast. The hotel is not the best in Ajaccio, but it is clean and comfortable and, most important, it is rather impersonal. You will be left to yourself.'

'Thank you, Jacques. Do you know why I am here?'

'I know only that you have fallen foul of the Union Corse and that bastard, Ricard, and that he holds your woman hostage. Claudia said you would tell me anything else I needed to know.'

'Did she tell you that this operation could be dangerous – very dangerous? Several people have already died.'

'There was no need to tell me that. Anything connected to those bastards is dangerous. It doesn't worry me. They are ruining my country and harming the people. Corsica is called the Island of Beauty, quite rightly so, but for many it is the Island of Fear. Tourists should flock to our shores and we should be prosperous, but the tales of bandits and criminals keep them away. Anything I can do to bring them down I do willingly – and if I die, well, so be it.'

'You and Claudia have a lot in common, each fighting your own battle against your own villains.'

'Yes. I have known her since she was a child. Her father and I collaborated often. We were both newspapermen with a mission. Alas, he is dead and I am old, but the evil is still there.'

The road twisted and turned up into the mountains, then down to Ajaccio, before there was any sign of life. Although it was still early, the city was beginning to come to life. Some cars and delivery vans were on the move. Bianchi joined the light traffic and wound his way skilfully through to a parking space in a narrow alley. He led Nick through a nearby doorway into an apartment block and up the stairs to the top floor. The apartment was small but, as Bianchi explained, he lived by himself so it was quite big enough. 'I think you should sleep. If you are going to go against Ricard you will need your wits about you. Use the bed. I will go out and listen to the gossip in the markets. Maybe I'll learn something.'

It was past ten o'clock when Nick awoke. He stretched and swung his legs off the bed. In the living room he found his host lying on the small sofa. He tried not to wake him but Bianchi opened his eyes and smiled up. 'I no longer sleep deeply; just the occasional nap. I have news for you.'

Nick caught his breath. 'Yes?'

'There is much talk about you in the markets. It would seem that Ricard is waiting for you to arrive – the talk is that he is wanting to do a trade.'

'Do you believe that, Jacques?'

'I believe there is too much talk for it to be idle gossip. I think the word has been spread deliberately in the hope that you will hear it.'

'If I had something to trade, would he keep his side of the bargain?'

'Very unlikely. I think he would kill you and the girl as soon as he got what he wanted.'

'Oh, God. What the hell do I do next?'

'Maybe God would have a better idea, but I suggest you arrange to meet him and insist that you see the girl is alive and well before you trade. He will have to produce her from wherever they are holding her and then, perhaps, you can rescue her somehow. Is there anyone else who could help in this? I'm all right for gathering information, but my days of storming castles and rescuing ladies are, unfortunately, past.'

Nick nodded his head slowly. He had hoped to manage this without turning to Harlow but now he knew that any attempt to rescue Sarah without him would end in disaster. He could not risk that. He asked permission to use the telephone and dialled the contact number Harlow had given him. It was the number of a hotel in Ajaccio. Harlow had booked in and was located quickly.

'Nick, I'm pleased you called. I'm told our friend wants to trade but I don't trust him.'

'And we have nothing to trade,' Nick replied sarcastically.

'That's right. Do you have any sort of plan?'

'First of all, are you operating alone as promised?'

'Nobody else even knows I'm here.'

'Good. I thought that I might meet the man and ask to see Sarah. That way we can find out where they are holding her. If they take me to her that will be easy, but if they bring her to me you will have to do a bit of shadowing. Do you think you're still capable of that?'

'I may be desk-bound but I'm still one of the best in the business.' It wasn't a boast – simply a statement of fact. 'The idea sounds good. Do you think you can contact our friend?'

Nick looked at Bianchi. 'Yes, I think I can do that. I'll call you back when I have some news.'

'Good. I've got a little bit of information which might prove useful. I'll follow it up while I'm waiting.'

Nick rang off and turned to Bianchi. 'Jacques, how do I go about meeting Ricard?'

'We let the word out that you want to talk and it will find its way back to him. Then we wait for a meeting place and time to come back to us. If it's suitable, we keep it; if not, we propose a place of our own. You say, and I will get it started.'

'I'm grateful, but you are getting more and more involved and I didn't want that.'

'I told you not to worry. Anyway, I'm protecting myself. I'm using several cut-offs, so they'll have quite a time finding my identity.'

'In that case, Jacques, start the ball rolling.'

Ricard looked across the big table at his master. For the first time in days things seemed to be going his way and he could look Debert in the eye. 'It is as I forecast: Byers wishes to meet me to talk about a trade. We should have no difficulty in recovering the disc now. It is plain that the girl is the only thing he cares about.'

'He'll probably want to see the girl before making the trade. Is she unharmed?'

'She is – and well cared for at Favone. There will be no problems there.'

'When you meet him, bring him to Bastia and have the girl brought here too. There is no point in giving away where she is being kept, since he will not bring the disc with him at the first meeting.'

'Yes, monsieur.'

Ricard turned to leave, but as he reached for the door Debert spoke. 'Ricard. When you have the disc, kill them both. Then find out who has been helping him and kill them too.'

Nick was growing impatient. It was the middle of the afternoon and there was no sign of Bianchi. He was frustrated because he could do nothing until he got the time and place of the meeting. Suddenly, the door opened and his host entered looking drawn and tired. He felt a wave of guilt at his own impatience.

'Jacques, you look all in. Sit down and tell me what has happened.'

'Yes, I am tired, but we have a meeting. You are to be in a bar next to the market at five o'clock this afternoon. I have let it be known that this is acceptable to you, but that you wish to see the girl is alive and well before you trade. I hope I have done the right thing.'

Nick crossed to him and gripped his shoulder. 'Jacques, you have done a wonderful job. Thank you from the bottom of my heart. Now your part is over. I shall go and book into the hotel, then keep my appointment. First of all, I must call Harlow.'

The call to Harlow was brief – just the information about the meeting and that he would be using the Hotel Napoleon in the future. Then he said farewell to Bianchi and turned to leave the apartment.

'May God keep a watch over you.' He turned and saw tears in the older man's eyes. 'I wish I could go with you.'

'You did your part well – now it's up to me and Harlow. And may God watch over you too.'

* * *

In the sparsely-furnished bedroom of the villa just outside the small town of Favone on the east coast of Corsica, Sarah tugged once again at the door but it was firmly locked. The heavy steel shutters on the window were secured on the outside and eliminated most of the daylight. There was a small toilet in one corner, with a bidet and wash-hand basin. The only other item was the solid wood divan. Sarah felt this room had been used as a prison before.

She had no idea where she was, or, in fact, what day it was. When she had recovered consciousness the previous day she had been lying on the bed. She had felt terrible and called for help. A big, butch woman had arrived and spoken to her surprisingly softly. In accented English she had assured her that no harm would come to her if she was sensible. She would answer no questions but gave Sarah some tablets to ease her headache and upset stomach. Then she left, promising to bring food later. Sarah caught a brief glimpse of an armed man outside the door. Since then she had been provided with good food and had not been harmed in any way.

When the door opened now, the woman came in to announce that Sarah was going to take a little trip. Seeing the fear in Sarah's eyes she smiled reassuringly. 'No, you have nothing to worry about. You are going to see your man.' Sarah's sharp intake of breath made her captor smile again. 'I'm afraid you are not going to be released just yet, but he wants to see that you are fit and well, and that I've looked after you. Now you must wash and make yourself look beautiful.'

Sarah's heart was racing as she was blindfolded and escorted to the car. She was going to see Nick again and she was certain he would find a way out of this mess.

Nick found the bar with no trouble. His watch told him it was five minutes to five. He went inside, found a table by the window and waited. When the waiter approached he ordered wine and paid for it immediately. At ten minutes after five Ricard entered accompanied by two swarthy Arabs, one of whom had his arm in a sling. Nick recognized Ricard as the man in the alley on that morning which now seemed so long ago. Ricard looked round the bar, spotted him and walked over to stand over him. Nick looked up but did not rise.

'Have you got it with you?'

'Of course not. Do you take me for a fool?'

'Where is it?'

'Somewhere where you will never find it. When I have seen the girl is well I will recover it for you.'

'No. When you have seen the girl you will tell me where it is and I will fetch it.'

'That is impossible. It will be handed to me only, no one else. What's more, it cannot be recovered until nine o'clock tomorrow morning.'

Ricard considered this carefully for a while, his heavy brow furrowed, before replying. 'Okay, but you had better not be trying anything foolish or both you and the girl will die.' The words were spoken softly, almost hissed, so that no one around could hear them. 'Come with me now. I will take you to the girl.'

He turned abruptly on his heel and walked towards the door, knowing that Nick would follow and not bothering to check. At the door the two Arabs stepped aside to let them pass and followed on behind. As they walked Nick looked down on the Corsican's thinning hair and realized just how much shorter he was. It somehow strengthened him mentally.

The black Citroen XM was parked in a 'no-parking' zone close by, the opaque windows giving it a menacing air. The uninjured Arab moved forward and opened the door. The Corsican waved Nick into the back and followed him in. The two Arabs sat in the front. The car moved away smoothly. Not a word had been spoken since Ricard had left the table.

They drove in silence up into the mountains and headed towards Corté, the home of the famous Foreign Legion and the old capital of the island. As they drove through the small town Nick gazed up at the fortress standing guard proudly on the hillside. He could quite understand Jacques Bianchi's feelings. The car passed out of the town towards Cap Corse, the finger of the island which pointed to mainland France, and the port of Bastia. Bianchi had told him that the top man of the Union Corse lived in a fortified farmhouse in a wild part of Cap Corse. He wondered if he was about to meet the boss, and if Sarah was being held in that farmhouse.

They drove into the centre of the bustling town of Bastia and down to the old port. The tall buildings rose up on three sides of the small fishing harbour, many of them sadly needing a face-lift. The car came to a halt in front of one of these, the ground floor of which was a rather seedy-looking bar. Ricard led the way to a doorway at one side of the bar and Nick followed. They climbed the steep, dark flights of stairs to the third floor, where Ricard knocked on the door. There was a short delay while they were checked through a spy hole; then the door was unlocked.

Nick's heart was beating fast. This was the moment he had been waiting for, the moment when he would see Sarah again. He had never even considered that she might be dead. The door swung open, a man with a machine pistol waved them in – and there she was. She sat in an upright chair on the far side of the room, which was otherwise clear of furniture. She started to rise, stifling a sob, but the large woman beside her put a restraining hand on her shoulder. Nick's anger nearly burst out as he started forward, only to be stopped by the man with the machine pistol.

His heart was breaking at the sight of her with tears streaming down her face. 'Sarah, my love, what have they done to you?'

She choked back a sob. 'They haven't hurt me, Nick. Have you come to take me home?'

Ricard answered. 'Not yet. He's got to buy you first. When he produces what we want he can take you home.' He turned to Nick. 'You've seen what you wanted. The girl is unhurt; she has said that herself. Now you will stop here for ten minutes while she is taken back to her lodgings. Then you will be released to find your way back to Ajaccio. I'm told the buses are very good. We will meet in the same bar at ten o'clock tomorrow morning, and no excuses. Have the disc with you.'

They looked at each other longingly as she was led out. She stretched out her hand, and as their fingers touched a thrill passed through him. Suddenly, he felt certain that they would win: they would be together again.

The ten minutes seemed like so many hours, as he stood in silence with the armed man watching him closely. After what seemed an eternity, the man moved to the door and opened it. He then stepped well back and waved Nick through, slamming it closed after him. Nick half tumbled down the stairs in his haste, though he knew it would be in vain and Sarah would have long gone. Sure enough, there was no sign of her or any stationary cars – just the normal bustle of traffic. He hesitated for a while, then walked back to the tree-lined square in the middle of the town. There he hired a taxi to take him to Ajaccio – for a small fortune, of course. On the way, he kept as close a watch as possible to check that he wasn't being followed. There was no point in revealing where he was staying. It might be important later. He stopped the taxi well short of the hotel and walked the last couple of hundred yards.

Maria came slowly down the steps of the hospital to find her landlady waiting, as arranged on the telephone. They embraced and the elderly woman gazed in horror at the young girl's face. The side of her jaw was badly bruised and swollen; X-rays had proved that the jaw and cheek bones had been fractured. One eyebrow and the side of her forehead were still covered by a light dressing. Her appearance was bad, but the real hurt and anger was deep inside her. She had given her favours freely in Ricard's service, but his act of rape had disgusted her and, in some strange way, she felt contaminated by him. Her terror of him had been replaced by a terrible rage. She was determined to get her revenge, even if she died in the attempt.

The drive to her flat in Calvi did not take long but she was filled with apprehension at seeing it again. When the woman had parked the car she spoke to the girl with sympathy and understanding, though she knew that by helping she was putting her own life at risk. 'Maria, I've had your apartment cleaned, but you don't have to go there. You can stay with me until you're properly recovered.'

Maria laid a hand on her arm. 'Thank you, madame. You have been so kind, but it will be better if I face the apartment now and get it over.' Her once beautiful face mustered a small smile of thanks as she turned and made her way slowly up the stairs.

At the top she tried the key in the door but discovered that it was already unlocked. Full of doubts, she pushed it open and moved inside. The sight of Harlow sitting in the armchair alarmed her but she took it in her stride. This was obviously one of Ricard's men come to kill her; her only regret was that she would be cheated of her revenge.

'You have come to finish the job. Okay – let's not hang about, let's get it over. Or do you plan to rape me too? Go ahead – it doesn't matter any more.'

Harlow smiled and spoke softly 'I'm not from Ricard, Maria. I'm from the opposition and I haven't come to hurt you. Nick Byers is my friend. I've come to ask for your help and, in return, I will get you safely out of Corsica to a new life.'

The girl was doubtful. 'If this is true how can I possibly help you?'

'Not only can you help us but, in doing so, you will be able to take your revenge on Ricard, because we intend to ruin him.' He watched the girl's eyes light up, and knew she was prepared to help. 'This is what I want you to do . . .'

* * *

In his room Nick lay back on the bed and waited in frustration. He could do nothing. Everything now depended on Harlow. If only he would hurry; maybe he had lost her – maybe he had been caught. The thoughts chased each other through his mind until, just after eleven o'clock, there was a knock on the door. Tensing himself, he flung it open. Standing outside was the figure of Harlow, wearing a black polo-necked sweater and a broad grin.

'Have you found where she is?'

'Of course I have, boyo. Now would I let you down? Let's go out where we can talk freely and I'll tell you how we go about rescuing her. But first of all pack up your belongings; you're checking out. After tonight it will not be wise to stay in hotels. I've organized a little hide-away until we can get clear of Corsica. Let's get on with it – we've got a girl to fetch.'

As they climbed into the car, Nick turned to Harlow and put his hand on the ignition key to stop him moving. 'Ricard mentioned a disc. What exactly did he mean by that?'

Harlow looked puzzled. 'Sorry, Nick, I can't help you. I don't know about any disc. What kind of disc are you talking about?'

'I wish I knew – and I wish I could believe you. Still, we'll get Sarah first and come back to the disc later, but I won't forget it.'

'All I can think is that it has something to do with Beardsley. Anyway, let's get on.'

With that he drove the Renault slowly out of Ajaccio, past the airport with its lights shining brightly and took the road to Propriano – the same road Bianchi had used when they had arrived early that morning. Nick could hardly believe it was still the same day, so much had happened since his return to Corsica.

About twenty-five miles along the winding road, Harlow turned off to the left along a smaller road, signposted to Zonza. Although Nick had never been there, he had seen it marked on the map and knew that it was high in the mountains. He had tried to curb his curiosity but could wait no longer. 'Isn't it time we cut out the mystery tour and you told me where the hell we're headed?'

'All in good time. Just remain patient for a few minutes more and I'll enlighten you fully.'

They passed through Zonza without really noticing. It comprised a church, a couple of hotels and a few houses, but not much more. Then they were heading for the Col de Bavella. It was there that Harlow pulled the car onto a small flat area of ground. He switched off the engine and stretched his arms to relieve the tension. 'It's been a long day.' He made a sweeping movement with his right hand. 'If it were daylight you would have the most magnificent view down there. Of course, during winter this road is often blocked by snow. There's actually a large sign at the bottom to tell you whether or not it's open.'

'Harlow, cut the crap. I don't want a guided tour. I want to know where we are going and what's happening.

'You are a very impatient fellow. When you went to meet Ricard in Ajaccio I kept a watch outside. I saw him arrive in the Citroen and when they left it I slapped a homing device under the wing. I followed you all the way to Bastia and waited outside until Sarah came out. Fortunately, they used the same car to take her back to her prison. I was able to follow again, at a distance, and I found they are keeping her in a villa just outside Favone on the east coast. Here, I'll show you.'

He put on the interior light and produced a map of the island. He indicated the spot with his finger. 'So far so good, boyo. You've seen how we professionals do it. Now we come to the difficult bit.'

'I'm sure you professionals will have a plan.'

'No need for sarcasm, boyo. Of course I've got a plan. I should warn you though – plans can go wrong; and if this one does we could all end up very, very dead.'

'I don't think we have much choice anyway, so let's hear it.'

'I agree with you. Whatever happens they will have you and Sarah down for elimination. Now, the villa where they are holding her stands in its own grounds and has a high fence on three sides. The other side opens directly onto the sea with a very rocky shoreline. From my observations, and chatting to a couple of locals, it seems the fences are wired to alarms, which rather rules them out as a first choice for entry. The gateway is similar. That leaves the seaward side. They've been a bit tricky there. They have strung out lengths of monofilament fishing net just below the surface. It's virtually invisible until you get tangled up in it; then the more you struggle the worse it gets.'

'So how do we get in?'

'That's where we have a bit of help from an unexpected source. A little friend of yours is coming to our assistance – a young lady called Maria.'

'What!' exclaimed Nick. 'She's one of them. We can't trust her.'

'She *was* one of them: now she's one of us. Ricard beat her up, then raped her. While she is quite happy to give her favours freely she objects strongly to being raped. She is determined to get her revenge and would prefer to see Ricard eliminated before he can get at her again. I approached her carefully when she came out of hospital and she agreed to help. It would seem that she was unwittingly involved in Beardsley's murder, and almost in yours. I promised I would do what I could to get her immunity and ensure her escape from the country.'

'At long last we have an admission that Beardsley had been murdered.'

'We only think he has. He has just disappeared.'

'How's that little bitch going to help us?'

'It's quite easy really. She's going to drive there on a pretext of carrying a message from Ricard. They'll open the gates to let her in and we'll sneak through with her.'

He reached into the back of the car. 'This is for you. It's an automatic with ten shots and a phosphorus grenade, which you will use to create a diversion while I nip into the house to fetch Sarah. On the road side of the villa there is a detached garage, a few feet away from the main house. You will make your way to it, hopefully without setting off any alarms, and, having pulled out the pin, you will toss the grenade through the garage window. As they pile out of the front door to fight the blaze, I will go in at the back and get Sarah. Once you've thrown the grenade you'll come back round the house and cover us as we come out. We should get clear before they know we've gone. There's one thing to remember. If you have to shoot anyone, shoot at the chest – it's the biggest target. Don't get all righteous and shout warnings. It's them or us. Do you understand?'

'What if they don't react as you expect them to when I set the garage on fire?'

'Then use your bloody initiative and do something else to attract their attention. No more "what ifs". It's time we moved.'

They motored down out of the mountains to meet the coastal road just north of Solenzara and turned to drive south through the town. The road was good but Harlow drove slowly until they came to a stretch where it was bordered on the landward side by a strip of gravel and a low cliff. He pulled onto the gravel and stopped the engine.

'We're here – or near enough. We leave the car unlocked with the key in the ignition. The first one back gets into the driving seat. If someone comes along in the middle of the night and steals the bloody car we can think ourselves right unlucky. There are only two guards, plus the woman, and I'm betting that they won't bother with a lookout at this hour of the night.'

They moved off down the road and hid in some shrubbery opposite the gate of the villa and waited for Maria to appear. About ten minutes later the headlights of a car came into view. It stopped by the gate and the driver got out and went to a post at the side of it. In the pale light Nick recognized the slight figure. He heard her talk into a microphone and then return to the car. After a short delay the gates swung open and she drove through.

Harlow tugged Nick's sleeve. 'Come on.' They dashed through the gate as it began to swing shut and dived into the shrubbery. 'We'll wait here until she goes out again.'

* * *

Maria spoke briefly into the microphone on the side of the gate. 'It's Maria. Will you open up, Jean, and let me in? I've a message from the boss.'

There was silence for a while. 'How do I know that it's you? You've given no password.'

'For God's sake, Jean, you can recognize my voice and I know your name. Of course it's me. Ricard was in a hurry and he obviously forgot about passwords.'

'I'm not sure.'

'Would you rather I went back to him and told him that you wouldn't accept his message?'

'Oh no, no. I'll turn off the alarm and let you in. As soon as you're through, I'll turn the alarm on again.'

Maria did as she was told and parked the car in front of the house, where she was met by Jean, an automatic rifle cradled in his arms. He shepherded her inside.

'God. Her certainly made a mess of you, didn't he. That'll teach you to be more careful in future.'

'That's certain. I won't cross him again.'

'Now what's this message and why didn't he phone?'

'That's part of the message. You're not to use the phones – they are all tapped. I think that Byers's Mafia friends have done that. The rest is to have the girl ready for collection at seven o'clock tomorrow. Now I'd better get back to him before he becomes impatient. I don't want another going over. You should be careful too – he's touchy at the moment.'

She turned on her heel and left as he locked the door after her.

They had to wait only a few minutes before she returned and took the car out through the gate. 'We'll wait a while to give them time to settle down again. Then it's all go.'

A quarter of an hour later Harlow nudged Nick and murmured that it was time. They made their way towards the house, keeping close to the trees and shrubbery which bordered the property. Harlow's main concern was that they might be being watched through closed-circuit television, but he said nothing to Nick. There was no point. As they drew nearer to the building he could see floodlights under the eaves but no sign of cameras. It seemed that luck was on their side. He unzipped his bag and took out the automatic, indicating to Nick to do the same. They were now close to the wall of the villa and the back door was plainly visible. He signalled to Nick to go round to the front, while he screwed a long silencer onto the gun.

Nick pressed himself against the wall and slowly eased his way along. At the corner he stopped and peeped round. All was clear. Across the driveway he could see his target, the garage. To reach it he would have to cross the front door. This he did quickly, without raising the alarm.

He stopped by the window of the garage and looked in. It was dark inside but he could just make out the shape of the car. He took out the grenade and, holding it in his right hand, pulled out the pin. Using the gun to smash a pane of glass he tossed the grenade inside. Immediately, he ran for the corner of the house and stopped behind it. In less than five seconds he was rewarded with a dull thud and a flash of intensely bright light illuminated the garden through the window.

There was still no sign of life in the villa. Nick had been sure that the breaking glass would have woken them, but apparently not. He was trying to figure out some other means of creating a diversion when there was an enormous explosion and a pillar of flame rose a hundred feet into the air. He crouched back against the wall as burning debris fell around him and onto the roof of the villa; some crashed straight through and the blaze soon spread to the house itself. He prayed silently that Sarah was well clear. At that moment the door of the villa burst open and two men rushed out, followed by the big woman. They stared in amazement at the garage, but there was nothing they could do to save that. In the light from the fire everything was bright as day, except where the smoke billowed across the lawns. Nick backed away into the shadow of the house and made his way carefully to the back of the building. The men by the garage lacked leadership and were obviously uncertain about their next move. Coughing from the smoke, they clearly didn't want to go back into the blazing villa, in spite of the woman's urging.

The back door was open but there was nobody in sight when Nick reached the rear of the building. His throat was burning from the acrid smoke and his eyes were streaming tears. He wiped them with the back of his hand and crouched low to cover the back door, his gun held high in a two-handed grip. He waited what seemed an eternity – though, in fact, it was only seconds – for the others to appear. At the doorway Harlow hesitated, taking a good look round, before leading Sarah towards Nick. Both were covered in black soot, the tears from Sarah's eyes already cutting channels through the dirt on her face. Nick lowered his gun, his heart full of joy, but it was short-lived, for beyond them the woman came round the corner opposite carrying a machine pistol. Seeing them, she raised the gun. Nick aimed at her, but hesitated. Deep inside him he knew he couldn't shoot. Harlow saw that and reacted quickly, pulling Sarah flat onto the ground. As the salvo of bullets passed over them, the automatic in his hand gave a soft cough and the woman was thrown backwards onto the lawn, the weapon flying from her lifeless grasp. By now the floodlights had come on and there was smoke and flame everywhere.

Harlow started for the front gate calling out, 'Let's get the hell out of here, and if anyone appears for God's sake shoot – don't wait.' He charged away, dragging Sarah behind him with Nick hard on their heels.

Harlow hesitated at the corner of the building to check that all was clear. The garage was a burning wreck, while the house blazed intensely, but there was no sign of the other two guards; leaderless, they had obviously fled in panic. They ran on to find the main gates open. They could hardly believe their luck as they dashed through and made for the car. Harlow jumped in, with

Nick on the passenger side and Sarah in the back, and drove off through the village and on southwards. Looking back, they could see the sky bright red over the villa, and people beginning to appear at doorways.

They continued until they came to Porto Vecchio. There they turned off to go through Ospedale and back towards Zonza. The road was winding and steep; far below them they could see the glow from the burning house.

'God,' breathed Harlow. 'I told you to set fire to the garage, not half the bloody island.'

'It wasn't my fault. They must have had a petrol store in there.' Nick felt lighthearted with relief. 'It was impressive wasn't it?'

'Don't get too pleased with yourself. You were meant to cover us as we left the house. Instead, you stood and stared like a bloody statue and nearly got us killed. I told you not to hesitate. Why the hell didn't you shoot the bloody woman?'

The memory of the woman being flung backwards, her face twisted in agony and rage, flooded back to him with sobering effect. 'I'm sorry. I guess it was just because she was a woman.'

'Unfortunately, they can kill you just as easily as a man – especially when they're carrying a bloody great machine-gun,' replied Harlow softly. 'We're safe now for the time being.'

Nick said quietly, 'That's good. And now, boyo, pull into the side and tell me all about a disc.'

'With all the excitement, I thought you'd forgotten about that . . .'

'You *will* tell me or I'll break your arm.'

'I don't think you could do it, Nick,' Harlow said quietly.

'Maybe not, but I could have a bloody good try.'

'Okay, I think you've earned it, but this is top secret stuff. Keep it to yourselves or, by God, I'll throw the book at you.'

'Too bloody true we've earned it. And we'll keep your little secrets. The last thing we want to do is endanger anyone else.'

'The disc is a computer disc which contains details of all the financial dealings of the Union Corse, including names of top officials and members of the police and judiciary who are in league with them. It's a bit of a bombshell.'

'It's a bloody atomic bombshell,' gasped Nick. 'No wonder they're desperate to find it. You devious bastard. You risked us to get it back. I suppose Beardsley is no longer with us.'

'Probably not. As I said, he has disappeared.'

'Why us?'

'I wanted someone who seemed innocent. I thought that way you would have plain sailing, so to speak.'

'And someone who was nothing to do with the Department if things went wrong, you lousy bastard. But why are you involved any way? This is French stuff.'

'Let's say it was a favour for my opposite number in French security. He didn't know for sure which of his men he could trust.'

'You lot disgust me. You're all the same.' This time the remark came from the back seat. 'And where is this disc that so many people have died for? And where do Dawson and Nixon fit in?'

'Sarah, believe me, I don't know where the disc is. Beardsley hid it somewhere and didn't tell anyone where. As for the other two, I really don't know about them any more than you do. I can only assume Beardsley was doing a bit of drug-trafficking on the side and they were in it with him. Now can we get on to our hide-away in the hills. I'm hungry – I haven't eaten all day.'

'One more thing first. Just before you arrived, there was a girl there. I heard the name, Maria, mentioned. Was she anything to do with you?'

In the darkness Nick felt himself flush deeply, but Harlow was quick to answer. 'Yes. She helped us gain access to the villa.'

'Who is she and why did she help you?'

'She was one of Ricard's girls, but he beat her up and raped her. She wanted revenge.'

'But she must have put her life in danger. They must know she helped you.'

'She certainly has. I intend personally to see her safely out of the country to a foreign hide-away where she can start her life anew.'

9

'What!' Debert's usual calm deserted him. 'You're telling me that the girl has got away, my villa and my car have been destroyed and Bella has been shot dead. I can't believe I'm hearing this.'

'They were taken by surprise and when the fuel store in the garage exploded they were confused. It was a very professional exercise. I will see that the two guards are punished severely. What's more I have reason to believe that the girl, Maria, was mixed up in this. I believe she betrayed us and assisted them to gain access to the villa. I will see she pays in full.'

'You are the one who should be punished. If she betrayed us it was probably because you misused her. However, this time she has gone too far. She is no longer useful to us. Eliminate her. Why were you not at the villa yourself?'

'I did not realize I was up against a professional. I was badly informed and I will find out why. Byers could not have done this by himself. He must have been supported by the man, Harlow. We were not told that he had entered Corsica; if I had known I would have been there myself.'

'I am beginning to doubt your ability, Ricard,' replied Debert. 'How do you plan to put matters right?'

'We are watching all the usual ways of leaving the island, paying particular attention to small boats. We are carrying out a check on all hotels and similar establishments. Finally, we are checking all holiday apartments. It will take time and many men but we will find them.'

'Pray that you do, Ricard – and when you do I will join in the final action myself. I want no further mistakes.'

They travelled north along the centre of the island. The road twisted and turned, dipped and climbed, through the mountains but the surface was good. Harlow drove carefully and no one spoke. They passed again through Corté and continued northwards. Then Harlow slowed down and became watchful, until he spotted a narrow road leading even higher into the mountains. Little more than a track, its surface had obviously been metalled at some time but that had long since broken up.

They bumped their way slowly uphill for about half a mile until the headlights picked up another dusty track leading off to the right. Harlow swung onto it and, immediately, a stone cottage appeared in the beams. He brought the car to a stop in front of it and announced proudly, 'Here we are – home sweet home, for the time being at least.' He took a torch from the glove pocket and led the way to the front door. Unlocking the door, he reached inside to turn on the light – nothing happened.

'Hang on here, I'll go round the back and start the generator. It usually comes on automatically when you switch on any light or appliance, but it's been shut down for some time.'

A few minutes later they heard a starter-motor whirring, followed by the cough of the diesel generator and then a rumble as it burst into life. The light in the cottage glowed and brightened and the generator settled down to a steady, well-muffled throb. Harlow came back, rubbing his hands proudly. 'Who's for breakfast then?'

'What I really want,' replied Sarah, 'is a bath. I feel smoked like a kipper.'

'I've started the boiler, but it will take a while to heat up. Come on in and make yourselves at home.'

He led the way into the small cottage. The living area downstairs was in an L-shape with the corner of the L filled by the kitchen. The stairs were against the kitchen wall. The room was sparsely furnished with a couple of easy chairs and a dining table with four chairs. The floor was of uneven slates. In the short leg of the L was a table bearing a very up-to-date computer and laser printer, quite out of place with the rest of the room.

Harlow's arm swept round in a flourish. 'Your home for the next couple of days.'

Nick took in the room and the computer. 'And whose home is it for the rest of the time? Not Beardsley's, I hope.'

'No, of course not. This place belongs to a friend of mine who has nothing to do with the Department. He's a writer, hence the computer, and spends a lot of time out of the country doing research. He's been in South Africa for the past four months – long before this operation began. No one will connect him with us, so you'll be safe here.'

'Harlow, I never know when to believe you, but I certainly won't feel safe until this whole thing is over and I'm back in England.'

Harlow shrugged. 'I can't help it if you don't trust me. It's understandable, I suppose. But whether you like it or not we're stuck here for the time being. I'll make some coffee.' He went through to the small kitchen while the other two flopped down into the old easy chairs.

Nick reached out a hand to Sarah and she took it in hers and squeezed it. 'Nick, you're a stupid bastard but I love you very much. Please don't let me be kidnapped again.'

'You bet I won't. I'm not going to let you out of my sight.'

'That might be somewhat inconvenient, but I get the point. I'm going up to have that bath. I don't care if the water's cold. Then I'm going to bed.'

Upstairs there were two bedrooms, a bathroom and a separate toilet. Once again, everything was basic, but the beds were comfortable and Sarah managed to find a pair of clean sheets. They didn't realize just how tired they were until they climbed into bed, whereupon they fell asleep almost at once in each other's arms.

The sun was shining brightly when they awoke and the house was silent. Nick looked at his watch – it was past ten o'clock. He swung his legs out of bed and pulled on a pair of slacks. Sarah lay with her beautiful black hair spread out on the pillow. He bent down and kissed her softly on the lips and she smiled up at him.

The door of the other bedroom was open and he looked in. It was empty but the bed had been slept in. He noticed that Harlow hadn't bothered with sheets. He went downstairs and found the place deserted. He was about to go outside when he noticed the note on the dining table.

Have gone to find out what's happening and get some news about the opposition. I also want to get Maria away as soon as possible. There's food in the kitchen. Don't leave the premises, and stay out of sight as much as possible. The track is hardly ever used but don't take chances. I'll be back this afternoon some time. H.

He took the note and, after a quick look round outside, went back up to Sarah and showed it to her. She read it quickly and nodded. 'He says to keep out of sight, so get those trousers off and come here.' She lifted up the bed covers and he caught a glimpse of her beautiful body before climbing in to join her. Their love-making was passionate and exhausting. Sarah wiped her hair back from his sweat-covered brow and chuckled softly. 'You need more practice.'

'I'm all for that.'

It was late when they eventually got up. While Sarah set about making coffee and toast Nick decided to take a look round outside.

'Are you sure that you should, in view of Harlow's note?'

'I'm just going to try and get the lie of the land. If anything happens I want to be sure of our surroundings. There are plenty of shrubs to give cover between the track and us.'

'Hang on. I want to see too. The coffee's ready and the toast is about there, so grab a mug and we can take it with us. There seems to be a good view down the valley; we can have breakfast alfresco.'

They left the cottage carefully, but it was soon obvious they were alone. The cottage was built on a bend in the track. In front of it was a mass of shrubs an entrance gateway on either side. A driveway curved round in front of the building. It was clearly intended for vehicles to come in by one and leave by the other. The track climbed steeply from left to right. Behind the building were more shrubs and a few trees, and behind them the cliff-face rose steeply. Away to the left were more shrubs and beyond them the ground fell away steeply in a sheer drop of some twenty metres. The cliff behind the cottage joined this and turned backwards away from the track, combining to form a jagged face of rock fifty or more metres high. The view down the valley was spectacular.

They settled down in a spot where they could see the track winding upwards and, leaning back against a huge boulder, enjoyed their breakfast in the morning sunshine.

'Y'know, Sarah. If it wasn't for the likes of Ricard, I could happily settle down here. The place seems to have everything.'

'I haven't really had a chance to see any of it but, if that view is anything to go by, it certainly is beautiful.' She waved her hand in a gesture which took in the valley below them. Then she stopped suddenly and sat forward. 'Nick, there's a car coming up the track.'

He felt cold fingers of fear as he leant forward and looked at the black Citroen XM as it made its way slowly up the hill. 'Come on. Let's get into better cover where we can see the people inside as it passes.' He took her hand and almost pulled her to some shrubs nearer the track. They sank down and waited, peering out through the branches. The car seemed to take a lifetime to appear and he could feel his heart racing. Suddenly, it was in sight. The windows were darkened but now they were wide open. The driver, a dark-skinned man, was taking it carefully, trying to avoid the pot holes. In the back seat the unmistakable face of Ricard scowled from the window. The car slowed down at the first entrance, but Ricard signalled to the driver to carry on, and Nick guessed they would use the second entrance, thereby facing the right way to leave. As the car moved out of sight, he stood up. 'Come on. The bushes behind the house are our only chance.' He crouched low as he ran, pulling her with him, and they had just time to gain cover when the car swung round in front of the cottage.

The car doors opened and they heard Ricard giving orders in French. 'Search the house first. Be careful and cover each other – he may have a gun still. If they're not inside, we'll search the grounds. They've got to be here somewhere.' The door of the house crashed open, and they heard raised voices inside.

Nick eased forward so that he could just see the car and, as he feared, Ricard was standing by it, keeping watch lest they make a break.

He edged back to Sarah. 'With Ricard on watch we can't possibly make it to the track. The only thing I can think of is to take him out and then run for it.'

'We wouldn't have a hope, but I think I know a way. You follow me for a change.' Keeping low, she led the way back to the cliff-face at the rear of the building.

'You don't expect me to climb that, do you?'

'Just have patience.' She turned left along the base of the cliff towards the lower end until she came to the spot where the ground dropped away in another sheer face. There she stopped and pointed out along the combined face to the left. A narrow ledge ran along at their level and disappeared round a cleft in the rock. The cliff-face towered thirty metres above it and dropped twenty below to the floor of the valley, which was littered with rocks.

Nick sucked his breath in sharply. 'I can't do it. No way can I go along that ledge. You know me, Sarah. I get dizzy standing on a stool.'

'It's up to you. It's either that or Ricard, and I know which I prefer. Just ease your way along and don't look down. Watch me – I'll go first.'

She edged her feet out onto the ledge and began working her way slowly along it. Left with no choice, he had to follow. He moved after her, feeling his way with his feet. He'd been wearing slip-on sandals, but had kicked them off into the valley below, preferring bare feet. The first few metres were easier than he had thought, with reasonable handholds, and he gained confidence. Then, as the handholds became fewer, he felt the stirring of panic, until he realized that Sarah had turned into the cleft and was out of sight – only a metre to go. He struggled round the corner to find Sarah huddled back into the cleft, leaving plenty of room for him to wedge himself in firmly. She leaned forward and whispered, 'Well done.' Then they waited in silence.

It wasn't long before they heard the sounds of the search on the plateau they had left. An English voice declared, 'They're not here. They must have gone earlier this morning.' Nick thought he detected a slight American accent.

'Not much earlier. The kettle was still warm. I agree there's no point hanging around here. Let's go back to Bastia.'

Nick leaned out slowly to try to catch sight of the American and, as he did so, a piece of the ledge gave way and his right foot plunged down into a narrow crevice in the rock. It twisted sideways and jammed agonizingly. He felt something inside break and the jagged rock cut deeply into his flesh. Waves of pain washed over him and he clung on desperately. Sarah leaned forward and held him to her.

'Hold on tight, Nick. We can start back as soon as you feel able.' In the background he heard the car start and it gave him new strength. He gently eased his foot out of the crevice: it was a mass of bleeding flesh. He tried to put weight on it but the pain was intense. He couldn't stay on the rock face indefinitely, and Sarah couldn't move until he did. He tried again, this time taking most of the weight on his handholds. Slowly, he edged back along the ledge, with Sarah supporting him and whispering words of encouragement, until at last he was able to collapse onto level ground.

'Stay there while I get something to bandage your foot.' Sarah was not away long, and returned carrying one of the sheets which she tore into strips and bound round his foot until he looked like a cartoon colonel with gout. She stood back to admire her work, then looked down the valley. She gasped – another car was making its way towards them. There was no way they could get away this time, not with Nick's injured foot.

'What's the matter?' Nick struggled to sit up and look. 'Oh, thank God. That's Harlow returning.'

Relief swept over her. 'I thought it was Ricard coming back. Now we can get you to hospital.'

'I think hospital is out – it's a bit too public. What I need is a private clinic of some kind. Maybe Jacques Bianchi can help us.'

Harlow's car pulled up in front of the cottage and, as he climbed out, Sarah called to him. He made his way across to them and stood over Nick.

'What stupid game have you been playing?'

All the pent-up anger and pain in him seemed to burst. 'This stupid bloody game was trying to get away from the bloody stupid trap you left us in. Your so-called bloody security seems to be completely and utterly bloody non-existent.'

Harlow was taken aback by the outburst. 'Whoa, boyo! Hold it. Tell me what happened.'

Nick collapsed back, while Sarah described what had happened. Harlow listened carefully without interruption until she had finished. Then he asked, 'This American voice. Did you recognize it? Had you heard it before?'

Nick shook his head. 'It sounded a bit familiar, but I can't say that I recognized it. I'm not saying it *was* American; it just seemed to have a bit of an accent.'

Sarah said thoughtfully, 'I certainly didn't recognize it. I can't recall ever having heard it before, but I'm not so sure about the American bit. Anyway we shouldn't just be sitting here talking – we've got to get Nick to a doctor.'

Harlow nodded. 'Okay. Let's get you to the car, Nick. With Sarah on one side and me on the other, can you walk that far?'

'I guess so.' Nick struggled to stand up, supported by the other two. As he looked over Harlow's shoulder he could see the track winding down the valley, and heading up that track was the unmistakable shape of the black Citroen. 'Oh, my God. It's Ricard, coming back.'

'What!' exploded Harlow, almost knocking Nick over as he swung round. 'Christ, we've got to get out of here.'

'What's up the track?'

'Nothing. It peters out a couple of hundred metres further on. We'll have to leave the car. It's on foot I'm afraid, Nick.'

Sarah gasped. 'He'll never get away – he can't walk by himself.'

'He must. Let's get across the track and down the slope on the other side. Then it will be on your bum most of the time. Quickly before they see us.'

With Nick in the centre, being half supported and half dragged by the other two, they got to the far side of the track and lowered themselves over. The ground fell away steeply into another valley, heavily wooded on both sides. They let themselves slide down, moving from tree to tree until they were completely hidden from above. On several occasions Nick was forced to use his injured foot to arrest his descent. Whenever he did so excruciating pain shot up his leg. Somehow he made it to the bottom, where Sarah waited for him.

'Are you okay, Nick?' The worry showed clearly on her face.

'I'll live – Providing Ricard doesn't catch us. How are you?'

She did her best to smile. 'Oh, I'm okay. I've scraped all the skin off my backside, but that's nothing. It would have been worse if I'd been wearing a skirt.' She beat a cloud of dust from her jeans.

Harlow chuckled. 'Much as I'd like to hear more about your rear-end, Sarah, I'm off to get another car. I'll go down this valley and try to find another way out. I don't much fancy climbing back up that slope, and Nick would never make it. And there's a possibility that they'll leave someone there in case we return.'

* * *

'Well, there's the bloody car but where the hell has the driver gone? Are you sure there was only one person in it?' Ricard spoke in English to the tall man by his side.

'Only one and it wasn't Byers. I couldn't see clearly because it passed too quickly, and it wasn't important until it turned up the track.'

'We'll give the whole place another going-over. I'll take the other two and search the grounds around and the rest of the track. You search the house for anything that might help us. Let's pray that something turns up or we'll both be up to our necks in trouble.'

Sarah and Nick huddled together in a small space shielded by a fallen tree. She prayed silently that their pursuers would not venture down the slope, and her prayers were answered. Although she heard voices at the top, they obviously decided that it was not practical to descend further. After about an hour she heard the car start and move away. At first she considered climbing back up to get water to bathe Nick's foot, for he was in considerable pain, but decided that the risk was too high.

It was another hour before she heard someone call her name softly. It was Harlow. She crawled out of their hideout and waved to him. She had not thought she would ever be pleased to see him, but waiting with the helpless Nick had taken its toll. She put her arms round his neck and hugged him. 'Thank God you're back. Have you got a car?'

'Of course. And, what's more, this valley is very short – about a hundred metres – and another road runs across the end. The car is there. All we have to do is get Nick to it.'

That proved to be a far from simple task. Although Harlow was strong, Nick was very heavy and the going was rough. However, slowly and with numerous stops, they made their way to the car and helped Nick into the back seat, Sarah climbing in with him.

'Are you sure that the people you got the car from aren't with Ricard? He seems to have agents everywhere.'

'It's all right. They are out of the country – I watched them get on an aircraft.'

'It's not a hire car then?'

'Oh, no. It's a stolen one. I stole it from the airport.'

'You what? God, Harlow, you are impossible.'

'I didn't see there was any alternative. Now to find a doctor, and this may be difficult.'

'You must contact Jacques Bianchi.' Nick whispered the words through clenched teeth. 'He will know where to go.'

'Is he the guy who helped you earlier?'

'That's right. Do you want to make a note of the telephone number?'

'Just tell me. I'll remember it.'

Harlow drove in silence towards Ajaccio and parked in the car park by the harbour. He left them briefly to buy a ticket. 'We don't want to attract attention to ourselves, do we?' Then he went to telephone.

In the small apartment, Jacques Bianchi sat gazing across the bay at the new developments around Porticcio. He didn't really like the idea of his island home changing under the influx of tourists but he was a realist. He knew they were essential if the people were to prosper. He looked up at the mountains beyond with satisfaction. They would never change. No amount of tourism could dull their beauty.

As he sat he thought about the Englishman and wondered if he had been successful in rescuing his girl. He hated the onset of age and wished he could have been at the younger man's side. Fear would have been there but also pleasure: the pleasure of striking a blow for his island against the forces of evil. He had heard about a fire at a villa in Favone, a villa belonging to Debert, the boss man of the Union Corse. Rumour had it there had been shooting, but somebody had put a clamp-down on the story and, while speculation was rife, there were no facts. He guessed that Byers had been involved, but had no idea of the outcome.

The ringing of the telephone startled him. He cursed it silently, but rose to his feet and lifted the receiver. 'Bianchi.'

The voice at the other end spoke in English. 'I am told by my friend that you are interested in horse riding.'

Bianchi's heart quickened. 'That's correct. Has your friend been successful in his enterprise?'

'Very much so, but he needs your help. Are you free to give it?'

'Of course. I will do all I can to help him. It will be an honour.'

'Are your previous activities suspected by the opposition?'

'Definitely not. If they suspected I would no longer be free to talk to you.'

'Good. Can you come to the car park by the harbour? I will be in a blue Alfa Romeo.'

'I will be there in five minutes.' He rang off and went to a cupboard in the corner to take out a light-weight jacket. He started to close the cupboard door, then had second thoughts. Reaching in to the back of the top shelf he lifted out a cardboard box, opened it and took out a service revolver, wrapped in an oily cloth. He put the gun, together with some cartridges, into a bag. He had no idea of what was required of him but he meant to be prepared.

As Jacques Bianchi left the apartment and made his way down the stairs, there was a new spring in his step and a smile on his face. He was going to do something useful. He wasn't too old after all. He was needed.

Harlow watched as the small, elderly man made his way towards the car and noted the jauntiness of his stride. He got out and met the other a few metres from the car. 'Are you the man interested in horses?'

'That is correct. Where is Monsieur Byers?'

'He's in the car, but he is injured and needs a doctor urgently. Can you direct us to someone who will help him without our enemies finding out?'

'I'll do better than that. I'll take you to a doctor who is very reliable. He is a friend of mine who hates the Union Corse as much as I do. Come. Let's not waste time.' He walked over to the car and opened the passenger door. The sight of Nick's pale, strained face caused him to draw in his breath quickly. He climbed in and slammed the door. 'You will soon have help, Monsieur Byers.'

'Thanks for coming, Jacques. I knew you would help.' Nick's words were little more than a whisper.

'Monsieur, do you know the way to Porto Vecchio?'

'Yes. I can go via Zonza and Ospedale.'

'That's good. When we get there I will give you further instructions.'

On the way, he asked Harlow about the rescue and was given a full account of what had happened. He expressed his delight to Sarah that she had come through unharmed, and was unashamedly captivated by her beauty. 'Ah, if only I were forty years younger.'

Their road joined the main coastal road just north of the small port of Porto Vecchio and Bianchi gave instructions to turn north towards Solenzara. 'Don't worry. We do not go as far as Favone.' In fact they had gone only a mile or so when he told Harlow to turn right towards the sea, along a small side road. After a few hundred metres they turned right through a pair of wrought-iron gates and headed down a wide driveway before coming to a stop in front of an imposing detached house.

Bianchi got out of the car. 'Wait here. I'll go and explain the position.' He walked to the front door and rang the bell. Moments later it was opened by a smart, middle-aged woman with dark hair brushed back into a loose bun. She greeted him warmly and ushered him inside.

He was led through to the lounge where a tall, powerfully-built man in his early sixties rose to greet him. 'Jacques, my friend, how are you? Welcome to my home. I hope this is a social visit.'

Bianchi shook his head. 'I regret it is not. Outside, in the car, I have a friend with a badly injured foot and he urgently needs medical attention.'

'We must not wait then. Let us fetch him in.'

'There is more. He and his woman are fleeing from the Union Corse. Ricard wants them badly and is prepared to go to any lengths to find them. I fear that he will punish anyone who assists them. Are you still ready to help?'

'All the more so. Anything I can do to hurt Ricard I do willingly.

Outside, Harlow was waiting by the car while Sarah sat in the back with Nick. Bianchi introduced the doctor briefly. 'This is Dr Philippe Azena. He will help Monsieur Byers.'

'Does he know the rest?' Harlow spoke in English and Azena replied in the same language.

'I know all I need to know for the present and it makes no difference. Let us get your friend inside to my surgery so that I can see what must be done. We will need a stretcher – your friend is a big man. Wait while I get one.'

Between them, Harlow and the doctor carried Nick into a modern surgery, which was spotlessly clean and smelled of antiseptics. They laid him on the bench and the doctor took the bandaging off his foot while the others looked on.

'The foot is badly injured, as you can see. The young lady can stay if she wishes but the rest of you must wait outside.' After they had departed he spoke to Sarah. 'I will give him a local anaesthetic before I touch the foot. You should comfort him while I clean the wound.'

Azena worked on the foot for a considerable time, as gently as possible. Even so, Nick's body tensed with pain on several occasions. At last he stood back and spoke to Sarah. 'I have done all I can. The foot is badly injured. The gashes you can see and the swelling from the strain, but inside there is at least one bone broken and probably more. I have no X-ray equipment to find out. I'm afraid he needs hospital treatment.'

'Is there a hospital where he can get treatment without Ricard finding out?'

'Not one that is one hundred per cent certain. You can never tell how far his influence has spread. Even the ones on the mainland are not without a small risk.'

Nick spoke in a whisper. 'Sardinia.'

'What do you mean?'

'If you know how we can get to Sardinia we'll be safe.'

'I can certainly get you there in secret, but I don't know how to go about arranging treatment confidentially.'

'Harlow can do that.'

'I'll see what I can organize. In the meantime, I'll give you something to ease the pain and you should sleep.'

'I must talk to Harlow first, and give him a contact in Sardinia.'

'There is no need. Give me the contact and I will work with him to arrange everything.'

Nick was inclined to be suspicious, but then he thought about Bianchi and felt there could be no better reference, so he gave Luciano Peretti's name and number. Then he lay back and surrendered to sleep.

Peretti sat at his desk and stared at the telephone. He was not happy. The request to provide assistance for Byers worried him and he knew that he must refer it directly to Scarfiotti. He liked an easy life, without difficult decisions – he preferred staying out of the limelight. Sighing deeply, he picked up the telephone.

The female voice was sharp and impersonal. 'The Scarfiotti residence.'

'This is Luciano Peretti. I would like to talk to Signor Scarfiotti.'

'Why?'

'About the Englishman, Nick Byers.'

There was silence for a little while. 'I will see if Signor Scarfiotti is in residence. Hold the line please.'

Almost immediately Scarfiotti's voice came on the line. 'Hello, Luciano. How are you keeping? And how is your mother?'

'We are all well, Uncle.' He was not related to Scarfiotti but, like everyone else, he addressed his leader by that term of affection.

'What is your problem?'

'It concerns the Englishman, Byers. I have been asked to provide hospital facilities for him.'

'I hope that he is not seriously hurt, but I do not see any difficulty. Of course we will provide all the help we can. Those were your earlier instructions and I have not changed them. Is there not a private ward free in the hospital at Sassari?'

'Oh, yes. We have the facilities available; that is no problem.' Peretti chose his words carefully. He knew he was on dangerous ground. 'I am not questioning your authority, Uncle, but the situation has changed. It would seem there was a battle in Corsica. Debert's villa was burned to the ground and I understand that at least one of his associates, a woman, was shot dead. There is an extremely high price on Byers' head. Debert obviously wants him badly and is prepared to go to any length to get him. Helping Byers could bring us into direct confrontation with Debert at a time when we are already having problems with the new families.'

'What you say is true, Luciano, and you did well to call me. However, Byers saved my daughter from the sea and returned her to me. I will not let him down and I will give him our protection from the scum which calls itself the Corsican Union. If anyone tries to collect Debert's reward they are to be dealt with severely – and permanently. Let the word be spread widely. Do as you have been asked, Luciano, and keep me informed. It is good to know that I can rely upon you to safeguard our interests in Sardinia.'

Peretti hung up the telephone and breathed a sigh of relief. He had cleared himself should anything go wrong and, at the same time, put himself in the big man's good books. He, like many others, had discovered that Scarfiotti's mild appearance was but a façade which hid a sharp and unforgiving mind – a man you fell foul of at your peril.

Nick slept soundly until the following morning. He awoke to find the sun streaming in through the open window. The bed was comfortable and the drugs the doctor had given him had eased the pain, but now his foot was throbbing again. He lay there, trying to collect his thoughts. At first he had trouble remembering what had happened and where he was. As the memories floated back to him he struggled to sit up and, in doing so, his elbow caught the bedside table and the lamp crashed to the floor.

'Whatever are you doing?' With a groan Sarah uncurled her cramped limbs from the easy chair which had been provided for her when she had stated her intention of staying with Nick.

'Sorry. I was just trying to sit up. What time is it?'

'It's half past seven. Try not to do any more damage while I go and see if the doctor is awake.'

'God, is it tomorrow morning? Have you been in that chair all night?'

'Yes and yes. Now do as I say and stay where you are.' She left the room, to return five minutes later accompanied by Philippe Azena.

'How is my patient this morning?'

'Other than an aching foot and a blinding headache, fine.'

'The headache is probably due to the pills I gave you to help you sleep. I will put a new dressing on your foot and give you something to ease the pain. You'll be pleased to hear that I have spoken to Signor Peretti and have obtained his assistance in providing you with medical care in Sardinia.'

'Good. I was sure there would be no problem.'

'Yes. He was most helpful. If Signor Peretti is who I think he is, I cannot say that I approve of your friends, Monsieur Byers.'

'Peretti is no friend of mine and I have no time for the people he works for. However, they owe me a favour and I am calling it in.'

Azena nodded. 'Good. I am pleased to hear that. I have arranged for a boat to pick you up here at midnight. It will take you to a cove in north-eastern Sardinia, close to Olbia. Peretti will meet you there in the early hours of tomorrow morning. There should be ample time to make the crossing. It is a fast boat and the sea is calm.'

'Won't Ricard be watching out for small boats?'

'Oh yes. One of his men has already seen the boat as it left this morning with a group of holiday-makers going cruising to Sardinia. They will be left there while the boat returns to collect you. Until then you should rest as much as possible, but before you do I believe your friend, Harlow, wants to speak to you.'

'That's another one who is no friend of mine, but send him in anyway.'

The doctor ushered him in, and they were left together. The look of deep concern on Harlow's face may or may not have been genuine, but Nick gave him the benefit of the doubt. 'Nick, I'm sorry to see you like this. You really do tend to put your foot in things, don't you?'

'Ha, bloody, ha. What is it you want? Remember I'm under doctor's orders and I can have you thrown out whenever I want.'

'I've just come in to tell you that I want to contact *White Albatross*, and I guess the only way to do that is to go through the Mafia – unless you've got a better idea. I don't want to use the police.'

'And why would you want to talk to Steve?'

'I would have thought that was obvious. You don't want to

travel back to Sicily to get the boat, do you? It would be much better if he brought it over to Sardinia.'

'What makes you think I'm going to ferry the bloody boat back to the UK? I might just get on a plane and fly home. After all, it will be difficult handling it with a dicky foot.'

'I know you too well, boyo. You're a stubborn bugger. You wouldn't give up a job once you'd started it and I'm sure you can talk Steve into crewing for you.'

'Maybe you're right. He's got a mobile phone which he can be contacted on. By the way, he should be in Sardinia already.'

'And you say that I'm devious. I'll leave you in peace now. Au revoir.'

'Where are you off to?'

'Back to the office. There are other things that require my attention. Anyway, I've got to return a car to the airport and a police helicopter is laid on to take me to Nice. Bon voyage.' He lifted a hand in salute and, with a broad grin, left the room.

The boat was ghosting along in the gentle breeze with the large genoa billowed out. There was only the quiet murmur of water passing along the hull and that was not enough to disturb Gina as she lay, topless, on the cabin in the warm sunshine. No other shipping was in sight as they headed on a course slightly north of east which would take them to Cagliari in the south of Sardinia. From there they would make their way slowly up the coast. If he had heard nothing on the mobile phone by the next day, Steve was resolved to ring the phone number he had been given by Nick earlier. He set the boat's self-steering and went below to fetch a couple of glasses of cool wine, then joined Gina.

She looked up at him with a smile. 'Thank you, but don't shade me from the sun.'

'Sorry,' he muttered and moved across to her other side.

'If you want to do something really helpful, you could put some cream on my shoulders.'

Steve shook some of the barrier cream onto his fingers and gently smoothed it across her tanned skin. She murmured softly with pleasure, then rolled onto her back. 'Please don't stop.'

He bent down and kissed her lightly on the lips. She reached up and put her arms round his neck, pulling him down onto her. He felt her bare breasts pressing against his chest and ran his hands slowly down to her bikini bottoms. Gradually, they became more passionate.

They lay side by side, at ease with the world, the sun warm on their naked bodies. Gina chuckled softly.

'What is it?'

She rolled on to her side and gently played with the hairs on his chest. 'If my father knew what we had done, he would insist that you marry me. He's old-fashioned like that and very, very persuasive. So, unless you are good to me, I might tell him.'

'Oh, I promise I'll be very good,' replied Steve. Then his brow furrowed. 'On the other hand, he might have the right idea.' Just then the mobile telephone rang. 'Don't go away – I won't be long.'

The reception was not good and Harlow's voice was not completely clear to Steve, but he was able to pick up the important points, which were repeated slowly. He understood what was required of him.

Before returning to Gina he worked for a while at the chart table, deciphering the message. Next he fetched a bottle of wine and went on deck, to find her sitting on the cabin-top, bursting with curiosity. 'Come on – don't keep me waiting any longer. Is Sarah safe?'

As he replied, he drew the cork from the wine bottle and poured two tumblers half full. 'Oh, yes. There's no problem there. It was Harlow and he kept things brief. Nick got hurt and is being taken to hospital in Sardinia. We've got to go to a place called Porto Torres in the Golfo dell Asinara at the north end of the island and wait there until we are contacted.'

Gina raised her glass in salute. 'Thank God she is safe. I know

Porto Torres well. There's a big marina there, so we should have no trouble in getting a berth alongside. Best of all, we've still got a couple of days to ourselves – so let's not waste them.'

10

Nick spent the day dosing fitfully; the pain-killer had eased the agony of his wounded foot but had not eliminated it completely. During his periods of wakefulness, he reviewed the events of the last few days. He should have followed Sarah's advice and told Harlow what he could do with his boat. He knew that, but it was too late now. Yet he felt strangely excited about what had happened. He had to admit that elation during the attack on the villa had been stimulating, unlike anything he had experienced before.

He also found he was giving much thought to the computer disc which had been responsible for all that had happened. In that semi-darkened room he gradually realized where Beardsley must have hidden it. His first thought was to contact Harlow and pass on the information, but then he reconsidered: the knowledge was a bargaining point should anything go wrong. He would keep it to himself until they were safely home in England; then Harlow could have it and do what he like with it.

At half past eleven that evening the doctor changed the dressing on his foot and gave him a pain-killing injection, then helped him to struggle into his clothes.

Dr Azena looked down at him as he sat on the edge of the bed. 'I can't carry you by myself – you are much too big. I will have to get help.'

'No. We can't involve anyone else – for their sake and ours. How far have we got to go?'

'Only a couple of hundred metres, but the ground is rough and uneven.'

'I could help,' said Sarah.

'Thanks, but I really feel that I can manage, providing you give me a pair of crutches and a steadying hand. Is there any moonlight out there or are we going to be in total darkness? I don't like the idea of flashing torches around.'

'We're in luck,' replied Azena. 'There's quite a bright moon. Enough light for us to see our way to the boat, but not enough to be seen. I'll get the crutches and we'll see if you can manage.'

'Don't worry. I'll manage – even if I have to crawl all the way. Incidentally, I haven't seen Jacques Bianchi all day. If he's still around I would like to thank him and say goodbye.'

Azena smiled. 'Jacques had some business to attend to, so he had to leave. You were asleep at the time and he didn't want to disturb you.'

'That's a pity. He proved himself a real friend.'

'I will tell him that.'

Nick had used crutches once before, following a rugby accident, and soon got the hang of them, but he moved carefully for fear of banging his already throbbing foot. Outside there was just enough light to make a steady progress. Madame Azena led the way, followed by Sarah. Next came Nick, with Philippe Azena bringing up the rear, ready to render assistance should it be necessary, and it was – on several occasions. Their track led them across the lawn at the back of the house and through a gate in a low wall. All this was easy, but when they headed off across the layers of rock the going got tough. Almost at once Nick's right crutch skidded away on the uneven surface. To save his injured foot, he twisted round and fell on his shoulder. His grunt of pain, coupled with the clatter of the falling crutch, caused Sarah to wheel round and she and the doctor bent over him.

'Are you all right, Nick?' The concern was clear in her voice.

'Don't worry yourself. I'll be fine. Just let's get on with it.' His irritation hid the pain he now felt in his right shoulder as well as his foot.

'Okay, but we must go slower. The boat won't go without

you.' The doctor bent down and took Nick's right arm to help him to his feet. He did not miss the grunt of pain as he did so, but he said nothing more. He did, however, move up very close behind Nick and slightly to one side, ready to catch him should he fall again.

The layers of rock carved out by the sea acted like a huge stairway, each layer dropping down about half a metre to the one below. Nick coped easily with the steps down by simply sitting, with the doctor's help, and swinging his legs round to stand up again on the lower level. At last they came to the water's edge. The sea glistened in the weak moonlight and there, lying alongside the rocks, was a fair-sized rowing boat with a small outboard motor on the stern. Nick used his sitting technique to get into the boat and Azena helped him to one of the centre thwarts where he sat with a feeling of relief. Sarah climbed in and was sent to the stern.

'I normally used the engine when I go out fishing,' explained the doctor, 'but I think we had better play safe, so I will row. We haven't far to go. My wife is remaining here.'

Nick took the hand which Madame Azena offered. 'Thank you for all you have done. I hope I have put you in no danger.'

'Do not worry. We will be all right. I only hope that you have caused damage to Debert and Ricard and their crowd of killers. We must get rid of them if our island is to grow and prosper.'

'I think we might have been able to help there,' said Nick, but his voice was more confident than he really felt.

Madame Azena released the ropes and pushed them off gently. She stood and waited while they disappeared into the darkness. When there was nothing more to see she walked slowly back to the house. Her words to Nick had been brave but deep inside she was scared. If Ricard found out that they had helped the fugitives he would show no mercy. Inside the house she went to her bedroom where she knelt and, twisting her rosary in her hands, prayed for God's help.

The sea was calm, only the faintest ripple breaking the surface and reflecting the moonlight. Azena's long, powerful strokes sent the boat surging forward with barely a sound. He rowed without checking his direction, in the manner of an experienced boatman. They had gone only a couple of hundred metres when he held water by burying the blades of the oars and, looking over his shoulder, Nick saw the sleek lines of the power-boat. Her gleaming white hull was some ten or twelve metres long. He could just make out a figure in the cockpit. It must be the person he was anxious to meet, someone who would take risks for no reward, the person who was prepared to carry them to the safety of Sardinia. Azena gave a couple of strokes with his oars then shipped the port one and held water with the other. They came to rest alongside the power-boat without the slightest bump. Azena grasped the gunwale, holding them steady against the cockpit ladder.

'This is the difficult bit. I'm afraid you'll just have to stand up and tumble yourself into the launch. You'll be safe now. Even if someone sees you there's no vessel around here that can catch you before you get to Sardinia. Now go quickly.'

'You have saved our lives by risking yours. How can I ever thank you?'

'If you can contribute to the downfall of Debert and Ricard and their kind it will be thanks enough. Now take care and go.'

Nick stood up carefully and held on while Sarah climbed into the launch. Squeezing Azena's shoulder, he muttered, 'Thank you. I'll never forget you.' Then he carefully swung his injured foot up onto the launch's gunwale and pulled the rest of his body after it. With the help of the other boatman he rolled over and fell onto the cockpit cushion.

'A bit undignified, but welcome aboard, Monsieur Byers.'

Through the pain in his foot and injured shoulder, Nick could not fail to recognize the voice. He looked up with pleasure and relief as he made out Jacques Bianchi's lined, grinning face.

There was genuine delight in his voice as he grabbed the older man's hand and said, 'Jacques, you old devil. I thought I'd missed you. Is this your boat?'

'Yes. It's a bit of an extravagance and I don't use it much these days but I'm reluctant to get rid of it. It reminds me of the old days when we were all a bit naughty.' He leaned over and spoke to Azena. 'Just like the old days, eh, Philippe?'

For the first time Azena laughed. 'True, but now you must be away. Bon voyage.'

He pushed off and rowed quietly into the night as they softly called their farewells.

As Nick made himself as comfortable as possible on the cockpit cushion, Bianchi went over to the helm and pressed the starters. The two powerful diesel engines rumbled into life and settled down to a steady tick over. Slowly he opened the two throttles and the boat surged forward at about twenty knots while he brought it round onto an easterly course. 'We'll head out to sea for a while before we turn south. Then I'll open it up and you'll see what this little beauty is really capable of.'

Debert sat with his elbows on the desk, fingers steepled, tips resting on his lips, and stared at Ricard with eyes as cold as steel. 'Well, Ricard, I hope that you have good news to report.'

'We are making progress, Monsieur Debert. We have found out that they had a contact in Corsica. An ex-newspaperman called Bianchi has been helping them. If you remember, a few years ago he wrote a series of articles about us. I said at the time that we should eliminate him.'

'And let the world see that what he said was true? You do not think with your head, Ricard. Where is Bianchi now?'

'Unfortunately, he too has gone missing. We are questioning people who know him. We do know that he has a large power-boat, but we understand that a friend of his took it to Sardinia on holiday. He was not on board.'

'Nevertheless, check on its present whereabouts and find out if he has friends or associates here. In the middle of all this I hope that you have not forgotten the yacht, *White Albatross*. Is she still in Sicily?'

'I'm afraid she too has gone missing. She sailed from Sicily with the Australian and the Scarfiotti woman on board and we lost track of them.'

'You are a useless fool. Alert all our men to keep a watch for her. It is my belief she will head for Sardinia too. That's where they will all gather and that's where we must strike them.'

'Yes, Monsieur Debert.'

'I'm worried about you, Jacques.'

'*You* are worried about *me*, Nick? I think you have your priorities wrong. You lie there, badly injured, being hunted by a team of psychopathic killers, and you worry about me. I can't believe it.'

They had been speeding south at over forty knots, but the bouncing of the boat on even tiny wavelets had caused Nick discomfort, so Jacques had throttled back a little and they were now travelling at about thirty knots. The Frenchman had explained that it was necessary to travel as fast as possible in order to lose any possible pursuers, not that he thought there were likely to be any. Now, while they talked, he held the boat steady as it skimmed across the surface.

'I mean it, Jacques. We are heading for Sardinia and then on to the safety of England. You will doubtless return to Corsica where Ricard may be waiting for you – and possibly for Philippe Azena and his wife.'

'You are right that I will return to Corsica, but not until you are safely in England. Then, if you complete your mission, you could do mortal damage to the Union Corse. They will be too worried trying to survive to bother about a small person like myself. You are, however, right about Philippe and his wife. I asked them to come with us, but they refused. They said they had too many responsibilities in Corsica. We can only hope that they are not traced.'

They raced southwards in silence, each one considering the dangers, but knowing there was nothing they could do to help the doctor and his wife – except hope and pray.

After a while Sarah grew tired with the monotonous drumming as the boat skimmed the surface of the water. Even the beauty of the mass of phosphorescence in its wake failed to keep her awake. She curled up on the cushions and fell asleep. Bianchi switched on the automatic pilot and took a blanket from the locker to cover her. He offered another to Nick, but he shook his head. 'I'm okay. I've had plenty of sleep. Sarah has been watching over me for a hell of a long time. It's not surprising she sleeps now. How long has she got before we arrive?'

'Not long. In about half of an hour we will see the lights of Aranci. That's on the headland to the north of Olbia. Once we've rounded that it's only ten or twelve kilometres to the landing place. We won't be going into Olbia itself – or rather, you won't. I'm dropping you off at an isolated spot before we get that far. I only hope your gangster friends are there to meet us.'

'Jacques, for the last time, these people are no friends of mine. I despise them as much as I do Ricard, but they owe me a favour – you know what it is – and I intend to make use of them. As I've said before, I'd make use of the devil if he got us through this.'

'As long as you realize they are little better than the devil, that's fine. But they put on a fine front of respectability, which can be very misleading.'

'Oh, yes. I've seen that myself. Don't worry. I wasn't taken in. I do wonder about Gina Scarfiotti. She seems so straight, it's hard to believe she is one of them.'

'In many cases the women are as bad as the men, if not worse. Oh, yes, they put on an innocent front, but don't be misled. Gina Scarfiotti is different. Her mother was a good woman and she did her best for the girl. Now her father has seen that times are changing and has tried to keep her out of things. If she could only find the right man and break away completely she would be all right.'

'You seem to know her well, considering she's not on your patch.'

'You forget that I'm a close friend of Claudia Bugiatti. When she asked me to help you she gave me as much information as she could. She is a very well-informed woman.'

'Except that she thought I was a Mafioso.'

Bianchi chuckled. 'Yes. She told me in detail how you two met.'

Nick couldn't think of a suitable comment, so he took refuge in silence. Sarah's sleepy voice came from under the blanket. She obviously was not asleep and sensed that there was more to the story. 'Who is this Claudia and how did you come to meet her? You haven't mentioned the name to me before.'

Nick was flustered and pleased that it was dark. 'Oh, it's just a girl I met when I was looking for you. With all that has been happening she slipped my mind. She gave me an introduction to Jacques. I ran into her on the road to the farm where you were kept prisoner and she assumed I was a Mafioso because of my association with Paolo.'

'When he says he ran into her he means it literally. Her motor scooter is a wreck and she has no insurance to cover it. Yes, you made quite an impression on her.' Bianchi chuckled again.

'When you speak of her again, tell her I will pay for a new one – and claim it back from Harlow. What the hell! He's going to have quite a bill at the end of this little venture, so he'll hardly notice a mere motor scooter.'

Sarah chuckled in the darkness. 'I always say that he's a terrible driver, but knocking girls off their scooters is a bit much even for him.'

'Let's clarify one point. She ran into me, not vice versa. I was stationary at the time.'

Sarah was about to dig for more information, when Bianchi interrupted. 'There are the lights of Aranci. It shouldn't take us long now. We round the headland, then go into a small cove. There's a jetty there and we can land you with no difficulty. There's a track down, so I hope they have a vehicle of some sort to meet you.'

'Jacques, you seem to know a lot about this kind of thing. Were you a smuggler or something?' Much to Nick's relief, Sarah had given up on Claudia and now scented a story in Bianchi's past.

He laughed. 'You might say a bit of both. It goes back a long way to the days of the OAS. It was all a long, long time ago. After terrible unrest in Algeria during the fifties, the military leaders wanted a firm leader and Charles de Gaulle was recalled. When he came to power everyone thought that he would keep Algeria for the French; instead, he gave Algeria a chance of independence and the Organisation de l'Armée Secrète was formed to oppose that decision. It was an organization of colonialists and some of the military. They began terrible reprisals against both Algerian guerrillas and French officials. Many lives were lost. A group of us got together to try and rescue some of the refugees – unofficially of course. Dr Azena and I were just two of the members.' He was silent for a while. When he spoke again the laughter had gone from his voice. 'The other members of the group are no longer with us. Regrettably the OAS held grudges for a long time, as even de Gaulle found out.'

Nothing more was said on the subject, but it gave Nick and Sarah an insight into the kind of men they had helping them.

Dr Azena came out of his patient's house in the small town of Porto Vecchio, climbed into his car and headed for home. It was still early morning but he was tired after the eventful night. He decided he was too old for these adventures. On leaving the outskirts of the town, he glanced in the mirror and felt a thrill of horror as he detected movement in the back of the car.

'Keep driving on the main road and don't do anything silly.'

The voice was familiar, but he was unable to place it for certain. He did as he was told.

When they were clear of the town the man in the back spoke again. 'Ricard knows that Bianchi helped the Englishman and has asked for a list of his friends and associates. Your name has been mentioned and it will be only a short time before he finds out that you helped too. For my own sake I must tell him soon, but I will hold off until this evening. Take your wife and leave Corsica today. Go on holiday – go anywhere, but go and do not return until this matter has been settled. If you stay you will both die.'

'Who are you and why are you risking yourself to tell me this?'

'Let's just say that I am in Monsieur Debert's employ. Last year you used your skill to save the life of my small son and I am now repaying that act. Now, pull in to the side of the road just round the next bend and let me out of the car. Stop just long enough for me to get out then drive on immediately.'

Azena started to thank the man but was cut short. 'Just do as I say.'

As the car stopped the man jumped clear and disappeared into the bushes by the wayside. Azena headed for home.

Madame Azena was waiting anxiously. She was always scared when he was away. He entered the house purposefully. 'Hurry, chérie – pack some clothes. We are going to visit your sister in Switzerland. I will cancel my appointments and arrange a flight. I think there is one from Ajaccio early this afternoon. Hurry now and don't argue.'

She smiled with relief and threw her arms round his neck. 'Oh, I certainly will not argue. The sooner we get away the better.'

The vehicle which met them at the jetty was a four-wheel drive and it was soon clear why it was being used. The jetty was dilapidated and the track leading away from it uneven and badly potholed. Now, however, they were on a better road, speeding towards Sassari with Peretti at the wheel.

The parting from Bianchi at the jetty had been an emotional one. Sarah had been unable to restrain her tears, while Nick had embraced him and extracted a promise that he would stay in Sardinia until things quietened down. Even so, he knew Ricard would harbour grudges for a long time and would not hesitate to take his revenge many years hence if the opportunity arose. He realized now that the only sure way to protect his Corsican friends was to produce the computer disc that would surely put the leaders of the Union Corse behind bars. There was no longer the option of flying away from it all – he had to get *White Albatross* back to England. While he was sure that he knew the whereabouts of the disc he was equally sure that there must be a back-up of some kind.

Peretti drove quickly but tried to keep the ride as comfortable as possible by slowing for corners and braking carefully. The motion of the car, combined with the drugs which Azena had administered, had a soporific effect and Nick dozed for most of the journey to the hospital.

On arrival, Peretti drove right up to the front door, into the space reserved for ambulances. The attendants inside were obviously waiting for them and rushed out with a trolley. With no fuss, and in complete silence, Nick was helped from the car onto the trolley. They wheeled him quickly inside with Sarah running along behind. The spotlessly clean corridor led into an open space where they stopped and a nurse in shining white overalls stepped forward to wave Sarah to one of the seats that lined the wall. She started to protest but the nurse indicated a sign announcing that they were in the X-ray department.

She smiled brightly. 'We will take care of him – do not worry. Since I am sure you want to wait someone will bring you coffee in a short time. The X-ray will not take long. Then the doctor must decide what to do.' She led the trolley through a nearby door and the red light above it shone brightly.

A few minutes later, a doctor walked up and sat beside her.

'Did the doctor in Corsica give you a letter for us?'

In the rush Sarah had forgotten it. She now reached into her pocket and passed the somewhat crumpled envelope across.

He opened it and read the contents, nodding with satisfaction. 'How thoughtful. It is written in Italian. It tells me what drugs have been administered and when. We don't want to overdo things. We will try to keep you informed as we go along so that you are not kept in suspense.' He flashed a brilliant smile at her before departing along the passageway, passing Peretti, who was just approaching, without acknowledgement.

Peretti took the doctor's seat and sat back with a sigh. 'We haven't really been introduced. My name is Luciano Peretti and I am Signor Scarfiotti's representative in Sardinia.'

'You mean you're Chief Mafioso here.' Sarah said it without thinking and immediately wished she hadn't.

The smile left his face and he bit his lip. 'Yes, I suppose you can say that. However, I would rather you looked upon me as a friend while you are here. I will do my best to make you comfortable until you are all ready to leave.'

'Please forgive me. I shouldn't have said that after all the help you've given us.'

'Think nothing of it. I quite understand your feelings and, if our positions were reversed, I would probably feel as you do. In the meantime, you must accept our protection. You are quite safe in the hospital – it is well guarded but, unfortunately, we believe Ricard is aware that you are in Sardinia. So you must be careful when you leave.'

There was no doubting the satisfaction in Debert's voice as he spoke into the telephone and Ricard, on the receiving end, did not miss it. 'I was right, of course, Ricard. They are all heading for Sardinia – Bianchi, Byers and probably the yacht as well. I understand that Byers has an injured foot and is in a Mafia-sponsored hospital near Sassari. You also let Azena slip through your fingers. He and his wife have flown to Switzerland.'

'It is not too late. My men can collect them all in.'

'You will do nothing of the kind. You will just keep watch until Byers and the boat are reunited. Then we must be decisive. In the meantime, you will take no action which would warn them off – and that includes killing Bianchi and Azena. We can get to that later. You will go to Sardinia now, and be prepared. I have an agent in the hospital who will tell us when they plan to leave.'

The operation on Nick's foot was carried out with the minimum of fuss and the maximum of efficiency and by midday he was lying back in a comfortable bed, feeling better than he had done since the accident. So much better, in fact, that he was already hassling the doctor about when he could leave.

'But, Doctor, I'm feeling fine. Surely another twenty-four hours here will be enough.'

The doctor was fast losing his patience. 'If you wish to go, then you can. You can go now, in fact. But you will end up in a lot of pain and probably be permanently crippled. It is my advice that you remain here for another seven days.'

'And very good advice it is too.' Sarah had listened to the argument with growing frustration. 'There is no need for hurry now and we are safe here. While they were treating you, Harlow phoned to say that he is sending one of his men to be with us – a Peter Cassells. He says you know him.'

'Yes, I know him – and if I'm going to be cooped up here for the next week he'll come in handy running errands.'

The doctor smiled. 'Am I to understand that you have accepted my advice?'

Nick nodded. 'I'm sorry. I'm the world's worst patient, so you'll be pleased to be rid of me. I should really have been thanking you, instead of bickering.'

'I was only doing my job.'

'There is one more thing you could do for me.'

'I will try my best. What is it you want?'

'I want a word with Peretti.'

'That's quite easy – easier than you might think. He is in the lobby next door, in control of a small army of guards. You must be the best-protected guy in Sardinia. I'll send him in to see you.'

Peretti walked through the door in his usual respectful way and Nick wondered what he would be like in an emergency, then thought he was probably putting on a similar front to Cassells.

'Signor Byers, I trust your injury is improving. How may I be of help to you?'

'I'm worried about Jacques Bianchi. I've a feeling this whole thing is big enough for Ricard to act against us here in Sardinia. I think Jacques is in danger. What can you do to protect him?'

'I'm not sure that we can. Don't get me wrong. We would like to help but it is difficult to protect someone who does not want to be helped. I asked him to stay in the hospital until you leave, but he told me in no uncertain terms that he didn't want our help or anything to do with us.'

'In spite of that, will you try?'

'I'll do my best. I will put a good man on to watch him.'

It didn't take Bianchi long to spot that he was being followed. He had been expecting it and had set a number of traps to expose his tail. He smiled to himself. Really, this was just like old times. It was late in the evening when he turned off the main street and waited in a doorway. As his tail came round the corner he drew a revolver from his pocket and stepped out.

The other man froze in his tracks and raised his hands. He started to bluster about being robbed but his voice tailed away as Bianchi slowly shook his head. 'This is no robbery, and you know it. It's a kind of introduction. You've been following me for some time now and I thought we should get to know each other. I assume you are one of Peretti's men.'

The other saw no point in denying it. He nodded sullenly.

'And, if we are to be together, what am I to call you?'

'My name is Vittorio. I was instructed to protect you.'

'Ah, I guessed so. May I suggest we go and have coffee together in the café along the road. It will be much pleasanter for you than waiting outside while I am comfortably inside.'

Vittorio grinned sheepishly and nodded.

They sat over the small cups of espresso coffee for some time, talking mainly about Vittorio and his family, for Bianchi had a knack of putting people at their ease. When they walked back to the boat together, they were chatting like old friends.

Bianchi invited his new friend on board. 'Come and see the boat and have a glass of wine until your relief comes.' Then he suddenly patted his pocket and cursed softly. 'I've left my spectacles on the table of the café. I must go back for them.'

Vittorio waved him onto the boat. 'You go aboard and stay in the saloon. I will run back for them – it won't take a minute.'

Bianchi thanked him and waited in the cockpit until he was out of sight. Then, with a chuckle, he ran ashore and cast off the moorings. The engines started at a turn of the key and the boat was away, leaving the furious Vittorio running back down the jetty, waving his arms in despair.

Bianchi manoeuvred the boat out into deep water, then set a course for the open sea. He was pleased with himself, for he had no intention of being nursed – especially by a Mafioso.

He shivered slightly in the cold night air and decided to go below to get a sweater. He set the auto-helm and checked around before ducking down the companion-way into the cabin. In the darkness he sensed, rather than saw, another presence. He stood still and tried to locate it, but he never saw the shadow that rose behind him, nor did he feel the knife that drove between his ribs and into his heart.

Hassan withdrew the knife from the body and wiped it on the clothing before returning it to its sheath. Then he hoisted the small body without difficulty and dragged it up to the cockpit. Having checked for other shipping and found all clear, he made his way to the bows and, opening the forehatch, dropped inside and searched around with his torch till he found a heavy anchor and a length of rope. Then he made his way back to the cockpit. He tied the anchor to Bianchi's feet and dropped him neatly over the side to his final resting place. Taking the helm, he set course for the Maddalena Islands off the north-eastern coast of Sardinia.

11

The days in hospital passed quickly and Nick's foot in its plaster cast became less painful. Sarah spent most of the time with him and, on other occasions, she found Peter Cassells good company. It was on the third day he came into report that *White Albatross* had arrived in the marina and was lying alongside waiting for them.

Steve had sent his best wishes but felt he should remain on board for security. Gina would visit as soon as she had completed a few odds and ends.

As they lounged in the garden in the bright sunshine, Nick asked Cassells whether there was any news of Bianchi.

'Not a thing. After he gave Peretti's man the slip, he disappeared from the face of the earth. He's a crafty old devil and Vittorio just wasn't expecting it. Still, if we can't find him the chances are that Ricard won't have any better luck.'

Nick nodded his agreement, but somewhere deep down he was uneasy. He thought for a bit, then shrugged it off. He was getting worse than Sarah with her woman's intuition. Of course, Cassells was right. The old man would turn up when he was good and ready.

Nick was becoming quite proficient with crutches and was even able to hobble short distances with just a stick to help him. He decided it was time to go back to the boat and make a break for it. Peretti had reported that there was no sign of Ricard's men in the vicinity. All strangers had checked out okay. It seemed everything was clear. Once again, he felt sad at not being able to say farewell to Bianchi. Maybe they would meet again some time.

*   *   *

'I gave you explicit instructions, Ricard, not to kill Bianchi. Yet you went ahead and did so.'

'It was not my fault, Monsieur Debert. Hassan did it before I could contact him.'

'Incompetence,' snorted Debert. 'As it happens it was for the best. Now we have the boat and, as long as they know nothing of his death, we have a means of approaching them at sea without scaring them. I would imagine that Scarfiotti's men are looking for the boat, but it is vital they do not find it.'

'They will not. It is well hidden in the Maddalena Islands.'

'Good. As soon as we get word that they are sailing we will make our move.'

Nick thanked the doctors and nurses and left the hospital able to move about with a certain amount of ease. He had to admit that the week he had spent there had not been wasted. If he had left immediately after the treatment he would have been a handicap on the boat, whereas now he could help in some minor ways.

Steve greeted him like a long-lost friend and almost lifted him onto the boat as it lay alongside the jetty.

'Come off it, Steve. I'm not a complete bloody invalid. I can get on board myself. When I move around on my hands and knees it may not be dignified, but it's practical.' The words were softened by the laugh that accompanied them.

Greetings over, they moved down into the saloon for a council of war. Nick began by asking Steve if he would be prepared to help sail the boat to England. 'There is a small risk we may still fall foul of the Union Corse, but all appearances indicate that they have lost track of us. If we stock up for a long voyage we could get clear of here and sail non-stop until we get to Portugal. We could time it so that we go through the Straits of Gibraltar at night. We should be safe then.'

'Just you try and stop me. I'd already made up my mind about that one. It's time I had a look at England – I've heard so much about it. It can't really be as bad as they say back home.'

Nick grinned. 'Thanks. I think you'll like it – for a short stay anyway. With the three of us we should be able to handle the boat with no trouble.'

'You mean the four of us,' I think.' Gina joined in. 'You don't honestly imagine I would let Steve go without me, do you?' As Nick tried to interrupt she waved him to silence. 'I know you are going to speak of dangers, but I am prepared for that. I probably understand them much better than you. Let me make it clear: I love Steve and I'm not going to lose him.'

Steve put his arm round her shoulders and pulled her close. 'That's right, Gina, you tell them.'

'Well, I think we can safely say that the party now numbers four,' said Nick.

'No.' The interruption came from Cassells. 'Five. At least, if you let me come along. Before you say no, let me point out that I may not be a good sailor but when it comes to dealing with Ricard, I'm the best qualified. Yes, I am carrying a gun and I know how to use it. Without boasting, I am extremely good with it. Furthermore, you, Nick, may be able to carry out light work, but what if we run into a real gale? I'm sure the girls are very competent but wouldn't a man's extra strength come in handy?'

'You've put your case very well, Peter. It will be a bit cramped but . . . welcome aboard. Won't Harlow miss you?'

'He suggested it,' replied Cassells with a grin. 'Don't forget that he is dead keen to get this boat back home.'

'Okay. That's the crew sorted out. Steve, what are the provisions like?'

'Fine. We're full of fuel and water. We've got all the food we'll need, except the fresh stuff, which I've left till the last minute. Then we'll have enough to sail to America.'

'Well done. I don't think we'll bother about America, though. We'll do the final shopping this morning. Peter, would you take the two girls and look after that? Remember, all of you, stay together at all times. There's no point in taking chances, even though we are probably under Peretti's watchful eye. We'll sail at midnight.'

The time passed slowly as they waited to set off. It was a time of stress, which seemed to affect Nick in particular. He became tense and spoke abruptly to the others, so that they tended to keep clear of him. Peter Cassells had taken Sarah and Gina shopping during the morning, as Nick had instructed. He was undoubtedly a good bodyguard but he was also a most chivalrous escort and soon won his way into the girls' affections. The party returned on board laughing happily, to be met by a sour-faced Nick. 'You lot seem to see the funny side of something. God knows, I can't see that there's anything to laugh at.'

The trio said nothing but, as soon as possible, found some excuse to go ashore again, leaving Steve and Nick alone together.

'Anyone would think we were on a holiday cruise, the way those three are behaving,' said Nick grumpily.

'And I wish that I could join them, mate, instead of baby-sitting a miserable old bastard like you.'

'Come off it. What the hell are you talking about? Anyway, there's no need for you to stay. I can look after myself.'

'Like hell you can. You're like a bear with a sore head and we're all a bit fed up with it. Why, man, why? We're on the last leg now – you said so yourself.'

Nick sat silently for a while before replying. 'Sorry, Steve. I guess I'm worried, that's all. Sure, I said that it was plain sailing from now on. That was for the others' benefit. In fact, I'm worried about the Union Corse. I honestly don't think they will let go so easily. I've got a nagging feeling that they know where we are and are just waiting for us to leave Scarfiotti's protective cover.'

'What makes you think that?'

'I don't know. Call it intuition, call it what you will – I just believe I'm right. Like *you* were about the storm.'

'Let's hope I'm a better prophet than you. Anyway, cheer up or we'll lose our crew before we sail.'

Nick forced a smile. 'I'll try.'

* * *

On board Bianchi's power-boat, as it cruised slowly off the north coast of Sardinia, Debert sipped his glass of champagne thoughtfully. He looked across the cabin to where Ricard sat uneasily on the opposite seat. He hadn't been offered a glass of the sparkling drink and was acutely aware of the fact.

'So, Ricard, the end of our problem is at hand and I personally will ensure that nothing goes wrong this time. We will wait just outside the harbour. Far enough away to be out of sight, but close enough to pick them up on our radar. Then we will follow them and, once clear of land, we will board them. They will have no alternative but to hand over the disc and, when they have done so, we will send them to join the thousands of sailors already at the bottom of the Mediterranean. It is all very simple, yet you have failed so often. Maybe you are getting too old. Maybe you should retire.'

Ricard shivered at those words. He knew that no one retired from the Union Corse, except very permanently. He decided to change the subject slightly.

'But they have the Scarfiotti girl on board. If her father ever found out we would have all-out war with the Mafia – a war we couldn't hope to win. Even their enemies in Sicily would join them if an outsider killed a member of the family. They don't mind killing each other but God help an outsider who dares to do so.'

Debert shook his head sadly. 'Ricard, Ricard. Just think. How will anybody ever know? We wait till they're clear of land and we are certain they have no means of transmitting on their radio. Then we make sure there are no witnesses left – on either boat – and we are safe. Yachts go missing all the time – why should we be blamed?'

Ricard shivered again. If Debert was about to wipe out his own men to cover the incident, then Ricard himself was in dire danger. He knew he would have to watch his own back. He looked at his wristwatch and stood up. 'It is half an hour to midnight. Shall I give orders to move closer to the entrance?'

'Yes, and tell them to darken ship. No navigation lights from now on.'

'Okay – it's time. We go out under engine and keep it running until we round the northern tip of Asinara. That should be about three o'clock in the morning. If there's no wind we keep it running as we head westwards. We should be clear of land by daybreak. I wish we'd got that damned compass adjusted properly while we were waiting. There was just too much to think about. Still, it isn't far out and Gina knows the area, so she takes the first stint at the helm. Maybe she can give us a course to steer. You, Steve, take the glasses and get up forward as lookout. I wish I'd had the foresight to get some proper night-vision glasses too, but we'll just have to rely on your eagle eyes. Report any shipping – and I do mean *any*. The rest of you let go the mooring lines, then get some sleep.'

The whole of the marina seemed deserted and the only sound was the muffled throb of their engine as they slid quietly out of the moorings. Nick would have preferred to go out under sail but he needed to get clear of land as soon as possible and there was insufficient wind to ensure they would do that by daybreak with sail alone. He hoped there were no hidden watchers to report their departure. It was a beautiful night, with a multitude of stars but little moon. The darkness meant they were soon invisible to any watchers ashore, but he was only too aware that they could be tracked easily by radar on a boat, which might be hidden from them.

They had been under way for about twenty minutes when Steve called softly from the bows. 'I'm not sure, but I think I saw a flash of some kind away on the starboard bow. I can't see anything now.'

Nick pulled himself to his feet and steadied his glasses on the edge of the doghouse as he searched the area that Steve had indicated. There was nothing to be seen.

'Maybe I imagined it. If so, sorry.'

'You did right. Keep a special lookout in that area, just in case.'

The flare of the match was bright in the cockpit as the crewman lit his cigarette. Almost by reflex, Ricard smashed his gun across the man's head, sending him senseless to the deck. The unconscious body rolled to one side of the cockpit as Ricard stooped to pick up the fallen cigarette and drop it carefully overboard.

'Ahmed, get the bucket and throw some water over that stupid bastard. Unfortunately, we may need him later – otherwise we could dispose of him properly.'

'What's going on up there?' Debert called softly from the cabin.

'Everything's okay now. One of your men, Fellini, decided to have a cigarette and light up the whole of the boat at the same time. I've dealt with him.'

In the cabin Debert was silent and Ricard suddenly realized that, out there, he had the upper hand. When the disc was recovered he, not Debert, could clean up. Then *he* would be the boss. He knew he couldn't run the whole Union Corse himself, but he could come to a settlement with one of their rivals, and retire properly as a wealthy man.

'Keep your distance from them. Just patiently follow on,' he instructed the helmsman.

As they ran on engine up the eastern coast of the island of Asinara there were very few lights to be seen. The island is some seventeen kilometres long and the site of a special prison, so no tourists are allowed. In fact, boats are permitted to land only in emergency or with a special permit. Nick knew he could have passed between the island and Punta Falcone on Sardinia itself, but that's what the Union Corse would be expecting and they could be lying in wait. If they were ambushed there, they would have less room for manoeuvre. He had decided on the longer, and possibly safer, route.

After a couple of miles Nick became a little more relaxed. Perhaps he had been imagining the dangers. The Union Corse had probably given up hope of getting the disc back and were busy working on damage limitation. Certainly, there was no sign of the enemy. Then Nick shook himself and muttered out loud, 'Hell, there wouldn't be, would there?'

'What's that, Nick?' Gina, who was still on the wheel, turned to him.

'Sorry, Gina. I was speaking to myself. Just imagining things. If you carry on at the helm for another hour, I'll relieve you then and you can get some sleep. Peter and Sarah can give Steve a break on lookout.'

Nick had chosen to keep as close to Asinara as possible, allowing for safety. Maybe if they were close to land it would confuse any radar operator who was following them. He also felt that being close to land might deter Ricard from launching an attack, should he be following them. Not that there was much sign of life ashore. He had seen the lights of only one car making its way along the road that ran the length of the island.

He tried to put thoughts of the Union Corse out of his mind. He had set lookouts and there was nothing more he could do except keep a watch and hope for the best.

Aboard the power-boat everyone was silent. Debert remained in the saloon and the others were in the large cockpit. The crewman who had been pistol-whipped sat to one side, holding a cloth to his head. Even so, the blood trickled slowly between his fingers.

Ricard broke the silence by speaking in a low voice to Ahmed, who was watching the radar screen. 'Can you still see them?'

'Yes, just. They are keeping close to Asinara and we are

getting a lot of returns from the land, but I've got them okay.'

'It's that bastard, Byers. He's a crafty devil. You take care. If you lose them, I'll lose you – permanently. Aside from the disc, I have a personal thing to settle with Byers and his Australian side kick.'

The light on the Punta dello Scorno at the northern tip of Asinara had been in sight for some time and, as it came abeam, Nick held his course for about half a mile before bringing the boat round ninety degrees to port. It was then three o'clock in the morning and he reckoned that he had nearly two hours more before daylight.

They cruised on under engine with the throttle wide open, the water rushing along the sides of the boat to mix with the bright phosphorescence in the churned-up wake. Speed was now more important than fuel conservation.

The first streaks of dawn coloured the Eastern sky a little earlier than he had anticipated and he called out softly to Sarah, 'Go below and wake Steve. I need him on deck right away.'

Moments later Steve appeared in the companionway, rubbing the sleep from his eyes. 'This is a fine time of the morning to wake a guy up. I thought this was to be a pleasure trip.'

'I need you to search the eastern area as soon as you can see clearly. If there's nothing there, we're on a pleasure cruise and you can go back to bed.' Nick passed over the glasses and Steve positioned himself against the after cabin where he had a clear view astern.

As the sky gradually grew brighter he swept the area carefully, well aware of the importance of the task. The island of Asinara was now a shadow on the horizon. Nick waited with pounding heart. Each moment that Steve stayed silent gave him hope.

Sarah and Peter sat in the cockpit with him and it was Sarah who spoke first. 'Nick, I thought that we were in the clear. What makes you think they are out there?'

'I'm not certain. I'm just being careful.'

'Quite right too.' Steve's voice cut in. 'It looks like we've got company. There's a power-boat of some kind out there and it's headed this way. It could be someone out fishing, or it could be our friends. We'll soon find out.'

Nick picked up the spare glasses and stared out astern. It was much lighter now and he soon spotted th white bow-wave of the boat following them. 'As you say, Steve, we'll soon know – they'll be up with us in fifteen minutes. Go and call Gina and let's get prepared.'

'If it's them, can't we just bargain, Nick?' Sarah's voice was full of anxiety. 'Can't we give them what they want? Then they'll probably leave us alone.'

'That would be all right if we knew what they were after,' said Steve bitterly.

Nick spoke quietly, but firmly. 'Oh, I know what they are after. What's more I know where it is – at least I think I do.'

Cassells was the first to ask. 'What is it? Where is it hidden?'

'It's a computer disc, holding information about the Union Corse – information which the French Government could use to smash it once and for all. As for where it is, that's something I would rather keep to myself for the time being. However, Sarah, you of all people shouldn't be misled about these bastards. If we give them the disc they will kill us out of hand. No, we've got to fight.'

'How do you know they won't let us go on our way?' argued Cassells. 'Let's be realistic, we've got very little to fight with. My little automatic will be useless against their fire-power.'

'Don't jump to conclusions, Peter. Bring on the artillery, Steve. We'll be prepared.'

A broad grin spread over the Aussie's face. 'Aye, aye, skipper. They're in for one hell of a surprise.' He almost ran down the companionway ladder while the others gazed after him with puzzled expressions.

Cassells, in particular, looked doubtful. 'I don't know what you've got, Nick, but it will have to be powerful if we're to have a chance.'

'Oh, it's powerful all right.'

At that moment, Steve reappeared brandishing a shotgun and Cassells' reaction was disparaging. 'That's not going to be powerful enough to save us, Nick. I thought you had a Bren gun or something. I recommend you hand over the disc and hope for the best.'

'Sorry, Peter, but no. The power of that gun is not in itself but in the cartridges, which are solid ball – and in the element of surprise. I plan to wait until they get close enough, then produce the gun and blow a hole or two in their bows. That should stop them, and we'll take it from there.' He broke open the gun and shoved in a couple of the cartridges which Steve had passed to him.

Cassells looked disgruntled, but the others were obviously willing to follow Nick's lead and watched while he wedged himself against the corner of the doghouse, holding the shotgun hidden from view, but ready to swing up to his shoulder. Astern of them the power-boat came on, closing the gap fast. Their worst fears came true for they could now see Ricard on the bridge, looking at them through binoculars. One of the Arabs stood on the foredeck, holding some kind of rifle across his chest. The white of the bow-wave stood out sharply in the early morning light. As they watched, the wave grew bigger and bigger, then suddenly diminished as the helmsman cut back the engines to glide alongside.

On the yacht they held their breath, thinking that Nick had left it too late. At that point he whipped the gun up to his shoulder and pressed the first trigger. He was unprepared for the huge recoil as the overloaded cartridges fired the heavy slug out of the barrel.

The effect on the power-boat was quite spectacular. Nick had aimed for the waterline but the recoil had pushed the gun upwards and the large slug had struck near the top of the stem, removing a large portion of the foredeck and part of the gunwale. The Arab was flung overboard. The power-boat veered sharply away and, as the gap between the boats began to open up, Nick prepared to fire the second cartridge.

'Enough, Nick. Drop the gun, or you're dead.' Cassells' voice cut through the cheering of Steve and the girls. There were instant silence as they turned to look at him. The automatic in his hands was pointed at Nick's head and it was clear that he not only knew how to use it but that he would not hesitate to do so. 'Hold the gun high so they can see it, then throw it over the side. Do it now.' His voice was no longer hesitant – it cut like a knife. Nick did as he was told.

Without taking his eyes off Nick, Cassells stood up and beckoned to the power-boat to come on. The others stared at him, unable to comprehend what was going on.

'But why, Peter, why?' asked Gina in a quivering voice. 'We had them licked. We could have got away.'

'Because the bastard is one of them. Don't you see? He's sold out to them. That's how they knew where we were and when we were leaving. Isn't that right, Cassells?'

Cassells bowed his head slightly. 'That's right, Byers. I'm sorry that it came to this. I was hoping we could get the disc without breaking my cover. This way it reduces my value a bit, but it still gives me enough to retire on.'

Sarah couldn't hold back the tears. 'But you've sacrificed us all just for money. Surely you can't live with our deaths on your conscience.'

'Oh, don't overdo it, Sarah. If I had to I would, but if Debert gets the disc I think he will let you go. It wasn't just for money either. I was the one who originally obtained the disc and gave it to Beardsley. Debert found out and I was given the choice: either I got it back, in which case I got a large reward, or I was a dead man. Now, seriously, which would you have chosen?'

* * *

On the power-boat, Ricard cursed as the shotgun slug crashed into the bows and the Arab went overboard. As the helmsman veered the boat away, Ricard roared at him. 'Circle round out of range. Then let Ahmed swim to us. It's time Cassells took a hand, and when he does we'll move in. But this time be careful. God knows why Cassells didn't tell us about that bloody cannon.'

He watched, and waited for Ahmed to swim to them. Then he saw Nick raise the gun above his head and throw it in the sea. He acknowledged Cassells' wave. 'Okay, it's all clear now but go in slowly. You, Ahmed.' He addressed the Arab who stood dripping beside him. 'Get the other gun and be prepared this time.'

There was no opposition as they manoeuvred alongside the yacht. The crewman, still a bit dazed from his head wound, held them in position with a boat hook – not a difficult task in the calm sea – as Ricard and Debert looked down from the bridge deck. Debert was unarmed but Ricard held a large-calibre revolver.

As the two boats bumped gently together, Nick, with a sickening feeling, recognized the power-boat. Obviously, they had killed Bianchi; there was no other way they could have got it away from him. He was more certain than ever that they would not be allowed to live. He kept the identity of the boat to himself, however. He could see no point in revealing what he knew.

Cassells called up from the yacht. 'Don't worry – they've got no more weapons, and Byers has said he knows where the disc is. It looks like I've earned my reward.'

Debert nodded. 'Good – you have indeed. We meet at long last, Monsieur Byers. I wish it could have been under better circumstances. You have proved very resourceful and have cost me dearly. However, I bear no grudge. I am a reasonable man and, if you give me the disc, I will let you all sail away happily. All, that is, except my friend, Peter Cassells, who has done such a good job rectifying his earlier mistake. Good – but not good enough.' He nodded to Ricard who casually raised his gun. The terror on Cassells's face was frozen as the bullet hit him in the chest, throwing him violently backwards. He was dead before he landed, a crumpled heap in the corner of the cockpit. His blood splattered the two girls.

Gina gasped and held her hands to her mouth. Sarah was violently sick over the side. A look of sheer disgust spread over Steve's face. Nick broke the silence that followed. 'You murdering bastard. Was that necessary?'

'Regretfully, yes, Monsieur Byers. I had to impress you with my determination to get the disc back at all costs. Cassells was expendable and his job was over. What's more, he was a traitor, and I hate traitors – you just can't trust them. Now you will tell me where the disc is or my friend here will shoot the young Australian. If you are still reluctant, charming Signorina Scarfiotti will follow, then your delightful lady, Sarah. I hope I shall have your co-operation, in order to avoid such bloodshed because, contrary to what you may have heard, I do not enjoy killing people.'

Nick nodded at the body in the corner of the cockpit. 'How do I know I can trust you to let us go after that?'

'You don't, but I am a man of my word.' He indicated the body. 'That man had it coming to him. He was nothing.'

'It seems I have little choice. Steve, go and fetch the tool bag. I need a small screwdriver.' As the Australian went down the companion ladder, Nick continued. 'I'm not a hundred per cent certain about this. I just *think* that I know where it is.'

Debert smiled. 'Let's hope for all your sakes that it is where you *think* it is.'

Nick took a screwdriver from the bag and crossed to the compass binnacle. He began removing the screws holding it in place. They came out quite easily, as he knew they would. He had earlier inspected them closely and noted the minute scratch marks where someone had removed them previously. He lifted off the compass itself and, nestled below it, was a computer disc – the thing that so many people had died for. He placed the compass on the cockpit seat and gently prised the disc from its hiding place, while the others watched, spellbound.

'Give it to me.' Debert's voice was no longer mild as it cut through the silence.

Nick knew he had no alternative. He passed the disc up to Debert who leant down to receive it. For a moment Nick considered grabbing the other man's wrist and pulling him down, but he rejected the idea at once. He would only have succeeded in getting the others killed by Ricard's gun.

'That was very wise of you. Ricard, is this the disc?'

Ricard took the disc and looked at it closely. 'Yes, that's ours. You can see the markings.'

Debert smiled. 'Excellent. Now we will sail away and let you continue with your voyage in peace. As I said before, I am a man of my word and you no longer pose a threat to our organization. I must thank you for your co-operation.' He bowed slightly and went below to the boat's saloon, leaving Ricard and the Arab to cover them as the power-boat pulled away and headed towards Corsica.

They stared after it. 'That's Jacques Bianchi's boat, isn't it, Nick?

'Yes, it was, Sarah – but I very much doubt that he needs it now.'

'You mean they've killed him?'

'That's right.'

'Then how can they let us go? They could deny all knowledge of killing Cassells and blame it on us, but they can't hide the fact that they are cruising round in a dead man's boat.'

'You've hit the nail right on the head, Sarah. They can't. This is all part of their sadistic game. I expect them to turn back shortly and come in for the kill – and we have no means of defending ourselves.'

'Like hell we haven't,' Steve remarked. 'When you told me to get that cannon, I thought I might as well ask for two. I always heard they came as a pair. There's another one of the little beauties down below.'

Nick's mouth dropped open and Sarah leapt up. 'Oh, Steve,' she said, 'I could kiss you.'

'You go ahead – don't let me stop you.'

'Before we start kissing each other,' said Nick, 'let's get the gun up here and load it. I'll feel safer then. And keep a close watch on that other boat.'

Steve ran nimbly down the companionway, leaving Nick deep in thought. What would Debert do? He would certainly return to kill them, but how would he go about it? Nick felt certain he wouldn't ram them; that would be too risky for himself. He could stand off and riddle them with fire from the automatic or he could come alongside and let Ricard do the job with his bloody handgun. Yes, thought Nick, that's what he would do. The sadist in him would enjoy watching their faces as they were blown apart, especially since he believed them to be unarmed. That could be his undoing. Nick grinned for the first time in ages – they had a chance.

Sure enough, as the other boat almost disappeared from view, the crew of the yacht saw it turn and head back in their direction.

'Do you think we've got a chance, Nick?' asked Sarah.

'I think we've got a very good chance. You saw what this weapon can do. If I can get two shots away quickly, I may be able to reload before they have time to react. Steve can stand by me with spare cartridges at the ready. You girls sit and look dejected – that shouldn't be difficult after all that's happened.'

'If we win, is there a chance of getting that disc back. I'd really like to break up that rotten organization once and for all. I'm beginning to appreciate why Harlow laid so much importance on it. If he hadn't involved us I might even sympathize with him.'

'Even if we could get the disc I doubt it would do us any good. You see, it's been sitting in the middle of a load of magnets for sometime now. It will almost certainly be wiped clean of all the information it held.'

'You mean this whole thing has been for nothing?'

'It looks like it. Now let's take up our positions and look as if we're beaten.'

He leaned back against the doghouse and watched as the other boat drew nearer. He could see plainly the damage his earlier shot had done. As he held the shotgun out of sight, he hoped they would not recognize that his position was the same as before, but it was the only place he could firmly wedge himself.

The other boat slowed and moved closer. Nick knew then that he had been right in all but one thing. Ricard was not going to use his gun. As he stood on the side of the boat, leaning back against the bridge, there was an evil grin on his face and a grenade in his hand.

A shot to the hull would not necessarily prevent the Corsican throwing the grenade. He had to take Ricard out. Praying that his aim would prove true, he whipped up the gun and fired as it hit his shoulder. This time he was prepared for the recoil, and his first shot crashed into the hull at Ricard's feet, sending him reeling backwards. The next hit him in the upper body, tearing it apart. The remains disappeared from their view. Nick reached for the spare cartridges, but Steve wasn't there.

He had dived for the yacht's throttle and, shoving it wide open, yelled to the others, 'Get your heads down, quick.' In that instant there was a loud roar, and a pillar of flame shot upwards. As they crouched in the cockpit of the yacht, pieces of debris from the other boat fell around them.

With Steve still crouched and holding the wheel amidships they moved clear of the danger area and were able to sit up and take stock. The stricken power-boat lay stationary, a flaming hulk. There was no sign of life anywhere.

'D'you reckon we should go and look for survivors?'

'We're not going near that wreck until it sinks – there may be more explosives on board. Then, with a bit of luck, there'll be no survivors. It looks very much as if the Union Corse is going to need a new leader as well as a new hit team. We seem to have done part of Harlow's work for him.'

Sarah spoke softly. 'I know that Jacques Bianchi would have approved of the way his boat went.'

'He would that,' agreed Nick. 'Now we had better go back to Sardinia and report things to the proper authorities – and unload that.' He indicated Cassells' body, which Gina had covered with a sheet.

'Oughtn't we go to Corsica, since that's where everybody came from?' Sarah asked.

'In theory I suppose we should, but I would hate to report to someone who was under the Union Corse's control. We've killed their headman, but there's probably somebody else ready to take over. No, we'll go to Sardinia. There, if the officials are bent it will be in our favour. We made use of the Mafia all along – there's no point in stopping now.'

Steve joined in the discussion. 'I don't know about you, but I think we should bend the truth a little in our report. Let's ditch the cannon and make no mention of it. Let's say instead that Ricard dropped the grenade when his feet slipped on the wet deck – early morning dew and all that. It isn't lying – as your civil servant said; it is being economical with the truth.'

'I agree. That way we should avoid trouble with the authorities. There we were on the high seas, stopped by pirates who shot one of our crew and then blew themselves up as they were trying to kill the rest of us. As for motive – some kind of feud between them and Cassells.'

That was the basis of the story they told when they arrived back in Sardinia, a story which was accepted readily – whether because of Scarfiotti's involvement or a natural hatred of Debert and Ricard, it was impossible to say. Either way, the formalities were remarkably brief and, by late afternoon, Nick was able to telephone Harlow. This time he had no trouble getting through the switchboard. As soon as he mentioned his name he was connected.

'Hello, Nick. I thought you would be on the high seas, heading homewards. What's gone wrong?'

'Just about everything. Your man, Cassells, was a double agent, working for the Union Corse. He was responsible for getting Beardsley killed, and nearly us too. Don't worry though – he's dead now.'

'What the hell! Did you kill him?'

'No. His new boss, Ricard, did that. But don't worry there either – *he*'s dead and so is Debert.'

'Great Scott, what the hell has been going on? Tell me all.'

Nick did just that, and Harlow didn't interrupt.

'Well, Nick, you certainly did well and I'm delighted to hear that you're all safe. We'll try to hide Cassells's doubling, if you don't mind – awkward questions would be asked. It's a pity about the disc. Beardsley was a bit of a computer buff, so it's strange that he hid it near the compass. He must have known about the effects of magnets. There's only one answer to that – he made a copy.'

'If he did no one has been able to find it so far.'

'Nick, you and the others move to a hotel for a week or so and have a holiday. We'll foot the bill, of course. I'll send a team of experts over and they can slip the boat and really go over it. If necessary, they can take it apart piece by piece.'

'Not too many pieces, I hope. I still want to sail her home.'

'So you shall. I'll make sure she's seaworthy for you. When you get back we may be able to do a deal with Beardsley's estate to sell you the boat at a good price. He's got no heirs to worry about.'

Nick and the others had been relaxing for a week in a luxurious hotel just outside Cagliari, at the southern end of the island. While the others were happy to drink in the sun and wine, Nick was beginning to get restive. He needed to do something. It was with a certain satisfaction, therefore, that he looked up from his sun-bed by the pool to see Harlow approaching him.

'Hello, Nick. We've finished and the boat is back together – as good as new. Better, in fact. You can have it whenever you like.'

'Did you find the disc?'

'No, not a sign of it.'

'So it was all for nothing. All those deaths. It was an ill wind that profited no one,' said Sarah bitterly.

'Yes and no. Some good has come from it. With the deaths of Debert, Ricard and that lot, witnesses are beginning to take heart and give evidence. With luck the power, not only of the Union Corse but of the other splinter groups as well has been broken. Let's get some champagne and drink to a good voyage home. You deserve it.'

EPILOGUE

The farmer was proud of his young son. He, himself, had had very little chance to do well at school. In fact, he was barely literate. His son, on the other hand, was remarkably bright, according to the teachers, and quite well ahead of the other twelve-year-old boys in his class. The farmer puffed on his long, thin cigar as he spoke to his wife in their stone cottage in the hills of Corsica.

'I think it's time to take Pierre out hunting. He has proved himself a good shot at the targets down the valley and we can reward him for all the hard work at school.'

'He would like that. He keeps asking me when you will take him. Since you gave him that gun he has thought of nothing else.'

'Tomorrow, then. We'll work our way up the valley and see if we can shoot a couple of pigeons for supper.'

The following day the farmer and his young son carried their guns up the valley until they were in a wooded area where the farmer had shot birds before. 'Okay, son. Load your gun now and put the safety catch on.' The boy did as he was told, but the farmer kept his unloaded. He was taking particular care to avoid accidents.

They progressed slowly, the guns held across their chests, until the farmer signed for them to stop. He pointed up to the branches of a nearby tree. There sat a fat pigeon, well within range. The boy took aim and fired. The glee on his face was clear as the shot struck home and the stricken bird fluttered down into some shrubs – his first kill.

'Well done, son. Give me your gun and go and fetch it out. You've got yourself a good supper there.'

The boy handed over his gun and wriggled his way into the shrubs while the farmer waited. After a few minutes he became impatient.

'Come on, lad, don't take all day.'

There was no reply. His impatience turned to worry and placing the guns against a tree, the farmer thrust his way into the shrubs. He frowned as he saw his son kneeling with his head buried in his hands. He was sobbing and had been very sick. The man looked further and saw the pigeon. It was lying on the decomposed remains of a man. The body was clothed in the tattered remains of a jacket and trousers, torn to shreds by scavenging animals. As he smelled the rotten flesh, he felt his gorge rise. Bending down he half dragged the boy away from the scene.

The remains of the body were stretched out on the operating table. The pathologist spoke to his assistant through the clinical mask. 'I don't think there's much doubt about how this one died, Jean. You could drive a bus through that wound. It would seem that the bullet went in the back and exited through the chest. Must have been heavy-calibre stuff.'

'Looks like our main job will be to try and identify him. We can check dental records of people who went missing early in the summer. The clothes were all English, but there was nothing else.' He pointed to one side of the wound. 'What's that? It looks like a bit of plastic.'

The pathologist looked through a large magnifying glass and picked out the object with a pair of tweezers. He laid it in the dish beside the body and, digging deeper into the wound, came up with several more pieces. 'Whatever they are they didn't get into the body from the front. They were obviously carried through from behind by the bullet. Go and have another look at the back of the jacket.'

The assistant walked across to where the remains of clothing were spread out on a table and inspected the jacket carefully. 'I've got it,' he exclaimed. 'There was a computer floppy disc in a pocket in the back of the jacket. I guess the bullet went straight through it. Strange place to keep it.'

'One thing's certain. No one will be able to read it now.'